Upon Destiny's Song

UPON DESTINY'S SONG

ഔ

Mike Ericksen
& Sage Steadman

UPON DESTINY'S SONG

Published by:
Empath Media, LLC
P.O. Box 1191
Farmington, Utah
84025

First printing 2013

Visit us at www.UponDestinysSong.com

ISBN: 978-0-9883604-1-9 (dj)
ISBN: 978-0-9883604-2-6 (sc)
ISBN: 978-0-9883604-3-3 (ebk)
ISBN: 978-0-9883604-4-0 (ibk)

Printed in the United States of America

This book is dedicated to Ane Marie.
With hopes that someday she will tell me that I got it right.

Mosiah 3:2–3

2. *And the things which I shall tell you are made known unto me by an angel of God. And he said unto me: Awake; and I awoke, and behold he stood before me.*

3. *And he said unto me: Awake, and hear the words which I shall tell thee; for behold, I am come to declare unto you the glad tidings of great joy.*

This is the story of how I awoke.

PREFACE

*A*t times researching my ancestor was like looking through binoculars at the moon, knowing there was a person there, and trying to understand what she was thinking. Other times it was as though she were right beside me softly whispering in my ear. I just needed to step back, close my eyes, and listen.

I was in my fifties when I met her, though my whole life I had carried inside me the result of all her hopes and dreams. Her name was Ane Marie Madsen. She left her native Denmark as a young girl in 1856 with her parents and siblings, crossing an ocean and a continent in pursuit of the dream of an American Zion.

This book tells two stories: The consequences of the Madsen family's choice, which launched them into the Mormon pioneer crucible that was the Willie Handcart Company, and my own obsessive search to give substance to that story, to make real persons of the statistics, and to create linkages that span generations. Like many Latter-day Saint families, we Ericksens were vaguely aware that pioneer ancestors had set a course for us in the American West, but we hadn't probed into the finer points of that fact. A truly miraculous event changed that in a matter of minutes. We suddenly were off on a quest that continues to this day.

In the search we found parallels to our own lives. Life consists of responding to challenges, whatever the age and the circumstance. But we also found, in the annals of the Willie Company, events so unique to the pioneer experience that we can only stand in awe and gratitude to those real persons who experienced them. We have respectfully trod the Wyoming hills and valleys where only the ubiquitous winds still nose through the remnants of memory from that era. But I will never know the reality of their suffering and sacrifices. I can only send a muted but sincere "thank you" back across the generations to my great-great-grandfather Ole Madsen. Because of his selfless acts, my great-grandmother Ane Marie lived to become a thread in the tapestry of Sanpete County in central Utah—and in our own lives.

Thousands of similar Mormon pioneers, un-noted and unsung, quietly slipped into the amalgam that became our modern world. In grateful memory to all of them and especially to my own ancestors, I have chosen to recall this history and to put their unsung stories, to the best of my ability, to life and to song.

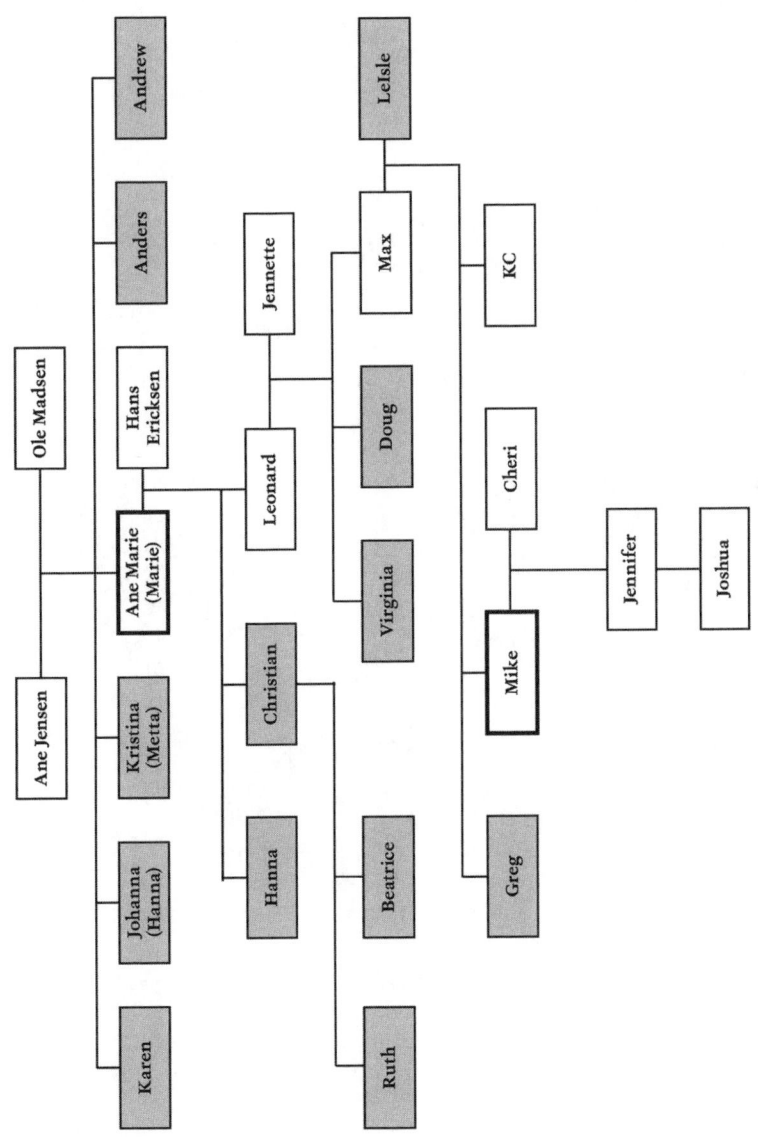

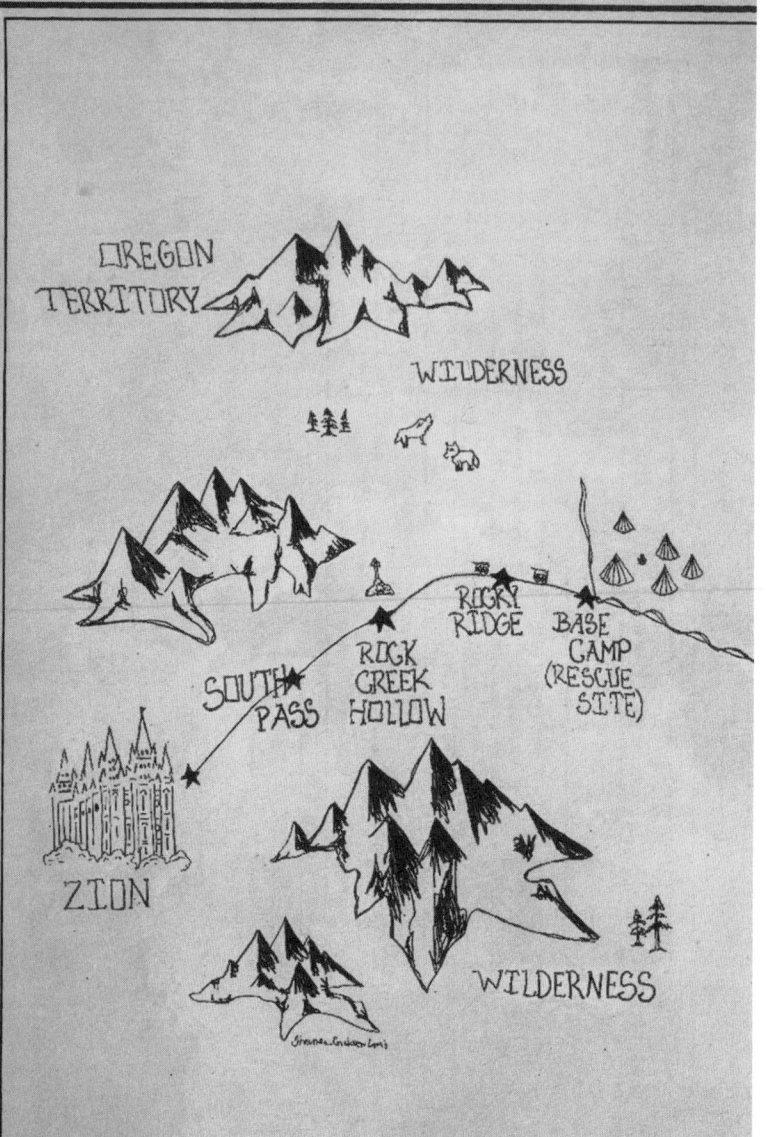

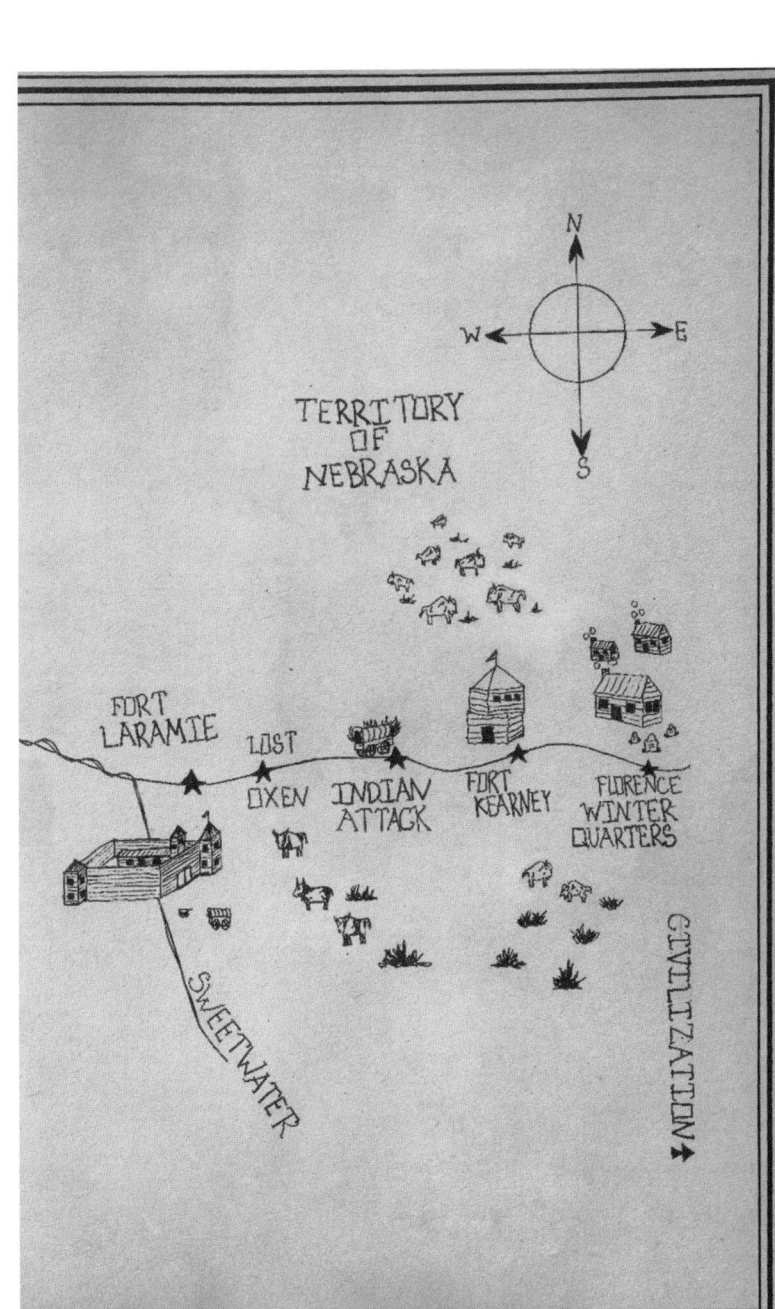

"We will gather experiences
that will follow us into eternity."
Peter Madsen,
Willie Handcart Co.

THEN

ℰ

September 1929

"With a slight hesitation /
I stand at the door…"
　　　　　　—Sonhar

*T*he day the Shoshone Indians came to town was the day Max's grandmother dropped dead at the dinner table. A passerby had announced the Indian's impending return, and although young Max was never allowed outside when they passed through town, this never ruined his excitement at their arrival.

Max, glued to the window, awaited any sign of their appearance—the thud of horse hooves against dry dirt or a moving dust cloud on the horizon. When he heard and saw nothing, he slumped back and restlessly bounced his hand on his knee.

Max lived in the small dusty town of Hamer, Idaho. It was the beginning of The Great Depression and many folks had abandoned their homes, farms and equipment, never to return. During this time, the Shoshone Indians were free to roam and usually passed through town twice a year.

As an adult Max later said his life in Hamer was not plagued with radios and televisions or other forms of fabricated entertainment and recreation. He relied on the wonders nature might offer to keep him entertained, and there were plenty.

Now, as a boy, he watched the cloud of dust form on the horizon miles out of town as the Shoshones' horses kicked up earth. They were headed to Camas Meadows as they had done for centuries to harvest the bulbs. In the spring and early summer the low-lying lands, wet with the spring run-off, came alive with blue-flowered camas so thick they created the appearance of a beautiful blue lake. The meadows were dry now, and beneath the camas plants were bulbs the natives used for food. It was a staple of their diet, one that helped them through the harsh winters of the high plateaus.

When the Shoshones came to town it meant trading time. The local townsfolk eagerly sought after the Indians' beautifully beaded gloves. The native women softened the glove's leather by chewing it, which eventually wore their teeth down to the gums.

In a few years Max would join the townsfolk in horse and merchandise trade. His father would help him pick out a beautiful bay pony with a deep black-brown hide that shone in the afternoon sunlight. For one silver dollar that pony would become Max's dream come true and make him a "real" cowboy. He would don his handmade black and white chaps, leather cuffs and bib overalls, retire the wooden broomstick that had once been his faithful sidekick and climb on his faithful pony, Topsy. In his imagination, they fought Indian wars and traveled on many cattle drives.

But today wasn't the day for those adventures. Today the only view Max got of the trading was from his bedroom window. He waited as patiently as a young child could until he was allowed outside to chase grasshoppers in the yard and visit his father at work.

Max's father, Leonard, managed the train depot. When Max came to visit he was always careful not to be near the tracks when a train passed. The train wheels kicked up rocks, making it dangerous. Some stones had previously splattered against the rough wood of the depot, and carved out their mark. Inside, his father tapped effortlessly on the telegraph key to contact other depots about the coming and going of trains and other news.

For many years the family lived in an apartment above the depot. At night, approaching trains shook their bodies, waking them long before the clanking of steel ever reached their ears. When the trains passed, their lights splashed against the walls of the family's upstairs bedroom, illuminating objects as all senses of sight, sound, touch and smell were awakened in the once-sleeping family. As time went on, they were eventually able to sleep through a train passing.

After Max visited the train depot, he took the eggs his grandmother, Ane Marie, had given him from the family's chicken coop, and traded them for hard candy at the local shop.

In the evening Max returned to the homestead for supper. He passed farm animals on his way: sheep, pigs, chickens and horses. He said hello to their mule, Napoleon Bonaparte, who helped work the farm. Inside, Max washed up before dinner. This meant removing his cowboy attire and washing his hands in the water basin in the front room. His older sister, Virginia, ran her fingers through his light brown hair to brush out any dirt. His mother, Jennette, had prepared vegetable stew and rolls for dinner. The stew was made with fresh carrots, corn and peas plucked from their vegetable garden, and dinner rolls were buttered with his mother's fresh-churned cream.

While the table was being set, Max played with his grandmother's music box by the hearth in the parlor. His grandmother had moved in with his family six months earlier after losing her husband, Hans, to pneumonia. Max opened the lid to start the cylinder turning and the steely sound of the song *Amaryllis* drifted through the house. The floor creaked and Max looked up to see his grandmother Ane Marie. Her gray hair was tied into a loose bun and eyeglasses sat on the end of her nose. She braced her fragile frame against a large brown sitting chair, lost in thought as she listened to the delicate sounds chiming from the box.

Max clicked the box closed as the song finished and saw a tear fall from his grandmother's cheek. "You okay, Grandma?" Max asked. There was a quiet nod. Jennette called the family to dinner and Max quickly scurried to the table with Grandmother trailing behind him.

It was a Tuesday in September, a day like any other, when Max had an experience he would never forget. They sat down to supper. His parents sat at either end of the table. Virginia and big brother Doug sat across from Max, who sat next to Grandmother Ane Marie. Max bowed his head and folded his arms as his father said a blessing over the food. After the prayer, and a resounding family "Amen," Max dipped his spoon into the stew and, careful not to spill, brought the spoon to his mouth. He took a bite of his roll and placed it on the dish before pulling his legs underneath him to sit on his knees, so he could more easily reach his meal.

"Did you get some candy for your eggs?" Grandmother Ane Marie asked. Max nodded, but decided not to tell them that the store owners also offered him candy for swear words. He didn't want to own up to the foul things he had said that day or he would get another mouth full of salt.

"Max, if you eat all your stew the dinner fairy will place a dime under your plate," his father said.

Max, wanting favor from fairies that rewarded good boys who ate their meals, gladly took another spoonful of stew into his mouth, careful not to spill. He glanced over at Grandma, who also was being careful to bring the spoon to her mouth without spilling. Her frame was small, and if Max sat up straight on his knees, he was easily the same height as his grandma, who slouched over her meal.

Ane Marie sensed Max's eyes on her and turned to look at him. The skin around her blue eyes drooped, but still hinted at a smile. She pushed her glasses up on her nose with the back of her hand and turned back to her meal.

She carefully dipped her spoon into the stew, paused, then with a sudden jerk her body stiffened, her hand went to her heart, and Ane Marie dropped dead. Her cheek smacked the edge of the stew bowl, its contents splattered on the dinner table and her head hit with a thud.

There was no one to call to carry her body away. Instead, the family laid Ane Marie in the parlor, placing silver dollars over her eyes and wrapping a towel around her chin to keep her head in place. Max's mother and sister were busy lighting candles and surrounding the body with blooming flowers picked from the garden both to beautify the simple bier and to conceal the bitter stench of death.

Max approached the parlor with trepidation. His grandmother's withered body, now dead and lifeless, lay before him. It was hard for him to understand how a person's life could disappear right before his eyes so suddenly.

His father stood in the middle of the parlor with his back toward Max, gazing at his mother lying on the table. His thin frame stood tall and his hands were folded over his chest. He watched his wife remove his mother's simple wedding band from her finger, careful to do so, as if Ane Marie could still feel pain or be bothered. Then Jennette carefully placed both of Ane Marie's hands on her abdomen, making it appear as if she were simply resting.

Leonard looked at the frown on his deceased mother's face and thought of the warm smile she had worn in life. That smile had offered him strength and courage over the years.

He recalled the times she had saved him from a whipping from his father when he got into mischief as a child—such as the time he told a neighbor that his mother was in want of chicken feed, requesting that she bring a bucket to their house. Earlier, as a practical joke, Leonard had emptied the bucket of chicken feed and filled it with heavy sand. The woman laboriously carried the weighty bucket seven blocks to his house and was rightfully angry when she realized the bucket had no feed in it. Then there was the time he had made Valentine cards and tied them to a string. He placed them on a person's doorstep and concealed himself in the bushes. When the person went to pick up the Valentine, he yanked it from their reach.

And always there had been his mother's smile.

Max watched his father carefully as he walked to the other side of the parlor. It gave the boy a better view of the focused features on his father's sad face. He studied his father's eyes. The usual softness in his gaze was there, but looked different now, and Max didn't understand the change. His father's thin lips pressed together and his hair, which was usually carefully parted in the middle and combed to each side, was disheveled, with strands falling into his eyes.

Max stared at his father, uncertain. Seeing his grandmother die before him was frightening, but not as upsetting as seeing his father in this moment.

"What is it, Max?" Leonard asked, seeing the fear in his son's eyes.

Max stared at his father, unsure. He didn't have the understanding or vocabulary to express his feelings.

Leonard crouched down and motioned to Max. He walked cautiously toward his father, who wrapped his arm around his son.

"Is this scary for you?" Leonard asked.

Max nodded and then looked into his father's clear blue eyes, "Grandmother is scary."

Leonard tightened his grasp around his son's small frame and looked into those anxious eyes, speaking intensely, "I have met great people, powerful men and prophets. But that lady, your grandmother, she is the greatest person I have ever, or will ever, meet." Leonard smiled and scooped Max into his arms.

Max didn't understand, but he knew enough to keep quiet. He looked again at his deceased grandmother, unable to see what his father saw. All he saw was a wrinkled, lifeless body.

Max rested his head on his father's shoulder and hugged his arms around his neck, letting the steady pulse of his father's heartbeat settle his fears.

Years later, Max would understand his father's words. His grandmother was totally unknown by the world's standard. Ane Marie was not a great leader, held no position, wrote not a single word about her life, wasn't heralded in a town history and was almost forgotten in time by most of her family. But everyone has a story. In time, through spiritual nudges and years of research, Ane Marie's story would finally be revealed.

NOW

ℰ❧

Winter 1996

"Sleep for both of us / All the night long."
—*Jenny's Lullaby*

*T*he little room in the basement didn't look the same. In reality, the world didn't feel the same. I slowly gazed around the small eight-foot square room lined with dark wallpaper lighted only by a small window to the backyard. With the bookcase, small roll-top desk, cheap keyboard and my guitar on an upright stand, there wasn't much room to turn around.

The room was my sanctuary when I had to write a talk for church, do family bills or, most importantly, play my guitar. Before claiming this room I had tried quietly playing my guitar while the family watched TV, or after dinner while the kids played, but my family grew tired of the background music. So this little room became that place.

I stood in the dark room feeling alone. It was very late and everyone else was asleep, if they were able to sleep. I often came to this room late at night to play the guitar or keyboard, but I didn't know why I was here now. I didn't feel like playing. I didn't want to think. But the thoughts lingered. "Where do we go from here? Are we going to be okay?"

I didn't think so.

My thoughts unwillingly retraced the days and months preceding this moment, like a song set to repeat. Then there was the horrid drive home today. A haunting emptiness had settled over the landscape as I drove. I'd have escaped into that emptiness if it meant I could leave the burdening pillars of weight behind. I naively thought returning home would bring me some comfort. I thought I could leave the past behind, by simply returning to the house with its familiar feeling of peace. I was wrong.

Driving home, I had watched the snow fall in a slow scattered pattern, between a dark winter storm and the sun breaking through. It was as if the earth were pausing somewhere in between summer and winter; it was a day to invoke no feeling, which is where I wanted to be—beyond feeling. It was late morning and my daughter Jennifer and I were driving home from the hospital.

Neither of us spoke, drowning in an unfathomable pain. We just stared at the random snowflakes. I couldn't muster up the simplest form of a sentence. To even attempt to put into words what I was feeling would be as difficult as describing the taste of salt.

After some time in this quiet void, I turned on the CD player. A soft and beautiful song called *Snow* drifted from the stereo and filled the car. It created a dreamlike ambience that could have lulled me to sleep as it spoke of a world disappearing under precipitation's white blanket. In later years, I would refer to it as *Joshua's Song* and it would be a long time before I would listen to it again. Even now it is difficult to think about Joshua, to imagine that he is out there and he doesn't know Jennifer, his lovely birth mother, or me.

I had thought that our family was moving along on the right path. I had always believed my girls would grow up living the ideal that I wanted for them. I had it in my head that they would do well in school, attend church, hug the guy on their first date, meet someone later, marry, have kids. Simple. Easy. Right.

We had the usual family struggles: getting our kids up and ready for school on time, inspiring them to attend church, struggling with them through homework and getting good grades. There were the expected teenage rebellions but no challenges that could derail us. We had a routine life that included our faith as members of The Church of Jesus Christ of Latter-day Saints and an outlook of hope and excitement for what the future held.

Jennifer always had a special way about her. She was, and still is, smart, bubbly and full of life. She is a very caring person and possesses a high level of empathy. Even at a young age she championed the downtrodden. She was always aware of social issues and challenged and corrected me on any comment I flippantly made about minorities or social injustice.

One day, Jenny and I were walking across a parking lot where we both worked, when a volcano of black tar erupted a hundred yards ahead. A crew was adding slurry to the parking lot when an explosion shot a black tar-like substance all over the street and a large swath of lawn. A walking blob of dripping goop staggered away from the truck. I turned to tell one of the workers, who had not noticed the accident, that one of his associates was in trouble. Jenny, on the other hand, ran directly to the injured man. My first thought was to tell her to stop, as I didn't know how dangerous it was. Instead I followed, running a few yards behind her.

The way Jenny ran toward the scene taught me once again the special nature of her spirit. While my first thought was to turn the problem over to someone else, Jenny's first thought was to run and help, regardless of who needed the help.

It's strange to think about that day, compared to the day I was walking home from church and saw Jenny waiting for me in the driveway, leaning up against the car. I smiled to myself as I saw her from afar. Her long brunette hair had a slight curl. She was wearing a long flower-patterned dress that accentuated her thin, young teenage body. As I walked closer, I looked for what I expected would be the familiar smile. Instead, there was a look of thoughtful concern. "I'm pregnant," she said.

I leaned against the car, my mouth dry with fear. Her words refused to register in my mind, but were painfully loud in my gut. In a matter of moments, I awakened to a life that wasn't mine. It was like peering into a dark hidden world that I wasn't supposed to know about and that my mind didn't want to believe existed.

I don't remember a word after that until I said we needed to go inside and talk about this with her mother. My wife, Cheri, was in the bedroom changing out of her church clothes. I think she knew in an instant, from the pale look on my face, that something was coming she didn't want to hear. After the words were spoken, she simply sat on the bed and wept. Jenny sat with her and cried.

Not a moment in the next several months was easy. Not only did we struggle to hold on to our relationship with Jenny and the continuity of our family, I also agonized over our place in the church and how our situation looked to others. It took a lot of prayer and soul-searching. My shattered expectations left behind festering splinters of my perceived failings as a father and I was sure everyone believed as I did, that I had failed as a parent.

Cheri was better at the rough spots and the moments when it was hard just to carry on. She taught me that dealing with problems takes time and a lot of focused attention; there are no quick fixes. Somewhere along the line, I really can't pinpoint the moment, I forgot about myself and what others thought and focused on the love I had for Jenny. After all, no matter how hard it was for me, I knew what she was going through was worse. It broke my heart when she cried, and all I could do was stay by her and stroke her hair. I had no words to console her.

I am still haunted by what I saw in the hospital on a very dark night just before our ride the next morning in the snow. It helped me understand what love truly is. Jennifer had made the decision, hard and painful as it was, to give the baby up for adoption. She had come to the same point we had come to, but it had to be her choice.

After the birth, Cheri and I had gone home, but not being able to sleep, we went back to the hospital late at night. Jenny lay in the bed holding her beautiful baby boy. How attached to this little soul she was and her love for him was obvious. She had a little smile on her face as she looked at his tiny face. The baby was asleep as she quietly hummed a song to him. I asked her if she was tired and needed sleep. She looked up and quietly said, "He will sleep for both of us. I don't want to miss a moment of my time with him." She paused, "I think perhaps if I hold him, and he hears my heart beat, that he will remember it, that he will remember me." Her touching words unglued me.

The following morning, we returned to the hospital and Cheri helped Jennifer as they quietly and carefully dressed Joshua in a special outfit they had picked out together. I wondered what his new parents would name him. To us, he would forever be Joshua.

Then Jenny held the baby, stroked his little head, kissed him and whispered something to him. She stood next to her mother, laid Joshua gently in the wheeled bed, then turned to me and said, "Please take him." The social worker was waiting down the hall.

Jenny turned and held her mother tight, burying her head into her chest while they softly cried together.

In that moment I lost my resolve to see the adoption through. I had been so sure of the path and was relieved Jenny had chosen adoption, but now I wasn't ready to give up my grandson. I wanted Jenny to be absolutely sure, because I wasn't. I wanted her to look at him once more. I started, "Jenny, please..."

"Please take him," Cheri said, and neither looked up.

I turned and wheeled the baby out the door as mother and daughter held each other and wept.

I was proud of my daughter and even more proud of the way our family gathered around her and each other. Our ward and its leadership had been doing what they could, but how easily the phrase, "It's going to be okay," was thrown around. I can say that there were times when it was not going to be okay, and I couldn't see my way ahead. I prayed hard for my daughter and for our family. I couldn't pray for myself because I didn't feel I deserved it. I wondered if we would ever sit and carelessly talk again. I wondered if we would hold together through this, if the inner struggles each of us went through would ever allow us to be a simple family again—talking about a test at school, an accomplishment or a funny show someone had watched.

I finally sat at the keyboard and turned it on the most ethereal setting it had and pushed the black and white keys, trying to get lost in the doleful digitized sound. My thoughts, though I tried to block them, kept going back to Cheri and Jenny holding each other while I, the confused idiot, took the child away, begging for them to look one more time.

I pushed the keys as the words slipped in with them, *It might be all right, if she just holds on tight,* I thought as I pushed the keys a hundred times over, *Then closing her eyes to hide the hopeless tide inside.* Was there an illusion that could hide this? Was there a thought that could take charge and make this one stop repeating in my mind?

Suddenly, I remembered Jennifer's smile as she lay in bed with that little baby, saying to me that she didn't want to miss a moment of time with him. The song unfolded and came out as a lullaby. For the first time I clearly saw the scope of what had taken place in the hospital room very late at night between a mother and little son as they came to terms with the sorrows of life. I thought of the incomprehensible ability we have to sacrifice at such a profound level of love.

I played the keyboard until the lullaby was finished, grateful for the role music played in my life. It seemed so simple in a lot of ways, to use a basic melody to pull away from myself. To ease the pain and hide my feelings deep within a metaphor that only I understood. I couldn't have foreseen that my quiet and dark night of the soul would start me down a path of expression through song.

When I went to bed that night, the rhythm of the lullaby still lingered in my thoughts. I slid over to my sleeping wife and held her tight.

The upcoming months were filled with grief, abated by my family's love and support, and my songwriting. In years to come, the grief dwindled, but the pain of the loss always lurked and opened its dark corridor when triggered. During these times, one family member in particular provided me the strength and courage I needed to let go of the past, and embrace life on the sturdy wings of faith. At this time, I didn't know who she was, or even her name, but within months she would step into my view to offer answers to some of life's hard questions. She would help me discover who I am, how I got here, and most importantly, who I want to be. She was my great-grandmother, Ane Marie, and though she lived before I was born, her life would speak loud and clear to my heart. Over time, she became the inspiration for more songs.

As I learned of her life, *Jenny's Lullaby* would later be dedicated to Ane Marie, and played at firesides across the nation celebrating pioneer heritage. The song, when played, went unsung. I never wanted to hear those haunting words again. I would play this music in reverence for Ane Marie and her legacy. For what I would learn of her life would put my own hardships into perspective.

NOW

&

Summer 1967

"We set ourselves to wander /
Across the span of years."
—*Set to Wander*

*A*s a boy, I lived the typical American childhood. I attended school, played baseball and learned to ride a bicycle. Music was important to me, and I spent a considerable amount of time spinning the records of Moody Blues and Moby Grape.

In 1967 I was seventeen, and despite being busy with sports, friends, and pulling weeds for my parents, I found time to visit my grandmother, Jennette. She was living alone, her husband, Leonard, having died years earlier. She lived just around the corner from my house. Her small apartment was added to the back of a house. Like the rest of the house, it seemed like an afterthought.

I was mostly there because she had Dr. Pepper in the fridge and candy bowls full of spice gumdrops and lemon teardrops sitting on the side tables in the living room. It reminded me of *Hansel and Gretel,* except my grandmother didn't want to eat me. Instead, she wanted to bribe me into staying so she could feed me stories, poems and songs she had collected through her 70-plus years.

She opened the door with a sudden surprised smile as if she'd just won the Publisher's Clearing House. I greeted her with a hug, and she smiled and called me Michael instead of Mickey, as everyone else did. Within minutes of being invited in, I was seated comfortably on her couch, one hand full of gumdrops, the other holding a nice cool Dr. Pepper.

Grandma sat next to me. She always dressed nice, usually wearing a button-up blouse and matching skirt. Her once-rich chocolate-brown hair was white with age. She wore it short and in small curls.

She asked me how my day was, and I responded, like always, as a typical teenager with short, non-descriptive answers: "good," "great," "fine."

On one occasion I remember visiting Grandma and seeing an algebra textbook sitting on her coffee table. When I asked her about it, she said she was studying it. I told her she didn't need to learn it. I mean, it was algebra. What use could it be to my grand-mother, who was in her late seventies? When I asked her why she was studying it, she responded, "Because I never learned it."

She was also an avid poet, and had been most her life. Every time I visited her she read aloud a new poem she was working on. She shared one, as I sat and slurped my soda.

> *Each day we live, we write a page*
> *A record all our own*
> *For God to keep or erase*
> *According to the seeds we have sown.*
> *For what you are, is God's gift to you.*
> *And what you take back to Him is your*
> *Gift to God.*

Once she finished reading, I told her I liked it. When I was younger she used to have me memorize poems and songs. I figured it was an old habit from her days as a Primary teacher.

She went on to tell me about my great-grandmother who used to have to carry buckets of water yoked to her like an oxen, taken from a stream to her house. I wasn't very attentive, as I was more focused on cooling off and gorging on treats. But like a good grandson, I feigned interest while popping another gumdrop into my mouth.

I grew up hating genealogy. It was stiff, old and musty—a project for old people. In those days it wasn't easy to trace your ancestors. You couldn't go online and search for your family history in the comfort of your own home. You had to pore over written records hidden away in books or listen to stories that your grandmother passed on to you.

"You know your great-grandmother emigrated from Denmark when she was only ten years old?" my grandmother said, adjusting her glasses as she launched into another story. I savored the imitation cherry-flavored gumdrop as my tongue swirled it in my mouth, and nodded in an attempt to show some interest.

"She once told me about a girl who was traveling with her when they crossed the plains who was so cold and starved she began eating her own fingers," my grandmother said. "She said that little girl died before they made it to Utah, and she used to say she was grateful that the Lord took that little child."

I looked at my grandmother, perplexed, and took a swig of Dr. Pepper. I had never experienced anything so horrific before. Because of this, the story was like a fairy tale—nothing I could relate to or possibly understand at my age.

My own first real experience with loss was when I was ten years old and Jennette's husband, my grandfather, Leonard, died. That was the first event that took me out of myself to a terrifying place where the world was no longer safe. Change became inevitable, and security a luxury you couldn't hold on to.

There were five of us kids in the family, four boys and a girl. Greg was the oldest, being eleven at the time and I was next at ten. KC was eight, followed by Robyn, the little sister and the princess, who was six. The baby, Steven, was five. I remember coming home from school and getting the news about my grandfather's death. After that, life felt different. Being only ten years old, I tried to figure out what that difference meant. All we kids knew about his passing was that he was gone and we wouldn't see him until the funeral.

I was confused as to where my grandfather had gone. I saw the sadness in my parent's faces, and experienced, for the first time, the uncertainty of change. I slowly began to understand that the comfortable and safe feelings of happiness that I was used to were not feelings I could hold forever.

That night, all of us kids slept together in a large bed in the basement, huddled with the light on. It was silent as my mother tucked us in, each of us lost in his or her own little world of thought.

"Mom," KC said, interrupting our reverie, "What would you do if you saw Grandpa?"

We all lay there, hanging on his words and bracing for her answer. Now, looking back, I would have expected her to say something profound about the Church's teachings, or that Grandpa was in Heaven and was fine. I later came to understand that her answer was more intricate and profound than I could have imagined.

My mother looked down at all of us and quietly replied, "I would give him a hug." Then she reached down and gave my brother a kiss and walked away.

Grandmother Jennette died twenty years later. At her passing, I thought of our visits and what Mother had said about Grandpa. A tinge of remorse hung in the air as I wished for the chance to see her again, to be able to give her a hug. Given the chance, instead of being concerned with Dr. Pepper and gumdrops, I would listen to her stories and hang on her every word.

THEN

ℰ

April 23, 1856

*"It's not how far you journey on /
Just with whom you walk along."*
—*Tyme*

*A*s the steamboat *Rhoda* pulled away from the dock in Copenhagen, Denmark, ten-year-old Ane Marie watched her sister, Karen, standing motionless on the dock. Ane Marie wondered if her sister would cry as she herself had done, but all she saw in her sister's eyes, as Karen grew smaller in the distance, was a blank stare.

Ane Marie stood with her father, Ole, her mother, Ane Jensen, and the rest of her siblings, Johanna, Kristina and Andrew, and watched the dock and its people disappear. With the steady pulse of the ship's steam engine all sight of land disappeared, leaving them surrounded by gray-green water.

Eventually the family would be forced to go below decks since their tickets were clearly marked "steerage." Until then Ane Marie would stay on deck with her family, feeling the slow rhythmic rock of the boat that pushed her far from home.

For Ane Marie, any excitement she previously had was replaced by a feeling of loss. Hours later her homeland disappeared completely and her tears stopped, leaving her skin dry and crusted. She was only ten but had an unrelenting tenacity. The loss of her sister was difficult to accept, but she would wipe her tears and move on. She drew on her faith, hoping that at the end of their journey, they would live in a place akin to Heaven on earth. A place called Zion.

On the dock, Karen stood holding her last few possessions and staring at the empty water. The morning wore on and the people around her disappeared. She tucked a few loose strands of dark hair into her bonnet, drew in a deep breath and turned away from the receding steamship that held her family. Only a few tears escaped her red eyes and she quickly wiped them away.

"Are you okay, Miss?" a woman asked.

Her black hair was wrapped in a bun with ringlets framing her face.

Karen nodded.

"Were you saying goodbye?" the woman asked.

"Yes," Karen regained her composure, "My family is traveling to America." She made sure not to mention they were Mormon converts traveling to "Zion," a place Karen deemed mythical.

"The American Fever." The woman nodded. "My brother and his family have it, too. Why did a young girl like you stay behind?"

"I am almost eighteen," Karen retorted, "and I have family here who need me." A tear escaped with those words. She quickly turned from the stranger. "I must be going."

"Good luck to you, Miss," the woman said.

Karen grabbed her belongings and left. She traveled to the heart of Copenhagen, bought a train ticket with the money her father had given her and returned home to Tornved, alone.

She had spent the past three years watching her family be absorbed into a religious fervor she did not understand. Unlike them she was not ready to leave behind everything she had always known. She would think of her family every day. She would think of the evenings spent reading together in the family room with her sisters, helping her mother cook and watching her father drink watered-down tea. Karen wished them farewell in all of her recollections and hoped, with all her heart, that they would make it safely to Utah Territory.

THEN

ಬ

Winter 1853

"Though I was awake / I started to dream."
—Requiem

$\mathcal{I}$n the winter of 1853, the children of the earth were striding their way into a new world. They looked past their collective parents to a carnival of endless rides and peered toward a midway of choices, as if all at once. The Age of Enlightenment had fully blanketed Europe and flourished in America. The debate was on about the proposed Gadsden Purchase from Mexico. It would add almost 30,000 square miles to America, comprising a large part of the nascent state of New Mexico. The first elevator with auto brakes would soon find its way into American architecture, facilitating what would be an endless rise in man's desire to build modern Babel towers. The gold rush to California and the call of westward expansion still lured thousands of Americans, while thousands from the European countries sought the blessings of the New World. As winter asserted itself in Europe, Charles Darwin received an award for his recent work on natural selection. The world was in frenetic motion.

Could this world of competing ideas and innovation provide meaning for a poor farmer from Denmark? It seems so, but perhaps in a subtler yet meaningful way than one might imagine. Certainly it became so with time.

Ole Madsen was that Danish farmer. He was poor, to say the least. When he married the widow Ane Jensen, he gained a small wheat farm and four stepchildren. Her children were grown, but Ole and Ane had six children of their own. Their children were smart, with unique personalities, yet still much like their parents. Karen, the oldest, was a spirited and independent girl who could spin quite a tale, just like her father—except Ole had the good sense to admit his stories weren't true.

Johanna, his second oldest, was a leader, much like his wife, Ane. At times, Johanna's determination came off as being bossy. Kristina came next and was considered the sweetest of the bunch. She still had bouts of stubbornness, just like her father and the youngest daughter, Ane Marie, called Marie for short. She was named after her mother, and was a lot like her. "Idealistic and determined dreamers," Ole called them. "Single-minded to a fault." Anders was next, but had sadly died when he was a baby. The youngest, Andrew, was only three years old, but showed signs of being another independent spirit.

Their small cottage in Tornved was enough for the five children. Beds were shared, with Ole and Ane sleeping on a pull-out bed in the living room.

After work one winter evening, Ole was leaving his job at the tavern and learned that two Mormon missionaries were coming to preach in a neighbor's barn the next evening. He mentioned this to Ane after dinner, and she suggested he go hear the preaching so they could better understand this new religion.

Ole was a seeker of truth. He spent time reading and studying the philosophies of The Enlightenment and reveled in the discovery of new knowledge.

Prior to The Enlightenment, Lutheranism had been the only religion in Denmark since King Christian III broke with Roman Catholicism in 1536. The Danes were seldom exposed to other religions, as immigration was rare. Landowners believed they had ownership over their workers, and peasants could leave this serfdom only by paying off the landowner, or by fleeing. The possibility of a new religion or new ideas was not considered. By 1848, a demand for democracy broke the bonds of Danish Monarchy. Wars for independence broke out across the country. With the end of absolute monarchy, there was freedom of religion, assembly and speech and the age of Enlightenment was entrenched in Denmark. Not only were Danish emigrating, but outsiders were coming in. Local ministers allowed missionaries of different faiths to preach at their church services. As Mormons began preaching, whole congregations were being converted and Mormons became unpopular amongst devout Lutherans.

In Denmark, it was believed that individuals were predestined to remain in the station into which they were born. Mormons preached otherwise and became quickly disliked. Their preaching was banned from local churches and relegated to farmhouses that folks offered as meeting places.

The next day, after Ole finished his work at the tavern, he walked to Jensen's barn to join in the novelty of hearing the Mormon missionaries preach. He enjoyed the silence and simplicity of his solitary walk. The snow fell lightly, with several inches of it on the ground. He took a shortcut across a field where he spotted footprints. He avoided getting snow in his boots by stepping in the previous tracks. The path let out onto the main dirt path that was both muddy and icy. Ole followed along the wooden fence, woven like a basket, until he reached an opening to the barn. It was growing darker now, the windows of the barn illuminated as lanterns were lit inside.

The barn held a gathering of neighbors. Ole brushed the snow from his hat and beard and greeted several friends with hand-shakes. He noticed some men had their pockets full of produce. Ole mused, no doubt as to where those spoiled goods would end up soon.

Dusk was upon them, and more lanterns were being lit as a hush fell over the crowd. The cold of winter deadened the sweet smell of hay that had previously filled the barn. A man introducing himself as Elder Petersen stood on a crate. He was dressed in working-class garb, wearing a dark, knee-length frock coat and a short-rimmed felt bowler hat. He clutched a small green leather-bound book with gold-trimmed pages. An ornate flower design was embroidered on the front. He held it to his chest, choosing to reveal it when the time was right. He knew that on a good day of preaching he risked being the target of spoiled goods and slander-ous remarks, and on a bad day, being beaten by a mob or jailed.

"Brothers, I thank you for gathering here tonight." The crowd of men quieted, and Elder Petersen scanned the room. He waited for complete silence before he spoke again.

"I call you brothers because that is what you are to me, just as Christ was our brother and our Savior. A Savior who would pro-vide a way for the church as it existed during his days on earth to be restored again in these latter days. The church, as organized by Christ in his time, did not survive the persecutions of the first cen-turies. But God has provided a way, with modern-day revelation, for His church to be restored so that He may gather His Saints together."

That was the clincher: "modern-day revelation." An addition to the *Bible* was unheard of, not to mention blasphemous. There was a brief murmur in the crowd.

"A prophet and apostles walk the earth today," he said with intensity, letting every word sink in. "They live in a country founded on a constitution that allows them to speak without censorship, to believe as they choose. God speaks today as in the time of Jesus, and He spoke personally to a simple farm boy, not a king or squire, but a simple farmer like you." Elder Petersen motioned to the audience. "And here are His words written in the *Book of Mormon*." He held up the book. An egg thrown from the back splattered on his left shoulder.

The crowd laughed. Elder Petersen spoke louder. "There is a prophet who walks among us today!" He shook the *Book of Mormon* in the air. A flung tomato smashed into the book.

Ole stood in the back and watched the scene unfold. "At least the men are putting their spoiled goods to use," he muttered.

Elder Petersen lowered the book, wiping off the remains of the splattered tomato with a kerchief he had retrieved from his inside jacket pocket. A man approached the Elder with a bottle of whiskey and demanded he drink. Elder Petersen ignored this attempt to belittle him, and the man took a swig for himself. The brief lapse in preaching stirred the crowd. They yelled freely as the produce flew.

"Devil!"

"Blasphemy!"

The crowd jeered.

Ole watched as the missionary stood soberly on the crate while the produce hit him. "If you would but pray to God you could receive the truthfulness of my words for yourselves!"

Ole scratched his head, losing interest as the crowd quickly grew into a mob. He tousled his short brown graying hair, matted down with sweat from a day's work, then ran a hand over his unkempt beard before donning his wide brown felt hat and leaving.

Ole's leather boots crackled as he strode through the snow away from the barn. The clouds had lifted on the horizon and the sunset's red glow peeked through. Ole had paused to admire the warm glow of light on the rolling white hills dotted with hickory trees when he saw two men climb out the side window of the Jensen barn. He recognized one as the Mormon preacher.

The two men quickly forged a path through the snow toward the main road heading east. Ole was no more than twenty feet from them when he called, "I think you are safe for now, but I don't expect that will last long."

Both men looked at Ole, unsure if he was with the mob. Assured by the smile in Ole's soft blue eyes, Elder Petersen spoke. "It would not be the first time." The dark-haired man with the Elder nodded in agreement.

"Tell me," Ole began, "What does he look like?"

The two men exchanged glances, "Who would that be?" Elder Petersen asked.

"The prophet," Ole said, "What does he look like?"

The Elder approached Ole with an extended hand, "My name is Elder Petersen. This is my companion, Elder Nielsen," he motioned to his companion.

"Ole Madsen." He shook the Elder's hand.

They heard yelling from the barn.

"It is getting dark." Elder Nielsen fidgeted. "We must go."

Elder Petersen nodded and turned back to Ole. "Joseph Smith is dead, Ole. He was shot by a mob nine years ago."

The men turned to leave when Ole said, "Doesn't sound like freedom to me."

Elder Petersen turned back, "I did not say there was not a price." He handed a pamphlet to Ole, touched his shoulder, and walked away.

Ole glanced at the pamphlet entitled *En Sandheds-Rest,* "The Voice of Truth." He tucked it into his jacket pocket and walked home.

*   *   *

"Mother, come look!" Karen called from the front room. Their white cottage had a sod roof covering a family room, kitchen and a bedroom the children shared. The outhouse lay nestled between cypress trees in the back. Karen had spent the greater part of the afternoon in the living room rearranging what little furniture they had.

Ane wiped her hands on her apron and stepped into the living room.

"What do you think?" Karen asked.

Ane's hair was parted in the middle and pulled back into two braids with the sides puffed out over her ears. The braids wound into a bun that was coming loose. She fussed over it as she surveyed the room. "You have scattered the chairs. How are we supposed to sit together as a family?" Ane stepped back into the kitchen to slice potatoes.

Karen huffed. Mother always encouraged her to think for herself, but when she did, mother was sure to have an opinion about it. Karen glanced down at the dirt collected on her green cotton dress and frantically brushed it off, smoothing out the folds and adjusting the matching ribbon in her hair.

The kitchen's heavy wooden door opened and clanked shut, signaling Ole's return. Karen rushed her father, bombarding him with questions.

"Did you see them Father? The Mormons? What did they look like? What did they say? I hear they are charming serpents that preach utter nonsense."

"Karen!" Ane chastised, "Do not repeat such gossip. Hush and let your father speak."

Ole took off his hat and set it on the table. A rooster strode along the table and pecked at the brim of the hat.

"Perhaps she would listen to what I have to say if my words were wrapped in a bow." Ole smiled and leaned down to kiss his daughter's cheek.

"Father, you're filthy," Karen complained.

Ole took his hat from the pecking rooster and hung it on a nail by the door, along with his old knee-length frock coat, revealing his dirty trousers and cotton shirt.

"What did they say, Father?" Karen persisted.

"They didn't have time to say much of anything. The mob was after them at the first sign of new thought. *Middag?*" Dinner? Ole looked to his wife.

Ane sliced an onion in half. "*Suppe.*" Soup. Ole rubbed his stomach in anticipation.

The rooster crowed as it strutted along the table.

"Karen, be useful and get that rooster out of here," Ane said.

Karen frowned, not wanting to go out in the cold.

Ane looked at her unwilling daughter and relented. "Finish chopping the onion then."

She grabbed the rooster by its feet and let it hang upside down, squawking and flapping its wings, as she carried it to the door.

"Let me take him," Ole offered, grabbing the legs and stepping back into the cold. He carried the rooster to its small shelter, a cage that sat next to a hen house covered in straw. He threw the rooster in and quickly returned to the warmth of the house.

Karen obediently chopped the onions as Ane set out bowls. Ole kicked the snow off his boots, grabbed the pamphlet the Mormons had given him and proceeded to his usual chair in the family room. He sat, unaware that his chair was facing a different direction due to Karen's new arrangement. His four youngest clamored about in the bedroom, but the noise didn't distract him from his thoughts.

The idea of modern-day revelation to a simple farm boy was both perplexing and stirring. He read the pamphlet cover-to-cover several times before dinner. Its claims were so far from what he had learned growing up he wasn't sure what to think of them. The pamphlet spoke of prophets and apostles on the earth in his day. It told of Joseph Smith's First Vision when Christ and God the Father appeared to him, and explained that the Godhead was made up of three separate beings: God the Father, and His son Jesus Christ whose images are the same as man's, and then the Holy Ghost who exists only in spirit. Separate beings, but joined together in unity and purpose. Ole had always been taught that God was a being without a body and that the Godhead was an entity incorporating Father, Son and Holy Ghost in one. What he read not only stated that God had a body but that man could obtain a God-like perfection through obedience and faith. The pamphlet did not speak of heaven and hell but of three separate kingdoms of glory where men would go after death and judgment, depending on their degree of worthiness. It also briefly mentioned a pre-existence, stating that men had once been spirits before they gained a body of flesh when born into mortality.

He read on as the pamphlet outlined the first principles and ordinances of the gospel. First being faith, something they said was sought through obedience and not given as a gift from God. Second was repentance, then baptism through immersion and receiving of the Gift of the Holy Ghost by the laying on of hands. How different this was from anything Ole had known as a Lutheran! The idea that baptism was done at the age of accountability, and that grace was given by obedience and not something simply afforded to the individual. And the laying on of hands? Did these men really have power from God to give the Gift of the Holy Ghost by the authority of the Priesthood?

He mused on the subject until Ane beckoned him to dinner.

"Are you thinking about the Mormons?" Ane asked.

"They do have some interesting things to say."

"Why not invite them to dinner? I would be interested to hear it as well."

"Ane, you have already married the bastard son of a tailor; do you really want to associate yourself with Mormons too?" Ole teased, "You are a lot braver than I thought."

Ane smiled. "Do you like what Karen has done?" She motioned to the furniture.

Ole glanced around, becoming aware of the altered surroundings. "I always told you she had talent."

"Do you ever take anything seriously?" Ane questioned.

Ole looked at his wife for a long time before nodding. "The men preaching said that God has restored His church on the earth as it used to be during Jesus' time."

"And how did God do that?"

"Modern-day revelation."

Ane lifted an eyebrow.

"They said that God appeared to their prophet and gave him new scripture."

"And who was this prophet? Their king?"

"No, just a man, a farm boy they said." Ole sat in silence for a moment. "It makes sense."

"The individual to whom God gives the office, he also gives the intellect," Ane said, quoting the Danish monarchy.

"I hope that is truer in this instance than it has been with our government," Ole smiled.

"At least the Monarchy has crumbled. Soon we may be able to purchase our own land," Ane said.

"I look forward to that day," Ole nodded.

Ane's figure became nothing more than a shadow as the fire dwindled. Ole added wood to the fire and Ane used the flame to light candles she placed in candlesticks on the dining table. The family gathered together to eat, and afterward they assembled around the fire as they always did.

Some evenings were spent with each one involved in his or her own craft, reading or playing with toys. Other nights, the family sat together and read stories from the *Bible,* but the girls' favorite stories were the ones Ole liked to spin.

Andrew sat comfortably in his mother's lap, his eyelids heavy. He let out fitful cries every few minutes as he resisted sleep.

"Do you wish me to take him to bed?" Kristina offered.

"No Metta." Ane stroked his soft curls. "He will be asleep soon."

Kristina nodded. She was only nine years old, but found comfort in being helpful, even though she often wished to help only when she could control a particular situation in her favor. In this instance, she preferred Andrew be put to bed so the girls could speak without whispering. It also gave her the opportunity to lean against her mother while she read. She was much like Karen in this regard, but Karen had the talent of sharing her opinions freely whereas Kristina dared not cross her mother.

Kristina sat on the floor next to Marie, who held her favorite toy, a porcelain doll, close to her chest. Kristina remembered when the doll had been hers, but upon seeing Marie's favor for it, she let her have it. The doll never left Marie's side. Kristina wondered if it was because the doll resembled Mother so much. It had the same brown hair and pale skin with brown eyes. The doll's hair was done up in a bun, just as their mother's always was.

"May I read aloud tonight?" Johanna asked her father. He had repositioned his chair back near the fireplace.

"What would you like to read?"

"*Den Lille Havfrue,*" Johanna said. It told the tale of a mermaid willing to give up her life in the sea for a human soul and life on land.

"But I want to hear one of Papa's stories," Marie protested.

"We will do both tonight," Ane said, "It is good for Hanna to practice her reading." Marie nodded in compliance.

Johanna grabbed the book, *Fairy Tales,* a compilation that included *Den Lille Havfrue,* from the end table and sat in a chair next to her father. The crackling fire provided enough light for her to read.

Andrew quickly fell asleep and the girls listened to Johanna read. Ole looked at his daughter with admiration, but his thoughts drifted elsewhere, pondering the pamphlet.

"'Your tail will then disappear,'" Johanna read on, "'and shrink up into what mankind calls legs, and you will feel great pain, as if a sword were passing through you.'"

"I don't understand," Kristina interrupted. "Why would she give up her family and life as a mermaid to feel such pain in hopes of living with a prince?"

"Because she was in love," Karen sighed. "People will do anything for love."

"Would you?" Kristina asked.

"Of course I would." Karen smiled dreamily.

"Is it time for one of Papa's stories?" Marie asked impatiently.

Ole smiled, "Yes, I think it is time I tell you about *The Master Fool.*"

Marie smiled with anticipation, as this was one she had not heard before.

"Once there was a woman who had a very foolish boy. One day the boy asked his mother if he could go to town to sell their butter."

"Did the boy look like Hans?" Kristina asked, referring to a boy from a neighboring farm.

Ole considered, "He looked similar to Hans in his eyes, but his face was much older and he was beginning to grow hair on his chin."

Kristina nodded and listened.

"So the boy—"

"Can we call him Hans?" Marie interrupted.

"Shush you two," Ane piped in, "Let your father finish his story."

Ole smiled and finished the story of the foolish boy who ended up lucky and married a princess. The girls interrupted him twice more, as was their way, before Ole finished the story and offered a prayer before bed.

The family hung their heads as Ole recited *The Lord's Prayer.* When he finished, the girls stood obediently, gave their father a kiss on the cheek and thanked him for the story before filing off to bed. Karen took a lit candle to the bedroom with her. Kristina carefully lifted Andrew from her mother's lap and carried him to the smaller bed he shared with Marie. The older girls shared the larger of the two beds.

Ole and Ane stayed in the family room sharing the silence of the house. They both gazed at the flames that licked the air. Minutes later, Ole spoke, "I often feel like the fool who is waiting for his luck to change."

"You are that fool," Ane teased. "You have more than what you were born into. Has God not blessed you?"

"He has," Ole agreed. "But I was born in a world where things did not change, and in my lifetime, everything has changed."

"Are you thinking about the Mormons?" Ane always knew where Ole's mind was going before he did.

Ole paused. A floorboard creaked near the bedroom doorway. The girls hovered unseen near the opening, listening, not quite ready to sleep.

"Hmm. I have been thinking, maybe I should have told the girls about the troll." He looked at Ane knowingly.

"You could not tell them that dreadful story, Ole. The horrifying truth of it would frighten them senseless!" Ane played along.

"Yes, but it is for their safety," Ole said.

"I suppose you're right," Ane sighed.

Ole quietly sneaked unseen to a chair paces from the doorway as Ane continued. "They should know about the gruesome, savage troll, with ears like a donkey and eyes like a wolf." The girls listened, not making a sound. "Who comes out at night to capture disobedient girls who sneak out of bed!"

Ole sprang from his hiding place and charged the doorway. The girls screamed and fled back to their beds, pulling blankets over their heads. Andrew awoke crying. Ole approached the straw mattress in the far corner and picked up Andrew, rocking him back to sleep. Ole smiled at his girls tucked away in one bed together, then returned to the living room.

Ane chuckled. "That is not going to work every time."

"It has worked every time so far." Ole laughed at the strange family tradition and kissed his wife on the cheek.

"*Natmad, vaersgo*?" They both turned to see the faint outline of Marie standing in the doorway requesting a snack before bed. She looked at her mother as she carelessly twirled the doll with one hand.

"Yes, but you must get to bed," Ane scolded.

Marie nodded and scurried back to bed, her teeth chattering from the chill air. The only thing providing them warmth was the fireplace. On occasion they would warm stones next to the fire and carry them to bed. Tonight, all they had to keep warm was each other.

Ane grabbed a handful of cookies from the kitchen and slid through the open doorway into the girl's bedroom.

"Can I have a lullaby too?" Marie requested.

Ane handed each girl a cookie and kept one for herself. "What lullaby would you like to hear tonight?"

"*Slaap kindje slaap,*" Marie requested.

Karen blew out the candle and Ane sang, "Sleep, little child, sleep, outside a sheep is walking. A sheep with white feet, it drinks its milk sweet. Sleep, little child, sleep."

* * *

Ole walked down *Skovvejen,* Forrest Road, the main path that divided Jyderup, the larger town near Tornved. It was early afternoon, but the gray skies made it feel more like evening. Christmas had already been celebrated and had offered a bit of light in the dark winter months. Ole's family had attended church on Christmas Eve and Ane handed out several different kinds of cookies to the neighbors.

The traditional rice pudding was made for dessert, and Kristina was overjoyed when she bit into the almond, for whoever discovered it hidden within the pudding was promised good luck in the coming year.

Before bed, the candles fastened to their small tree were blown out and Andrew helped his mother put out the bowl of porridge for the *Nisse,* the mythical inhabitants of the lofts and attics of homes. After the holiday had passed, Andrew asked every night if he could put out the porridge again and Ane reminded him he would have to wait until next Christmas.

After the celebrations had ended, they settled into the bitter winter. The ground was cold and hard that day and a storm was threatening.

Ole walked past the road that turned off and led to his church and took the next turn into Jyderup, heading toward the tavern.

Before he could disappear into the streets and buildings of Jyderup, elders Petersen and Nielsen walked down the path toward him.

"*Goddag.*" Good day, Elder Petersen said in their native tongue.

"*Hej.*" Hello, Ole responded. "Quite a chill we are having."

"Yes, it is quite cold," Elder Nielsen agreed. "What brings you to town?"

"Besides working the farm, I also lend a hand at the tavern here in town," Ole responded.

"You are a busy man," Elder Nielsen said.

"With mouths to feed," Ole responded. "Where are you headed today?"

"We had business in town," Elder Nielsen responded. "Now we are headed to the church." Ole assumed they were meeting with the pastor to seek permission to preach to his congregation.

"Where are you staying?" Ole asked.

"We sleep and eat where we are welcome."

"How much does the church pay you for preaching?" Ole didn't mind being forward.

"We travel without pay," Elder Nielsen said.

Ole examined the men with some curiosity. Despite their uncertain circumstances, they were quite content.

"I live in Tornved. Where are your travels taking you today?" Ole asked.

"Are you inviting us into your home?" Elder Petersen asked.

"I guess I am," Ole replied. "But just to give you a hot meal. You can ask where my house is when you reach Tornved; someone will direct you."

Elder Petersen replied, *"Tak, Gud velsigne."* Thank you, God bless.

"We would be happy to join you later and are very grateful for the offer," Elder Nielsen said.

Ole nodded and added his farewell, *"Pa gensyn."* See you later. *"Farvel."* Goodbye, the elders called.

Ole pulled his collar up and turned into the cold wind. With his hat on and head down, he walked toward the tavern where he found warmth.

*   *   *

Frikadeller was Ane's favorite dish. Pork meat balls with cabbage. She prepared it especially for the Mormons.

When they arrived, Ole welcomed them in Danish, *Velkommen.* They shook hands with everyone, as was customary. There were a few minutes of kind conversation in the front room before the elders were escorted to the kitchen and the family crammed themselves on the mismatched chairs and benches around the small wooden table.

They blessed their meal with the customary prayer, "Come Lord Jesus, be our guest; and let these gifts to us be blest. And may there be a goodly share; on every table everywhere. Amen."

The elders echoed their "Amen" loudly, but graciously before eating.

Karen had been eyeing the Mormons suspiciously since they arrived. Ole introduced the children, who stared incredulously, having heard the most awful things about Mormons from their schoolmates.

"Karen is our oldest. She is fourteen, Johanna is twelve, Kristina is nine, our youngest daughter Marie is almost seven, and our son, Andrew, is three."

"Would you like more bread?" Kristina offered.

"Yes, thank you," they both replied and she served them another roll.

"Thank you so much for having us in your home," Elder Nielsen said.

"We've heard stories," Karen blurted.

The elders chuckled and Ane gave her daughter a reproachful stare.

"I am sure you have," Elder Petersen said.

Ole finished swallowing, "What people do not know, they must assume. I guess now would be the time for me to ask what you believe so I can separate truth from myth."

Elder Petersen cleared his throat and set down his fork. He repositioned himself on his chair and faced Ole. "We believe that the Lord Jesus Christ and His Father appeared to the Prophet Joseph Smith with revelation that allowed God's true church to be restored here on earth."

"That is not true," Karen said.

Elder Nielsen smiled. "Perhaps we can speak about this later after the children have gone to bed."

"They have a right to hear and make up their own minds," Ane said.

Elder Petersen nodded respectfully. "A wise woman."

"I am often in need of her counsel." Ole smiled. "You say this prophet of yours died?"

"Joseph Smith was murdered by a mob, yes." Elder Petersen confirmed.

"Did Jesus not die during His time for His revolutionary thought?" Elder Nielsen added.

"Are you saying this prophet is equal to Jesus?" Ole asked.

"No," Elder Petersen was quick to respond. "He was simply a messenger who was willing to die for his message."

"Why would our Lord speak to a simple farm boy?"

Elder Nielsen looked sternly at Ole, "Because he asked. 'If any of you lack wisdom, let him ask of God, that giveth to all men liberally, and upbraideth not; and it shall be given him.' *James,* chapter one, verse five."

The family listened, unable to eat.

"After reading this verse," Elder Petersen added, "Joseph, as a young boy, went into the woods to pray and that is when the Lord revealed Himself to Joseph. You also can pray about the truthfulness of our words and receive your own answers."

"I do not suppose I would be ready to receive an angel," Ole said.

The elders laughed, "I doubt any of us would," Nielsen said, "but the truth comes to you here," he said, placing his hand over his heart.

"We will leave you with this." Elder Petersen set a *Book of Mormon* in front of Ole. "It is scripture, meant to be a companion to the *Bible.* We ask that you read it and find the truthfulness in it for yourself."

Ole's rough hands grasped the leather binding. Ane and the girls watched intently to see his reaction.

Ole flipped through the book, and set it next to his plate with a shrug. "I'll look at it."

The Elders nodded. They ate and discussed the weather, Ane's fine cooking and Ole's farming secrets.

Before the Elders left they asked if they could visit later in the week. Ole knew their intent to convert him and his family. He also knew that being friendly with them would create discord between him and his neighbors. With all this weighing heavy on his shoulders he intended to tell them they weren't welcome back. But as he spoke he found himself saying, *yes, you are welcome here anytime.*

*   *   *

Ole lifted the straw-filled cushion of the loveseat. The bottom was made of wooden slats lined up in a tight row. He pulled the edge of the wood out and the slats separated into every other one, making a bed. He pulled the cushion down into a mattress and sat on the bed. Dishes clanked in the kitchen where Ane was cleaning up; the girls and Andrew were fast asleep in the room next to him. He knelt down at this bedside and prayed, "God, if there be any truth to these words, please help me know it."

After a few moments, he sat on the edge of his bed, kicked off his boots, opened the book the missionaries left him and began to read.

THEN
❧
April 15, 1853

*"You will hear a name / To sing to your soul /
And ease your pain."*
—*Along the Path*

*O*le stood ankle-deep in the stream's freezing water. The throbbing pains in his feet were no longer a bother, as they had gone numb. He crouched down and firmly grasped the edge of a large rock, braced himself and lifted. The rock came inches off the ground before slipping from his wet grasp and slapping back into the water.

"Elder Nielsen, I am going to need some help," Ole said. Elder Nielsen stepped through the shallow water to his side. They bent down together, on the count of three, *"En, to, tre."* They lifted the large rock with a grunt, and strategically placed it near the others to dam the water enough to create a small pool deep enough for one person to be immersed.

"If you do not hurry, Father, people will see us and soon you will have people jeering at you and throwing food," Karen said nervously.

"Never mind what other people are going to think, Karen." Ane touched her daughter's shoulder. "Let the men work. Did you remember towels?"

"I have them," Kristina said, lifting the bundle.

A cool breeze swept past. "It is going to be cold." Karen shivered and hugged her arms.

"It will be fine," Ane said. Her heart fluttered with anticipation.

"I think we are ready," Elder Nielsen said. "We will baptize Brother Madsen first."

Ole had never witnessed a baptism like this. Lutherans were baptized as infants. Mormons believed baptism should take place later in life when a child could be held accountable for his or her actions.

Ole's conversion to Mormonism had been subtle but quick. He had opened his mind to the possibility of new truth and inquisitively studied the *Book of Mormon* nightly. He pondered his reading and prayed to know the truth. As he did, the truth came alive in him. There was a knowing both in his heart and in his mind. He understood he had free will and chose to receive the gifts that God offered to all His children.

Ane's conversion was less logical and more emotional. For her, it was a strong knowing in her heart, akin to the feeling of love she had for her family.

Ole and Ane had been told that complete immersion in the water was symbolic of a washing away of their sins. They would become new so long as they were repentant.

Ole held to Elder Nielsen's left arm, as the Elder raised the other. The prayer was quick. Ole bent his knees as Nielsen placed his right hand on his back and lowered him under water. The rush of the cold water enveloped him. Moments later Ole emerged from the water, laughing.

Elder Nielsen shook his hand, and Ole climbed from the stream. Kristina offered Ole a towel, which he hugged around him. The sun provided little warmth, but Ole could still feel its rays on his wet face.

Amid the sound of sheep bleating nearby, birds chirping and the babbling of the stream, Elder Nielsen offered the prayer for Ane's baptism, "In the name of the Father, and of the Son, and of the Holy Ghost." There was a splash of water as she was submerged. Ane sprang from the cold stream and wiped her face with her wet hands. Her dress was heavy with water and she labored to move from the creek. Kristina threw a towel around her. Ane wiped her face and looked at Ole and smiled. Ole opened his arms for her and they embraced, cold, wet and happy.

NOW

ॐ

Summer–Fall 1968

*"Do you dream? / Does it seem / That part of you /
Lives in between?"*
—*Sojourn*

*M*y three brothers and I sat perched at our usual station, on the shed nestled in our backyard, watching the screen of the drive-in movie next door to our house. Of course we couldn't hear anything. To rectify this, we asked the patrons nearest us in the dark part of the drive-in to turn on the speakers closest to us. These particular movie-goers were usually happy to oblige since the reason they were in the darkest part of the drive-in was because they were taking their friends out of the trunk of their car. The drive-in charged by the head. On days when a good show was playing and we were desperate to hear, we would hop the fence and turn the speakers on ourselves.

Our family never had a good relationship with the theater owner, mostly because of the noise the drive-in made late at night as the patrons impatiently honked for the second feature. And of course there were the speakers on the back row that were occasionally turned up too high. There also was an incident involving my brother's band that made relations significantly worse.

Greg played in a band called The Grimm, named after *The Brothers Grimm*. With its distinctive rock sound, it was no ordinary garage band. The group won just about every Battle of the Bands contest they entered, and they developed a strong local following.

One evening, The Grimm decided to play a show on our back patio before the start of the first featured movie. Moviegoers flocked toward the sound that emanated from our yard, lining the back fence to hear the concert. Soon there was quite a crowd, all enjoying an outdoor summer evening concert. The drive-in's patrons were mesmerized by The Grimm's music and disenchanted with buying popcorn for the movie. That's when the owner of the drive-in called the police and the concert abruptly ended.

For a time, The Grimm had a real run at the big time. They had a couple of record companies looking at them. In the spring of 1968 they released the first of two records. One of their songs, *The Darkness and the Night,* rose to the top ten in Salt Lake City within a couple of weeks from its release.

I had just turned eighteen and The Grimm was my world.

Greg and I had started guitar lessons at the same time when we were kids. I was on an Hawaiian steel guitar, which is one that you hold in your lap and play with a bar, while Greg played the Spanish guitar. I remember making our debut at a Primary program for our church. We played a song called *Sleep Walk*. After it was over, I was traumatized from having to be onstage, but Greg loved it. After that, I was content to leave the stage to Greg, and watch from the sidelines.

My favorite Grimm concert was in Big Springs, Idaho, near Yellowstone. Just being in that place was an adventure—the mountains, the crisp air and the rustic lodges. At Big Springs there was a large slab of cement set under the pines as a make-do stage and kids from Idaho Falls to Cody, Wyoming, would show up for a summer concert.

The night The Grimm were set to play, the disc jockey from the town of Saint Anthony, Idaho, got up on stage after the opening band finished. He spouted some drivel about the radio station and announced The Grimm. When he called them to the stage, the audience responded with the normal polite applause, but no one came up. The band was announced three more times and after five minutes the stage remained empty and the crowd grew frustrated.

The DJ acted a little nervous and asked if someone would go and see what was keeping the band. Then he asked if someone would like to come up and play something on the instruments that were already set up on stage. No one volunteered and there was a growing murmur of irritation in the crowd. After the offer was repeated a couple of times, a reluctant hand went up in the crowd. A guy slowly walked to the stage and picked up one of the guitars, putting the strap around his neck. He timidly played an uninteresting group of notes and chords; more focused on the guitar in hand then the audience's want of music.

The DJ continued his offer until there were a drummer, bassist and two guitarists playing, with hardly anyone paying attention. The cacophony they played sounded terrible and the tension was building. People had come to dance.

Unknown to everyone, The Grimm had been dancing to the last couple of songs from the opening band and now were comfortably on stage, incognito, tuning and checking their instruments.

An instant later and all at once, the stage came alive as the tight blend of five instruments hit at the same moment, like unorganized matter going super nova. Heads turned in curious disbelief. No one danced. Instead they all gathered around the stage, mesmerized and captured under the moonless night with the Milky Way overhead.

Six months later, The Grimm was only getting better. The group was just releasing its second record and planning to play back-up to a national group at a larger venue in a couple of months. Then something happened that seemed at odds with the excitement. The drummer, Lane, called and informed Greg that he had turned his papers in and accepted a call to serve as a full-time missionary. He was quitting the band!

This was a gigantic blow to me. I knew The Grimm had the potential for being the next great American success story. I remember looking out our front window and seeing Lane drive up to the house to talk to Greg. I thought maybe I could convince Lane to stay, so I met him halfway between his car and the house.

"What do you think you're doing?" I blurted, "You can always go on a mission later. You're going to be famous."

Lane and I had been friends and I looked up to him. He had a great disposition, but I wasn't sure how he'd take my hassling him. Even though I had traveled with the band, I wasn't officially a member of it.

He smiled calmly, looked me in the eye and pointed to his car parked on an angle across the driveway. "You see that car?" he said. "I drive where I want, I have everything I want and all my life I have had three meals a day. I have nice clothes and a good place to live. I've been given everything and it's time I did something for someone besides myself."

Not the answer I had expected. I thought he'd say he had promised his parents, or that he would be back and not to worry because he would still be a rock star. But that was all he said. He placed his hand on my shoulder and quietly walked past me toward the house without another word.

Instead of following Lane into the house, I walked past his small cheap car that I always made fun of. You could barely fit two people in it, and you wouldn't want a bicycle to run into it because the bike would win. Lane was not rich by any stretch of the word and yet he wanted to give back. All I had really been aware of up to that point was my car, my hair, my music and my clothes. My attitude had revolved around one thing: impressing those around me, especially girls. My clothes and my car were empty possessions to be seen and admired by others. It was a strong wake-up call.

An opportunity was presenting itself to me. I was given a reflection of who I was versus who I wanted to be. I went back to my house and started preparing to serve a mission.

THEN
﹩
Winter 1856

*"He could set his spirit free / To look for the answer /
To all that he could be."*
—*Set to Wander*

*A*ne aggressively kneaded the bread, working out her frustrations as she pushed the heels of her hands firmly into the dough. After a few minutes, she pinched the over-kneaded dough's firm edge and grunted her annoyance. She cleaned her hands on her apron, and wiped the flour from her cheeks with the back of her hand. She turned her attention to cutting vegetables and tried to forget her overworked bread.

Her frustration had been growing since their baptism. Their neighbors and acquaintances spat the name "Mormons" with the same tone they used to condemn the devil.

Ane, in hopes of containing her growing frustration, began to hold others at bay. Her family only saw a glassy-eyed smile or observed a deep silence in her eyes that held the depth of her sorrow and dissatisfaction.

She heard the front door open as Ole entered the house just in time for dinner. He greeted the children first. Ane heard snippets of their dialogue amidst the chaotic thoughts that swam through her head. Karen asked how his day had been, Marie asked for a story later, Kristina shared the poem she was memorizing. Within minutes, Ole was by her side.

"Metta says *The Maid as a Hind and a Hawk* is her favorite ballad. Just like her mother."

"That is not my favorite." Ane chopped the vegetables, not looking at Ole. He noticed her remoteness but said nothing. "Maybe when I was girl, but not now."

Ole nodded once in understanding. "Why are the girls not helping you with dinner?"

"They have had enough to deal with today. I am letting them play."

Ole sighed. "It happened again?"

"About a dozen or so eggs they had to clean up this time."

"Idle hands will not make it better," Ole said, hanging his frock.

Ane chopped more aggressively. "Maybe you're right."

Ole turned to his wife. Her shoulders were tense.

Chop. Chop. Chop.

"What is your true concern, Ane?"

Ane shook her head, irritated. The knife sliced through the carrots and smacked the counter. "With the children unable to attend school it is getting harder for me to take care of what I need to here. I cannot be their teacher and their mother." The sharp knife came down, nicking the edge of Ane's finger. "Ahwe!" Gritting her teeth, she grabbed a small towel and wrapped it around her finger and returned to her slicing.

"Ane?"

"I am fine." The knife's blade thwacked the counter loudly.

"What would you have me do, Ane?" Ole shook his head as he sat at the table. "America is not the solution."

"The Elders say that the Prophet has commanded us to gather to Zion."

"The Mormons are persecuted in America, just as they are here."

"But there will be more of us," Ane countered. "Thousands of people immigrate to the Utah Territory every year. And in Zion, President Brigham Young leads us. At least our children would be able to go to school without risk of being mocked or called names or having eggs thrown at them!"

Ole threw his hat down on the table and rubbed his forehead.

"Not to mention the farm," Ane began. "With the import of cheaper grain from Russia..."

"I will turn to pork and dairy to keep up."

Ane sighed.

Chop. Chop. Chop.

"It is not enough!"

"Papa." Marie stood at the edge of the kitchen. "Will you tell me the story of *The Girl Clad* before dinner?"

"Not now," Ole said, keeping his eye on Ane, who stood facing away from him.

"Papa, please."

Ole slammed his hand on the table, both Marie and Ane jumped. "I said not now!" Marie scampered away. The room fell silent. Ole gritted his teeth in frustration. "I want to be able to protect and take care of my family."

Ane silently added the vegetables to the soup.

"If we sail to America, we will be nothing but second-class citizens. We won't know the language. We will have to give up everything. Who is to say America will be better than here?"

"We will never know if we do nothing. Here is a chance to dream of more than just making a poor man's wages and working someone else's land. If you believe in what the Brethren have taught us, as I know you do, then you will do this," Ane said sternly. When she spoke like this, Ole knew there was no arguing. He also knew she was usually right. "We will never behold the glory of the Temple and its covenants if we stay here," Ane continued. "Is it not God's will that we be sealed together as a family for eternity? That is what you want, is it not?"

Ole stood, the chair scraped the floor and fell backwards. He clenched his teeth and said nothing. Ane did not move. She knew he was not mad at her, but at the circumstances. He went to her side, but she turned away from him. He wrapped his arms around her. "Of course I want that," he whispered.

She stopped stirring the soup.

Ole, remembered a verse from *The Maid as a Hind and a Hawk,* and recited it to her, "'He took her so gently within his arm, and then her lips he kiss'd.'" He kissed her cheek. "Let us wait. We cannot emigrate until spring, we will decide then," Ole said.

"I am not going to change my mind."

Ole paused. "I know."

Ole grabbed the injured finger she had wrapped in a towel. He softly loosened the towel and examined the superficial cut, dabbing the wound a few times with the cloth. Seeing that the bleeding had stopped, he took her hand in his. "'Thank God! I find thee so sound and fresh,'" Ole recited. "'So long as I thee have miss'd.'"

Ane rested her head on his shoulder. He always smelled of earth and barley with a hint of leather. She took comfort in the familiarity of his smell, knowing that if she lost all her possessions and her home, at least she would have her family.

*   *   *

Ole stood in his living room, head bowed, as Brother Jensen offered a prayer before their Sunday service. Ole was getting used to a very different kind of worship. Instead of attending church in a white chapel connected to a red brick bell tower, surrounded by luxuriant gardens, they were home. Ole missed the formality of Lutheranism, sitting with their community on wooden benches in a room with white arched ceilings, the pastor preaching from an ornately carved wooden pew. He recalled seeing the christening font at every service, and remembered his children's baptisms as water was poured over their heads. He was accustomed to looking upon the shrine that had a baroque-style painting that covered the wall and ceiling, with a carved wooden backdrop depicting Jesus on the cross.

In Great Salt Lake the Saints gathered in churches. Here, in the small town of Tornved, there was no opportunity for this. Membership in the church, although growing, was still small. Many who were baptized were immigrating to Utah Territory to be with their fellow saints.

Johanna shifted uncomfortably as she sat on the floor with the younger girls. Chairs were limited and offered to the guests. The congregation included Brother Garff, the Jensen and Sorensen families, Brother Christiansen, Brother Hansen, Elder Lars Madsen, and his sister, Miss Karen Marie. Every family had a *Bible* and *Book of Mormons* were shared.

As the meeting commenced with a song, Ole prepared the sacrament. How different the sacred experience of the sacrament had become. As a Mormon, he partook of a sacrament, but only in remembrance of Christ's body and blood, not as a Real Presence. During Holy Communion at the Lutheran Church, Ole had knelt before the shrine, and the pastor stood before him wearing an alb. The bread was received from the pastor's hand. Here, in his home, Ole was the one to bless the bread and water in remembrance of Christ, and it was his hands that offered it to others in the congregation.

After the sacrament service, Ole watched as Elder Lars Madsen weakly stood to speak. He had arrived earlier, pale and sick with a fever. Ane immediately offered the girls' bed for him to rest in, but he was resolute on preaching today. When Brother Hansen and Brother Sorensen arrived, Lars asked for a priesthood blessing. "I feel strengthened already!" he exclaimed after the blessing, and insisted on addressing the small congregation during service.

Ole leaned against the back wall, his *Bible* splayed open in his hands as Elder Madsen directed them to a scripture in John, regarding Christ's atonement. Ole's view of the atonement was becoming very different as a Mormon. As a Lutheran, Ole had believed that until God opened a person's eyes, he was a slave to his sins, living without free will. Only when God chose to give the sight to see or the ears to hear, through the Holy Ghost, could a person know the truth of God's grace and salvation through the atonement alone. This truth, once felt, could never be denied. In some small way, Ole still believed in this Divine Monergism, even though it was contrary to what Mormons preached concerning free will and having the choice to know truth and still deny it. Except now, the truth Ole felt and couldn't deny resided in Mormon doctrine.

Ole was studying the passage in John, thinking on his new faith when an egg hit the window with a startling thwack. Ole charged the door with an angry grunt, slinging words hardly appropriate for a church service. A group of teenaged boys immediately ran off laughing and throwing their eggs blindly behind them. Most of them hit ground. One egg shot toward the house and was intercepted by Ole's hand. The yolk splattered on his clothes. He held his tongue and wiped his hand on his shirt and turned around. The brethren stood in the doorway with looks of concern. Brother Sorensen beckoned him back to the house.

Ole trudged inside, glancing briefly at Ane; her furrowed brow mirrored his frustration. He took his place in the back of the quiet room, opened his *Bible,* and nodded at Lars to continue.

Lars looked at the ground and sighed, "Has it been getting worse?"

Ane and Ole exchanged glances, "No," Ole said. The persecution hadn't gotten worse. It was the same harassment they had endured since their conversion.

"I wish we could attend school," Johanna sulked.

"Hanna!" Ane scolded.

Johanna had said what all the girls were feeling. They wanted to attend school without being shamed or humiliated by their teachers and friends for having been baptized Latter-Day Saints.

Johanna had been baptized a year earlier along with Kristina. Karen was the first of the children to be baptized, eight months after their parents, in the dead of winter. They had to break the ice to baptize her. There was some concern she would fall ill, but she never did.

"Karen has been helping us with our lessons," Kristina offered as consolation.

"The Lord appreciates your sacrifice," Lars said.

The children said nothing, and Karen simply nodded.

Lars cleared his throat. He gripped the chair for support and considered his thoughts. Lars was a fellow Danish convert and young missionary for the church. He had come to know Ole's family well over the past few months. He searched for words that might comfort them.

"The Lord understands you have been afflicted. All of you," Lars said addressing the small congregation. "And I bear testimony to you that I know that the Prophet Joseph Smith spoke to God and His Son, and I know that America is a place blessed for us to gather. The commandment to gather in Zion is just as important as is the commandment of baptism. The Prophet Brigham Young has said to 'Gather up to the land of America,' and he is providing a way. Many of our brothers and sisters have donated money to the Perpetual Emigration Fund to allow you to go to America and build up God's Kingdom on Earth." The small congregation listened silently to Lars' words. He let them hang in the air before closing his testimony in the name of Jesus Christ.

Brother Garff, who was leading the meeting, stood to bring it to a close. "Brothers and sisters, I am happy and grateful in all things."

Such an agreeable thought for such tense circumstances, Ane thought. She admired his optimism.

"I propose," Brother Garff continued, "that Ole Madsen be ordained an Elder." The decision had previously been made, but would now be put to a vote. "All in favor," Brother Garff spoke, raising his right hand to the square. The assemblage followed in agreement. "We will take care of the ordination before we have our closing song and prayer." Brother Garff pulled out his chair and motioned for Ole to sit. The elders placed their hands on Ole's head, and the ordination through prayer was made.

Though the circumstances were bleak, the small band of Danish Mormons knew how to rejoice, and the remainder of the evening was spent in song and dance.

After everyone left and the children were put to bed, Ane and Ole climbed under the covers. Ole held out his arm and Ane rested her head on his chest. "Okay," Ole said, and it was all he needed to say.

Shortly after, Lars ran into Ole, who was traveling to the nearby town of Odsherred.

"Why are you traveling to Odsherred?" a curious Lars inquired.

"I am purchasing a travel chest," Ole responded. "My family and I are sailing to America."

* * *

Marie lay awake as the house creaked and groaned for no reason she knew of; perhaps from a gust of wind, someone rolling over in bed, or a mouse scurrying from one room to another. Marie clung to the covers, unable to sleep without her doll. It rested in the trunk in the front room. Each child was being allowed to bring one personal item to America. Aside from a few items of extra clothing, Marie had nothing but her doll. Her clothes were ragged with wear and she watched her mother carefully fold and place them in the trunk.

Johanna packed her favorite book, *Fairy Tales,* and Andrew brought his favorite toy, a carved wooden cup-and-ball game. The toy could keep him transfixed for hours, and Marie was sure if he hadn't thought to bring it, Mother would have packed it anyway, for her own sanity in keeping a six-year-old boy entertained.

Karen chose a hat she had crafted herself with lush red ribbon. She had never had occasion to wear it, except for sometimes around the house when she was feeling fanciful. Kristina clung to her own collection of poems, *The Maid as a Hind and a Hawk* being her favorite. Mother brought her silver heart-shaped jewelry box, along with a locket given her by her mother.

Now all they were able to take for the journey was boxed up in two trunks. In the morning they would leave everything except those trunks and each other behind them.

Marie shut her eyes tightly, listening to the hum of the wind as it blew past her window. She begged for sleep, but within a few minutes her eyes opened, unwilling to shut again. Marie set her bare feet on the cold floor and tiptoed quickly to the sitting room where the unlocked trunks sat. Marie carefully lifted the lid to the larger trunk and slid out her doll that lay at the top of the heap. Then she quietly lowered the lid and tiptoed to bed.

Kristina and Johanna lay next to each other asleep. Karen was not in bed, but sitting awake by the window, gazing at the moon.

"Metta," Marie whispered. Her sister stirred awake and upon seeing Marie lifted the covers for her. Marie scrambled into bed and slid over Kristina so she could lie between her and Johanna.

"What is it?" Kristina asked.

Marie stayed mute.

"Are you afraid?"

Marie paused, unwilling to admit her fears.

"There is nothing to be scared of," Kristina murmured sleepily. "We are going on a big adventure, and we are going to be with people who will be kind to us."

"And not throw eggs."

"Of course not. That will all be behind us."

"And you will be there?" Marie asked.

"Of course I will be there," Kristina whispered.

"We will all be there," said Johanna, who had been wakened by their voices.

"Good," Marie let her eyes close, "I want you to be there. I want all my sisters with me."

"What about Andrew?" Johanna asked.

"I want him to be there, too, and Mary."

"Mary? Who is that?" Johanna asked.

Kristina smiled and held up Marie's porcelain-headed doll.

"Of course, Mary will be there too." Johanna examined the doll that Marie held so close to her. She watched as Marie, now ten years old, clung to the doll as if she were still a little girl.

The girls had been told to see their emigration to America as an adventure, like the stories their father told them. Still, they all understood Marie's fears of leaving everything they knew behind. They were unsure of the changes, but were eventually convinced that living in Zion would be worth the sacrifice. "We will all be there together." Kristina found the words that would comfort all of them, "We will all be there," she repeated.

Johanna stroked Marie's hair until they fell asleep.

The moon hung framed by the single windowpane in the girl's room. A ray of light peeked through the glass and illuminated the floor where Karen sat, silhouetted against the night sky. Karen had listened to her sisters' feeble attempts to find comfort as she sat by the window staring at the moon. She didn't wish to go to America, but the thought of being separated from her family was enough to swallow her opposition. The prospect of giving up everything to travel to a foreign land where they would have close to nothing didn't interest her.

What once had been their home was now a shell that would soon exist only in memories. Any furniture that did not belong to the landlord had been sold to pay for passage. The only thing remaining were the trunks holding their last possessions. The whole idea made Karen sick.

Karen heard her sisters' breathing deepen as they fell asleep. Although she was tired, her mind refused to rest. She closed her eyes and imagined that her father would wake the next morning and change his mind, that they would stay in Denmark, denounce Mormonism, work the land until they had enough money to buy it and she would have the opportunity to marry and secure a good home in familiar surroundings.

She lost herself in such dreams until sleep overcame her. She awoke the next morning with a crick in her neck and the reality of her present situation shining down on her with the brazen morning sun.

THEN

&

April 22–23, 1856

"I set myself to wander."
—Set to Wander

a lot of things constitute adventure. Many revolve around moving to new frontiers and exploring the unknown. The spring of 1856 saw the births of Sigmund Freud and Robert Peary. The former would expand the understanding of the mind and the latter would find the North Pole. But with adventure comes risk, and as Ole moved his little family toward adventure, perhaps going to the North Pole would have been safer.

Ole's family gathered with a group of emigrating Danish Saints in Copenhagen, Denmark, under the charge of Brother Johan Ahmanson. Ahmanson was a Danish convert and missionary in his late twenties, traveling with his wife and young son. It was his duty to make sure they arrived safely in Liverpool, England, where they would join other Saints traveling to America. Ahmanson was clean-shaven and wore his dark hair long so it hung just over his ears. He was energetic, and at times, impatient. The night before they were to depart on the steamship *Rhoda,* Ahmanson gathered the emigrating Saints together and gave them specific travel instructions. They would take the steamship to Kiel, Germany. From there they would board a train to Hamburg and board another steamship, *Morsdoe,* to Grimsby, England. Then they would travel by train to Liverpool. From there they would set sail to America.

After the Copenhagen meeting, Ole and his family stayed the night in a boarding house near the dock. The room was small for their family of seven. They shared beds, and the smaller children, Andrew and Marie, slept on the floor, using their wadded clothes for pillows.

Marie awoke from a fitful sleep to hear her parents whispering and Karen crying, muttering something about her aunt.

"It was only a dream, Karen; you do not know for sure," Mother said.

Karen sobbed, "She is sick. I know it."

"Even if she is sick that is no reason for you to stay," Ane reasoned. "I know this has been hard on you, but we need you to stay steadfast. Before you know it we will be in Zion."

"What does that mean?" Karen retorted. "Zion cannot fix everything, Mother."

"Karen, that is enough," Ole said, raising his voice.

"Please," Karen pleaded, "I am old enough. I will stay with family here. I will promise to write and maybe join you later, but I know Uncle needs me right now."

"That is not an option," Ole started.

Ane placed a hand on his shoulder. Neither of them wanted to lose their daughter, but Ane knew it wasn't their choice. "It is her decision, Ole. We have to let her go."

Ole clenched his teeth in frustration. "We will see how you are feeling in the morning." It was Ole's last attempt to try to change

Karen's mind. Perhaps if she had more time to think, she would find reason.

They went back to bed, although sleep was difficult as they anticipated their journey.

Despite the lack of sleep, they woke the next morning fully alert. Karen's decision to stay in Denmark had not changed.

Just before they boarded, Karen announced to the family her intention of staying.

"Why?" Marie looked confused.

"I have to stay," Karen said. "Something has happened, I think Mother's sister is sick, and I need to go back to Tornved."

"What do you mean she is sick? How do you know?" Johanna questioned.

Ane looked into the faces of her distraught daughters. She hid her pain behind an emotionless expression. "Karen dreamed last night my sister died and that they were preparing the funeral."

"I know it was not just a dream," Karen insisted.

Johanna shook her head. She knew Karen had a talent for dramatics and had never wanted to go to America, but this? Johanna held onto Karen with mixed feelings of anger and sadness. She pulled away, letting the rest of the family bid her farewell. They all knew there was nothing they could say to change her mind.

Marie's heart broke as her family was torn apart. She cried, hugging Karen, not letting go. Finally, Johanna offered Marie her hand, and Marie reluctantly took it. Together they watched as Mother hugged Karen one last time. Karen promised she would write and perhaps sail to America next year.

They never saw each other again in this life.

NOW

ဆ

Spring 1997

"To the mountains / Set off by chance, / In constant yearning /
I start the dance."
—*Requiem*

*I*t had been twenty-five years since Greg had picked up his guitar. He had long ago given up the dream of being a famous musician. He had traded in his guitar, along with his t-shirts and jeans, for a briefcase, suit and tie, to practice law.

When I first learned that Greg was quitting The Grimm I was on my mission and I remember calling him in hopes of changing his mind. Only a couple of years earlier I was sitting in an office with Greg as a recording contract was offered to him by an executive who told him that they were taking him but not his group. Without hesitation he told them either they took the group or nothing. They took nothing.

I believed in his music and the gift he had for songwriting. On the phone that day Greg told me he didn't like where the music business was taking him. He had friends who were using drugs and was surrounded by people who were fake. He had chosen, he said, to have a family and a life.

So when Greg walked away he was grateful for the opportunity to raise a family and stay connected to the church. That, to him, was happiness and for a time, music played a distant role in his life.

On this particular spring evening all of that changed.

Greg had spent the day in Afton, Wyoming, for work and was driving back to Utah. As Greg drove, a wondrous glow lighted up the horizon. He assumed it was lights from a nearby town, although there were none in the area that could give off that amount of glow. Just then, vibrant music began playing. It grew louder, filling the recesses of his car. Confused, Greg reached for the radio to turn it off, but it wasn't on. This confirmed what he thought he was hearing—a song yet to be sung.

The song replayed in his mind as Greg drove west of South Pass, growing louder with each turn. Greg became overwhelmed with tears and wished the music to stop, as he was already tired from the day's work. But the music didn't stop. When he arrived home at one a.m., he burst in to wake his sleeping wife.

"You have to hear this song," Greg said, stirring her awake.

She was justifiably annoyed at being awakened in the middle of the night, and told Greg to forget it before falling back asleep.

So Greg took the guitar that he had barely used in the past twenty-five years into another room, and in the still of the early morning he wrote *Light up the Land.*

*   *   *

I had just arrived home from work when the phone rang. Jennifer answered it as I kicked off my shoes.

"Dad, the phone's for you," she called.

"Who is it?"

"Uncle Greg."

I took the receiver and said hello.

Greg said, "I've written a song and I'd like to play it for you."

I smiled, happy to hear he was playing again. He invited me to his home to hear it.

Greg had written about fifty songs in his heyday. An executive once told him he was one of the greatest songwriters since John Lennon. Greg isn't arrogant enough to agree, but I do think he is a very talented songwriter. I was anxious that day to hear what he'd written.

Before playing his song, Greg briefly recounted what had happened to him in the car. I really liked the song, and I couldn't believe he was writing music again.

At this time, Greg was active in a local youth anti-drug movement. He called the high school his kids attended and talked to the choir director about doing an after-school concert with the school choir. This was to be an awareness assembly. Greg called his old band buddies and told them they were going to perform again, one last time. He sent the music to them and set the concert date. This wasn't an easy task as the drummer who had replaced Lane lived in Denver; the lead guitarist lived in San Francisco and the others in Salt Lake City.

The assembly was scheduled for a Monday after school. The band reunited the Friday before to practice. The once-teenaged band was now gray-haired and middle-aged, but eager to play again.

The day of the concert I went to the high school from work, expecting not to find anything but a few kids and a middle-aged rock band. What occurred took us all by surprise. The auditorium was packed with students, and two local television stations had gotten wind of the concert and were set up for what they thought would be a filler story on a slow news day.

Some of the students had passed out keychain flashlights that flickered among the seats as they restlessly awaited the start.

I went backstage to talk to Greg and see if he needed any help from his former roadie. He told me to sit in the mixing booth and make sure the balance was right. The lead guitarist asked me to make sure that his guitar on *Light Up The Land* was at the right level: LOUD.

The announcer came on stage to welcome the band. "They were originally known as The Grimm, with a top ten hit, *The Darkness and The Night.* You can ask your parents about that," he smirked. "And now I think maybe I'll rename them Mid-Life Crisis. Please welcome to the stage the reunion of The Grimm." The crowd cheered, and their screams echoed through the auditorium.

The band took the stage, picked up their instruments and made a few tuning adjustments.

"Rock, baby! Rock!" A few students screamed.

The Grimm finished their tuning and started playing as the crowd cheered. Behind The Grimm was a large screen with a psychedelic light show transporting the audience back to the sixties. The Grimm started with a couple of older rock songs they believed the students would recognize and a couple of their vintage Grimm songs.

The students went wild. It was as if they were watching the latest group on MTV, not a group of old has-beens.

Suddenly the stage lights came up and the music stopped. The musicians left the stage and a picture of a water droplet falling in a pond, creating a ripple, appeared on the screen. Greg walked to the center of the stage alone, with a microphone in his hand. He asked the teens if they had enjoyed the music so far and a thunderous cheer arose.

"I wanted to share with you a few things that I've learned over the years, and one of those things is that from little things, big things come."

The crowd cheered as Greg continued, "People were activists in the sixties and seventies." Some hoots from the crowd, "And they stood up for what they believed!"

The crowd applauded, and Greg called the rest of the band back on stage.

All the lights went dark, suddenly a lone guitar started and a spotlight fell upon a stool as a girl sang "You offer me light..." Then the light pulled out and the whole band joined in. The small flashlights flickered in the audience.

Something special was happening as the lead guitar rose in the break. I remember feeling that the music had pulled me in and carried me above myself as I looked down on the auditorium. Next, the school choir walked onto the stage. Their voices carried the song to its very last note. When the song ended, the students leaped to their feet, screaming, clapping and waving their key-chain lights.

It reminded me of that night, long ago, in Big Springs. Greg's music had captured the crowd. But instead of being hidden by the forest, it was about to go out to the world.

The Olympic Games were coming to Salt Lake City in the winter of 2002. What started in Wyoming as Greg drove near South Pass was about to enter into the worldview.

What was meant to be a filler story became a big story. Someone said, "You know, *Light up the Land* should be the Olympic theme."

The song did become the theme of one of the Olympic albums, and a top seller at the Winter Games. It went out to the whole world and was sung during the closing ceremonies at the Utah State Capitol Building for dignitaries from all over the world.

Greg never considered his experiences unique. He understands that people don't write music, that music writes itself. Listeners find their own meaning in it. He never expected the song, after its moment of Olympic fame, would become an important element of remembering a group of faithful pioneers who were caught in severe winter storms in Wyoming and those who risked their lives to rescue them. The song was included in many programs and firesides dedicated to honoring their memory. It was considered the official song commemorating the rescue of the Willie and Martin Handcart Companies.

At the time, Greg didn't know his song would become a spiritual landmark for a holy place he'd driven by the night he'd heard it. It was in this place that, 150 years earlier, thirteen people battling starvation and a massive snowstorm, eventually collapsed from exhaustion. Their bodies, frozen stiff, were placed in a large but shallow grave. Some of the men who dug the graves for their friends died themselves only a few hours later as one and then another of the members of the Willie Company succumbed to starvation and cold. The bodies of the thirteen were placed together in the ground and the grave was covered with coals and rocks in hopes of discouraging the wolves.

At this spot, Ole Madsen ended his quest for Zion, leaving Ane and his children to finish the journey without him.

THEN

ജ

June 14, 1856

"I set my mind / Across the great beyond."
—Eutaw

$\mathcal{T}$he sea air pushed the *Thornton's* massive sails, blowing the ship into port at Castle Garden, the landing depot in New York City. The port held a round red granite building that had previously been used as concert hall, theater, church, saloon and finally an immigrant depot.

The main deck was crowded. Everyone was anxious to see New York City for the first time. The immigrants had seen the lush green pastures of Long Island as they sailed by, and were reminded of home. The Madsens secured room on the open deck, leaving the musty air from below decks behind. Ole and Ane stood next to each other on the crowded main platform with their children. As soon as the Manhattan skyline came into view, the girls jumped onto their trunks to get a better view. There were some hoots and hurrahs from the group as they approached their new land. The travelers looked in awe at the vast rows of three-story buildings that stretched for miles deep into the heart of the city. The Trinity Church on Broadway cast its spire above the rest.

Once the ship was moored, Health and Customs officers came aboard. Every member on board would be inspected and accounted for. They would be asked nineteen questions on board and then the same questions after they debarked. It was important that their answers be consistent. Ole was grateful for his family's clean bill of health or else they would be sent back to Liverpool without stepping ashore.

The inspection process was lengthy and arduous. Every person was inspected, along with the ship itself. The inspectors had learned that a ship carrying mainly Mormons would be in better condition than others. The Saints traveled in organized groups under the direction of an appointed leader. During the trip, the Saints worked together to make sure below decks stayed clean and orderly, and that they themselves stayed clean and free from disease. While sailing, watchmen were posted by the hatchways in the evening to ensure there was no inappropriate or disorderly conduct. During the trip, when the watchmen learned that some of the young people were meeting inappropriately and in secret, the situation was rectified immediately.

Because of this orderliness, the company formed a friendship with the ship's captain, a Mr. Collins, who on many occasions joined them in song and dance and even attended one of their religious services. As the company sailed they experienced births, deaths, the finding of a stowaway, weddings, violent storms, burials at sea and even a fire. Stowaways were usually flogged, but in this case, he was forgiven.

At the last meeting before they reached port, Captain Collins bid them farewell with tears in his eyes and wished them luck. The excitement of the first leg of their trip was over. They had got their sea legs just in time to need them no longer. Now they were anxious to be on land—the Promised Land. Despite the excitement, they waited patiently for the inspection of the ship to be completed and for the inspector to move on to individual inspections. After they had waited several hours, the inspector finally reached Ole and his family.

"Name?" The inspector asked, not looking up from his clipboard. His sandy blond hair was slicked to one side. Ole waited for the translation before replying.

"Ole Madsen."

"Occupation?"

Ole looked at the translator, who made it easier, "Job."

"Farmer," Ole said in his best English.

"How many in your family?"

The questions continued. Ole stated the first and last names of every member in his family to the inspector, who wrote them down on his list along with the date of arrival and name of the ship.

"One last thing." The inspector looked up from his clipboard now. "Your family will go by the last name of Madsen instead of Olesen or Olesdatter. And your wife will take your last name instead of Jensen."

Ole shook his head, not understanding.

The inspector explained, "I know that in Denmark the children take the father's first name as their last name, but here in America your sons and daughters cannot be known as Olesdatter or Olesen. Every American son or daughter must take the last name of the father, which, in this case is Madsen." The inspector handed Ole a tag, and the translator instructed him to present the tag to the examining officer on shore.

The inspector moved on to the next immigrant as Ole stared in disbelief. His astonishment turned to annoyance and quickly crawled to the surface as laughter. He hadn't even stepped ashore and had already lost one tradition of his Danish homeland. This meant only one thing to Ole: he was officially an American.

Once the inspection was complete, the baggage was barged from the ship, the gangplank descended and Ole and his family walked ashore, feeling a rush of excitement as they experienced their new land for the first time. They moved as a herd with their fellow Mormon immigrants. Their legs adjusted slowly to being on land as they continued to feel the rock of the boat as they walked. Although a journey to America had ended, a new journey for the Madsen family was about to begin: The journey to Zion.

THEN

∞

June 27–July 12, 1856

The rain beat down upon the people of the Willie Company as they waited in Iowa City. Thick droplets spattered on the dry dirt of the campsite, turning it to mud. Canvas cloth lay strewn about as women sat rain-soaked sewing the rough material into tents that would be their only shelter on the trail.

It had taken the company eleven days to travel to Iowa City. They had journeyed by rail, steamboat and ferry in conditions that were grueling and often appalling. They had stayed in unventilated railroad baggage cars and filthy cattle trains to save money. They were left to sleep in the unruly streets of Chicago after the train conductor booted them off one evening because they were Mormon. Luckily, they secured shelter in a warehouse for the night.

Such persecution never birthed any doubt in the hearts of the Madsens. They now had something they didn't have in Denmark—the freedom of possibilities. They remained steadfast and arrived in Iowa ready to begin their journey on foot across the open land.

While swarms of flying locusts blanketed wheat fields and lay bare the Saint's crops in Utah, Ole stripped unseasoned wood to make handcarts for the traveling company. The traditional method of travel by an ox-drawn wagon had been retired for some immigrating groups in favor of the cheaper handcart plan. The locusts had also fed on Utah's crops the previous year, devastating their production, and donations to the church's Perpetual Emigration Fund were scarce. Handcarts were a less expensive option and deemed preferable to unbroken and potentially dangerous oxen and untrained teamsters.

Many pioneers were reluctant to travel without wagons, since they provided better shelter from storms, relieved them from walking and could accommodate more of their personal belongings. Their criticisms were met with a romanticized view of the handcart plan. Their leaders told them that pulling handcarts was faster, more efficient, less expensive and resulted in fewer deaths. Their leaders also told the pioneers that pulling a handcart would make them physically stronger and give them better health.

After sending three earlier companies of nearly 800 people on their way west, the church's agents in charge of receiving and outfitting the immigrant companies in Iowa City received about 700 immigrants from the *Thornton*. Even though they were expecting the great influx of immigrants, they still weren't prepared to receive them. There was not enough wood to make the carts. Builders were forced to use unseasoned green wood in their construction, as they had nothing else. Ole examined the design of the handcart as he assisted in its production. It was like an oversized wheelbarrow he would be pulling some 1,300 miles across an irregular terrain.

Tents had not been constructed in Iowa City to house the newcomers and no other lodging was available for the company. Ane and the girls joined other women who helped sew tents while the men assisted in the construction of the handcarts. Together they weathered rainstorm after rainstorm without shelter while tents were being made and handcarts were being thrown together.

James Willie, the leader of their company, was in his early forties. Willie and his sub-captains, Millen Atwood, Levi Savage and Johan Ahmanson, held frequent worship meetings with those who were traveling under their direction. The company gathered together every morning and evening for prayer during their stay in Iowa City.

When Captain Willie addressed his company, he liked using words and phrases such as, "Obedience," "Faith in God," and "Perseverance." He was a straightforward and confident man. Being captain, he was given the opportunity to travel by mule, but Willie was not the sort of man who led without example. Upon seeing the mule he simply proclaimed, "I will never get on its back. I will show the example; you follow it." The meetings he conducted with the company were spiritual and instructional. Here the details of the trek were disclosed, as well as rules of conduct to be observed:

> *1. The bugle will blow at 4 a.m., and the company is expected to rise, pray, attend to their assigned teams in taking down tents and packing up carts. Breakfast is fixed, and the company is ready to leave by 6 a.m.*

2. The invalids will be sent on ahead as not to slow down the company.

3. Each man is to have a loaded gun within reach. A piece of leather should be kept over the firing device to guard against moisture.

4. The company will stop at noon to rest the animals. Dinner will be pre-cooked as to not delay setting up camp.

5. The bugle will blow again at 8:30 p.m. signaling the return to the tents to pray, except the night guards. Fires will be extinguished by 9 p.m.

6. The company will remain together while traveling, and no man is allowed further than 20 rods away from camp without permission from his captain.

Five people were assigned to a cart three feet wide and five feet long. The cart itself weighed seventy pounds. All food was carried in the wagons, along with the tents. That allowed each adult member seventeen pounds of personal belongings to take with him across the plains. Children were allowed ten pounds. Captain Willie knew if people attempted to carry more, they would suffer delays from broken-down carts and fatigue from pulling the extra weight. It had to be done.

Ane was tying her last sewing knot when a man arrived in camp with a scale as promised by Captain Willie. Ane's clothes, still damp from the persistent rainstorms, sagged heavily from her shoulders as she labored to move. She sent Johanna to retrieve Ole from the woodshop and met him at the edge of camp where they had stacked their trunks.

"Let us hope we are under weight," Ane said.

"The trunks are going to be the biggest problem," Ole remarked. He sat pondering for a moment. "Let us see what the scale says before we get rid of them." Ole and Ane, with the help of the girls, carried the trunks to the line that had formed in front of the scale at their campsite.

When it was their turn, Ole lifted the trunks onto the scale and watched the dial flip way too far. The man was patient with them as they pulled their belongings from the trunk and haphazardly stuffed cloth sacks full of clothes, blankets, cooking utensils and personal items. Still, the scale showed they were carrying too much weight. Many of their belongings would have to be left behind.

"What about our dishes?" Ane wondered, "What will we eat our meals on as a family when we reach Zion?"

Ole scratched his head and sighed. He turned toward Ane. His eyes conveyed his message to his wife.

She sighed.

"If I can sell it, we can buy new and better dishes when we get there," Ole said.

She nodded. "Yet, we still have so much, and what if we cannot sell it?" She began rummaging through the trunk, "We can do as the others are doing," Ane suggested, "Double up our clothes, sew our belongings into our skirts and then put them on the cart. I am sure we can manage the extra weight."

Ole shook his head, "The carts are unseasoned wood. As soon as it heats in the sun we risk it cracking and breaking. And the journey will be too hard on Andrew to walk the whole way; even the girls will struggle. They will need to ride on the cart occasionally..."

Ane turned away. She drew in a quick breath and turned to Ole. "Fine, then sell it, all of it." Her face was cold and determined. Ole nodded in agreement.

Ane rummaged through her sack of extra clothes and bedding. She placed a few sheets and extra things into the trunk. She pulled out an ornate heart-shaped jewelry box and lifted her silver locket from it. She strung the locket around her neck and tucked it safely beneath her top. Her hand rested over her heart, willing the necklace to stay with her as she journeyed. She handed the box with the remaining jewelry to Ole.

"I wish..." Ole began.

Ane smiled at her dear Ole, "I can trade jewelry for Zion." She walked toward the women who were finishing the tents. Ole knew his wife was strong, competitive and overly determined at times. He often joked that she wasn't happy unless there was a battle to be won. But he also knew her sadness was like a deep well just beneath the surface of her determination. He looked at the box she had handed him, a family heirloom. The necklace she kept had been her mother's. He reluctantly placed the jewelry box in the small trunk. He placed the smaller trunk within the larger one and turned to his children.

He wanted an eloquent way of telling them they would have to sacrifice even more. How could he make the trials worth it to them? How could he make them understand that living in Zion would make up for any sacrifice they had to make? "We have to get rid of anything we do not absolutely need. We can only keep clothes, the bedding and cooking utensils."

The children looked at him, confused, as if he were speaking a foreign language. Surely he could not be serious?

Ole considered reprimanding them to get them to hurry. Maybe if they got it over with quickly, they wouldn't have time to feel the loss. He hated doing this, but there was no other choice.

He looked away from their sad faces. "Hurry," he motioned for them to come forward and release their last possessions. His children stood quiet, each reluctant to release the personal item he or she had brought from home.

"We have to do this," Ole told them sternly.

Johanna acted first. She reached into her cloth sack and pulled out *Fairy Tales*. She slowly rolled the book over in her hands, memorizing the cover as she said goodbye. She flipped through the pages, feeling the air on her face and breathing in the smell of the paper. Ole watched patiently, until she finally handed the book to him.

Ole nodded, acknowledging his daughter's sacrifice. Ole looked to Kristina, who shook her head in defiance. Ole's eyebrows rose. He had never seen her like this; the ever-helpful servant of the family was now refusing to offer up her beloved collection of Danish ballads, a strand that kept her connected still to the home she had known first.

"I will carry it," she insisted, "I will tie it to string and sew it to my skirt. It will not be a problem. We should not have to do this."

Ole looked at her firmly. Tears welled in her eyes. This was one battle she would not win and she knew it.

"Give it to me, Kristina," Ole said, his tone harsher than he wished.

Kristina pulled the collection from her bag and reluctantly handed it to her father. She watched as he dropped it in the trunk, then left in tears.

In a couple of years Kristina would be busy with finding a husband and taking care of a home, Ole reasoned. She wouldn't miss these. He turned to his two smallest children, Marie, who refused to make eye contact with him, and Andrew. Ole watched as Johanna whispered something in Andrew's ear. He pulled out his carved wooden cup-and-ball game and handed it to his father.

"*God dreng,*" Good boy, Ole said, patting him on the shoulder. Ole looked at Marie, who stood frozen in silence hoping to be overlooked. Johanna smiled encouragingly to her as if these sacrifices were equivalent to hard candy. A treat. Marie reluctantly relinquished her doll, which her father placed in the trunk. He then pulled out the family *Bible* and went to place it in the trunk. Johanna stopped him.

"No, Father." Johanna stopped him. "This we must keep."

Ole paused. Tears formed. He could feel them in his heart and in his throat. Marie and Andrew too, nodded their heads.

Ole smiled. Johanna dived into the trunk, grabbed the collection of Danish ballads, found Kristina's favorite poem, and ripped it from the collection. She stuffed it in the *Bible* and walked away. Ole, without speaking, put the *Bible,* with its precious addition in his sack and closed the trunk.

Ole traveled to town with several members of the Willie Company who also hoped to sell their extra items before the trek. This was not the town's first encounter with Mormons. They had interacted earlier with the three other handcart companies that had passed though in the spring and summer.

Ole approached people on the street, offering his goods for sale. The language barrier was difficult and he used gestures to convey meaning.

He had several interested buyers. But after looking over the objects they made ridiculously low offers. When Ole attempted to negotiate a price, they suddenly became disinterested and refused to purchase. He was able to sell the dishes and his wife's jewelry box at prices below their worth. Had he known about the weight limit before he set sail, he could have gotten a better price in Denmark and had less to carry.

"They are not going to buy," a fellow Danish immigrant commented. "They know we must abandon our belongings where we are camped before we move on. Why would they buy something today that they can have for free tomorrow?"

Ole shook his head. Not only did they have to leave precious belongings behind, but they also couldn't sell them. Ole couldn't abandon his things only for them to be swept up by someone who didn't understand their worth. The alternative was to ship his belongings to Great Salt Lake at prices that were too steep for his means.

Ole returned to the campsite. He wondered if he should hide the trunk in the bushes. If the children were to see that he hadn't sold their things, they might be tempted to sneak them along, and Ole wouldn't object. He deliberated over his options until he heard a commotion near the river. It sounded as if someone had fallen in. He turned to see a traveling chest bobbing in the water as the current carried it away.

He watched as other men and women dumped the remainder of their belongings in the river. The sentiment was that if they couldn't have them, neither would anyone else. Ole considered this for a moment. He knew there was no other way. He could either leave his belongings in the dirt for a local to discover or he could throw them in the river.

Ole carried his trunk to the edge of the embankment. He placed a few rocks inside to make sure it would sink. He took a moment to say goodbye and give what remained of his former life a proper burial. For a moment he thought perhaps he should take the trunk back to camp, somehow sneak the items onto his handcart. They were so few. The extra weight would be no problem, he was sure. Even as he thought this, a humbling peace descended upon his heart. Something told him it was going to be fine. He closed the lid of the trunk, latched and lifted it. He was moments away from pushing it into the water when he was interrupted.

"Ole! Stop! *Afholde!*"

Lars Madsen, a fellow Danish emigrant he had met on board the ship, ran toward him yelling and waving. "I have another idea," Lars offered. His black hair was tucked behind his ears. "Some of the men would like to purchase a wagon together to carry the rest of their belongings. Are you interested?"

"I have some money but not enough to help buy a wagon."

Lars patted Ole on the back. "Then I will lend it to you."

Ole nodded, "I will pay you back as soon as we reach Great Salt Lake."

Ole was elated to tell his family he had secured a share in a wagon for their crossing. The trek would be difficult but now he was able to supply this small comfort to his family. Not only could they keep their treasures, but Andrew could also ride in the wagon when he was tired. Ole smiled, assured he had received a blessing from God.

Anxious to return to camp, Ole grabbed hold of the trunk handles.

"Let me help you," Lars offered. They grabbed either side of the trunk and lifted it, struggling for just a few paces.

"What do you have in here?" Lars asked.

"It feels heavy." Ole agreed and then chuckled. He set down his side of the trunk. Lars did the same. Ole lifted the lid and pulled out the rocks.

Lars laughed. "Mystery solved."

"Just preparing for the pull," Ole joked.

"Then you will easily be the strongest Dane. *Øvelse gør mester.*" Practice makes the master.

Ole laughed.

With the blessing of a wagon, his spirits were renewed.

THEN

℘

July 15–31, 1856

"Take my hand / And walk with me."
—Sonhar

*I*t was morning of the first day of the journey west. Ane sat quietly with her thoughts, as she slipped on leather shoes that extended above the ankle. They had a slight heel and came to a round point at the toes. She laced up the inside and secured the pewter clasps. She had never imagined she would someday wear this pair of shoes to cross America. They pinched her toes and rubbed against her heel. She stood, adjusting her apron, and grabbed the edge of the handcart. Ole stood ready to pull.

They left their encampment with dirt-covered linen strewn about the abandoned grounds amongst clothes, shoes, children's toys and other discarded belongings. The handcart wheels crunched over them, and the dry wheels screamed as the Willie Company started for Zion.

In the beginning there were many in the company over-anxious to complete the journey. They stepped out of line and hurried forward, leaving others in a cloud of dust, forgetting they were all in this together. But as the journey wore on, those Saints too eager to reach Zion learned to pace themselves. The days grew hot and the garish sun tanned their faces, blistered their noses and cracked their dry lips.

Some days they journeyed only five miles, usually on a Sunday when they held services before starting. Most days they tallied ten to twelve miles or more.

The father of the family pulled the handcart, being relieved or helped by the wife and older children. The Madsen girls had a difficult time keeping up. Although they were given an occasional reprieve riding in the wagon or on the cart, they still had to endure miles of walking. By the end of the first day, they couldn't comprehend doing this every day for months. They no longer thought of Denmark or of Zion, but simply focused on putting one foot in front of the other. The children sympathized with those in the company who had turned back as reality set in.

The bottoms of their feet were too tender to stand on. Every joint in their bodies ached and side aches would come and go. There was always a point during the day's walk when they experienced sudden fatigue and questioned the ability of their feeble legs to take another step forward in their inadequate, cracking shoes. Yet they did. They had to. Just one more step. One step closer. Closer to camp, closer to rest, closer to Zion. They found strength they didn't know they had to move forward.

Flies and gnats swarmed over them during the day and mosquitoes pestered them at night. They began their journey batting them away, but tired of this and decided to save the energy it took to swat them off. All manner of insects buzzed in their ears and coated their bonnets and hats. Horseflies nipped their skin, leaving it swollen and irritated.

Every night the company arrived at a new campsite and busily went about their duties of cooking, washing, fetching water, setting up tents and fixing broken handcarts. They even enjoyed some merriment. Zion was ever nearer.

Before bed the Madsens rubbed the aches from their legs and stiffness from their joints. They wrapped their feet, now ripe with blisters, with wet cloth to help cool the burning. Their bodies, covered in dust and sweat, were toweled off. The children were disinclined to complain. They whimpered, or even cried, but they knew better than to complain.

After a hundred miles, the endless walking began to consume Marie. The sweet smile she usually wore was difficult to find as she was on the verge of swooning. She imagined Zion to be the most beautiful place on earth. Rich soil to farm, blossoming trees in spring, golden fields in the fall and a spring of fresh water in which she could cool herself during the sweltering summer months. Her imaginings helped carry her through the day.

When she felt dizzy she held onto her sisters. When horseflies bit, she cursed them and was reprimanded by her mother for using such language.

Finally, one day when the dream of Zion could not carry her through, she threw herself on the ground and begged for rest. The company walked on. She had no choice but to stand and move or be left behind. She found the strength to get up and run to her family.

"Take my hand," Johanna insisted. "We will give each other strength."

That night the children whimpered as they tended to their aching muscles and blistered feet.

"My darlings," Ole whispered so as not to disturb the other four families in the tent preparing for bed. "Can you be strong for God?" he asked. They had tears in their eyes, but they nodded their heads. Of course they would be strong for God.

"What about your family? Can you be strong for each other?"

Again they nodded and held onto each other.

"So we can reach Zion together?"

They nodded. Ane smiled, happy to see that although their bodies were weak, their spirits remained strong.

"Soon you will adjust to life on the trail and your feet will heal and callous and your bodies will grow strong and resilient and it will get easier, I promise," Father told them.

Again they nodded, believing him.

"Do you remember the story of *The Girl Clad in Mouse Skin*?"

Marie managed a smile, and nodded. This was her favorite.

"Can you tell it to me?"

Marie wiped her eyes. "The princess is locked away in a secret place for her protection."

"And what does she do when she runs out of food and clothes?"

"She eats rats and makes clothes from their skins," Kristina answered.

Ole nodded, "She does not give up when she knows her father is dead, does she?"

The girls hung on his words.

"Instead, she is strong and resourceful, just like you, and even though she is covered in rat skin, she makes it to her kingdom to reign once again, doesn't she?"

Four little heads bobbed in agreement.

"So it is with us. We may be covered in dirt, our skin scorched by the sun's rays, and we may not be seen as the royalty we are, but when we arrive in Zion, we will know our birthright."

Ane led them in a family prayer, "Thank you for the blisters," she said, "for they make us strong."

Ole and Ane kissed their children and let sleep silence their soft cries.

*   *   *

After a week and a half, the Madsens, along with the rest of the company, quickly grew accustomed to life on the trail. The work was difficult, but they found comfort in the routine. Still they remained alert for the unexpected. There was never a moment when a ridge, an outcropping of foliage or a rock formation would not be carefully regarded and approached with suspicion. With the increase of travelers on the pioneer trails west, Indian attacks had also increased and there was always the threat of attack by wild animals, such as wolves. Armed guards and hunters rode parallel to the train at all times to provide protection. Before the trek, the Latter-day Saint travelers had been ordered to arm themselves. Ole had a loaded rifle that never left his side.

Men greatly outnumbered women on the plains and occasionally men from the nearby towns came around the traveling camps to try to talk the women into staying. "Come on lassie, I can provide you with a nice home. You need not carry on with these Mormons!" was the usual proposal.

The townsfolk's knowledge of Mormons relied heavily on rumors. The Willie Company had a few men from nearby towns threaten to stir up trouble or come into their camps at night and tear down their tents. About a week into their travels, the local town sheriff, who had heard women were tied up and being held captive, searched their tents. Some believed the Saints were devils, hiding horns underneath their bonnets and wide felt hats, and called out to them, "Ye devils!" Other locals were more congenial, offering gifts such as shoes or extra bedding for the journey.

Many townsfolk stood outside their houses churning butter or hanging laundry and watched silently as the pioneer men and women rolled through town in their soiled slacks and skirts that had once been vibrant in color.

Some men were too busy gambling in the saloons to pay any mind to the Mormons, while others flanked the streets yelling, "gee-haw" at the sight of the handcart pioneers pulling their own "pretend" wagons like oxen, and mocking them as they laughed and pointed.

"It is an honor to be reviled in such a way," Ane said to her children. "It is a vindication of our faith. Just ignore them and keep walking."

"*Tomme tønder buldrer mest,*" Ole joked. Empty vessels make the most noise.

*   *   *

One hot afternoon a couple weeks from Iowa City, the company stopped for lunch and to rest. They were nearing Iowa's western state line, having traveled nearly 150 miles. In a couple weeks they would board a ferry that would take them across the Missouri river and into Nebraska Territory. The Madsens snacked on dried apples and jerky while Ane oversaw the preparation and cooking of the skillet bread and beans for lunch. They drank heavily from their wooden canteen, but continued to thirst because of dehydration. Ole was prepared to refill the canteen with stream water when some of the townsfolk came by, offering food and well water. A young woman, no more than sixteen years old, approached Ole. Her blonde curly hair was pulled back into a loose bun. The girl's mother walked by her side, carrying a bucket of water and offering sips from a ladle to the weary travelers. The young girl handed the ladle to Ole, who first gave drink to Andrew and the rest of the children before drinking himself.

"Thank you," Ole said. It was one of the few phrases in English he had mastered.

The girl nodded and spoke, "You should not keep going. It is too dangerous."

Ole didn't understand. He looked at her and wiped the beads of sweat from his face with a kerchief.

"Soon there will be no towns, and you will be alone and vulnerable to the red faces. You have been led astray and you will risk your life for this nonsense."

He could tell she was concerned. Ole nodded again and said, "Thank you."

The girl nodded and walked on, offering water and pleading for the pioneers' souls as she did so.

Ole turned to Peter Madsen, the 62-year-old Danish company clerk, who was scribbling in his deep brown leather-bound journal. Sweat drenched Peter's clothes, and his thick and wiry facial hair, gray with age, glistened with sweat in the sun.

"What did she say?" Ole asked.

Peter looked up from his journal, first at Ole then off into the distance as he replied, "She was begging you to stay, to turn back. Said it was too dangerous."

Ole nodded, scanning the rolling hills that smelled of sweet grass. "I thought that's what she said."

NOW

❧

Spring 1997

"Holding on to what came in a dream."
—*Rainy Day*

J had a dream.

As I dreamed, I was divided between two places: what was and what is. I saw my grandmother Jennette, and I thought, *I'm just dreaming this, and I know she should not be here.* I was caught in the middle of deciding whether I should wake myself up or move forward. I hesitated, not sure if it was safe to move forward in the dream. Then I decided to go with it.

I found myself standing outside a room. As I dreamed on, it amazed me how detailed the dream was, both in texture and color. My grandmother stood in the center of the room. She was very clear and bright. She didn't shine, but there was sufficient light on her that I could see every detail. I could see the softness of her wrinkled pale cheek, and the light bouncing off her curly short white hair. She was wearing glasses and had a soft smile. I remember thinking she looked so real—exactly as I remembered her.

I stood there for a time and just looked at her, remembering the times I'd spent with her in my youth. How I wished I had spent even more time with her and really listened to her stories.

As I stood in my dream reconciling my thoughts, I remembered the words of my mother from when I was just a boy, words that she had spoken almost four decades earlier. She had said then that if she ever saw Grandfather Leonard again, she would give him a hug. I, too, wished to give my grandmother a hug.

I considered this as I dreamed and saw this as an opportunity to do just that. As I walked up to my grandmother she smiled at me, as she always did, and said, "Hi, Michael." I just looked at her, and without saying a word, moved forward to give her a big hug.

Then I awoke.

THEN

&

August 13, 1856

*"And she said / You can get there /
If you travel / With a friend."*
—*Tyme*

*I*t took the company nearly a month to travel 270 miles and they had more than 1,000 miles to go before they reached Great Salt Lake. The trail wasn't always pleasant. The road was often rough and hilly. Handcarts teetered on broken bridges when crossing rivers. Other times the travelers waded through streams with water up to their knees. The company always stayed near a river so they would have plenty of water. In the beginning the trail ran through trees that provided enough wood for fires. But as the trail moved into dry rolling prairie, sage and buffalo chips were used instead.

In the first four weeks only two deaths occurred along the trail. One was a girl who died late one morning after a strange rash was discovered in her mouth. The other death was an older woman who collapsed from heat exhaustion. The very young and the very old were typically first to succumb to the trials of the journey.

Provisions became low as they had little tea, coffee, sugar, rice and apples left. They mainly had flour, and occasionally meat.

The company stopped in Florence, Nebraska, to purchase new supplies, fix broken handcarts and prepare for the journey ahead. Beyond Florence, there were no towns along the trail where they could gather supplies. There were only widely separated and unreliable military forts.

Camp was set, and the family was busy erecting the tent for their group, starting a fire and cooking dinner. Ane made her way to the river with a brass pail. She dunked the pail under, letting it fill entirely. The river flowed softly and was smooth as glass. Her feet ached and burned with blisters, and she paused to consider soaking them in the river.

She looked around and saw others fetching water farther off. She slipped off her shoes and stockings, lifted up her skirt and stepped into the cool, soothing water.

She closed her eyes and listened to the soft whispers of the wind. She thought of Denmark and how far she was from home. Except now, it was no longer home.

She considered what had made Denmark home to her anyway. Was it the sense of familiarity? That wherever she went there were echoes of a hundred memories she could pluck from her thoughts?

She thought of her abandoned life in Tornved with sadness, but also peace. The memories of her former life were growing distant and for a moment, this new and unfamiliar land felt more like home than Denmark had. She smiled briefly, stepped from the river, donned her stockings and shoes and carried the water back to camp.

Ane prepared dinner while Ole and the girls foraged for fuel. Ole watched his daughters skip ahead of him, amused by their renewed energy that popped up each time they made camp.

Johanna led the way, scooping up twigs for the fire. Kristina held her apron out, creating a hammock to place sticks for the fire and also rocks she thought were pretty. She would examine the rocks' colors by the light of the fire at night, and leave them on the trail by morning.

Ole gathered his own basket of firewood as he kept an eye on the girls, making sure they didn't stray too far.

"Metta!" Johanna scolded, "Stop picking up rocks. The weight will burden you and make it difficult to carry anything else."

"You cannot order me, Hanna, not if Father says it's okay."

Ole, overhearing the girls' argument, intervened, "If you sincerely wish to carry the heaviness of rocks, Metta, how am I to counsel you otherwise?"

Kristina smiled at her victory.

"Perhaps you can share your stones with your mother. She could use them in the fire to heat up your dinner."

"I can spare a few." Kristina nodded.

"A few?" Ole chortled, "That's a good girl." Ole stroked Kristina's hair and continued walking, accidentally kicking a rock with his boot.

Ole glanced down at what caught his foot. It was a large flat stone with a name carved on the face. A strange chill ran up his leg as he recognized the stone as a grave marker. Ole glanced around at the other randomly placed stone slabs sporadically dotting the green pasture.

They were gathering kindling in a graveyard.

Ole and the girls returned to camp. Ole fashioned a fire with some cloth by striking a steel handle against a flint stone until a significant spark lit the fabric. He then nursed the heat with tree bark, softly blowing the flame until it blazed. He left Ane and the girls to the cooking and went to see sub-captain Ahmanson as he was curious to know the history of those who had come before him and were buried on this site. He discovered Ahmanson manning a wagon, yelling at the oxen.

Ahmanson scolded, tsk-ed and clucked, waved his arms and flapped the reins, but the oxen stood firm as rocks. He rocked forward a bit, as if this would get them moving. "Move! Move!" he commanded. It was his last resort before he sighed and climbed off the wagon.

"Brother Ahmanson," Ole removed his hat.

"Brother Madsen," they shook hands. "What can I do for you?" Ahmanson removed his gloves.

"What is the history of this place?"

Ahmanson studied Ole. "You have heard of Winter Quarters where the Saints spent the winter ten years ago, preparing to go west?"

"I have heard it mentioned."

Ahmanson spoke, "A darker time in our history, as I am told. When we Saints spent the winter here, hundreds died from starvation, the bitterness of winter and disease. We are in that area now."

Ole thought it curious that Ahmanson said "we," but he understood the reference. Mormons were few and their faith bonded them.

"What sort of disease?" Ole asked.

Ahmanson busied himself unhooking the wagon from the yoke. "Blackleg, among other things."

"Thing I don't understand," Ole said, "is why the first group of pioneers traveled here during the winter season? And across the Mississippi River, no less."

"They had no other choice, Ole. Besides it was prophesied."

"What was?" Ole asked.

"Joseph Smith, before he was killed, said we would move west and find a resting place among the Rocky Mountains. After Joseph died, we lost the right to a standing militia for our protection, and as the mobs grew, Brigham Young had no choice but to move fast."

"So many senseless deaths due to senseless hate," Ole shook his head.

Ahmanson shrugged. "Let it be a reminder of your faith, and what was sacrificed so we could come and settle in a Zion already prepared for us."

Ole nodded.

Ahmanson loosened the yoke and Ole lent a hand in lifting it over the oxen's heads. They set it on the ground, and Ahmanson thanked Ole. "We will be meeting soon." Ahmanson used his whip to direct his oxen towards the others that were grazing. "Best get fed before."

"Ane's preparing dinner. She's finally getting used to cooking with the baking kettle over a fire."

"I am sure by the time she has mastered it, we will have arrived in Great Salt Lake and there will be no use for it," Ahmanson laughed.

Ole nodded and watched absentmindedly as Ahmanson and the other men wrangled the oxen. Ole felt fond of his captain and crew. He didn't regret the decision he had made, but he still felt an unsettling concern. What if America was no different from

Denmark? Would his family suffer here just as his fellow Saints had in previous years, or would they be safe in Great Salt Lake as was prophesied?

Ole brushed the dirt from his brown felt hat, and with it any doubts.

The fire crackled and an orange glow danced on the faces of Willie and his sub-captains as they stood before the company. The group met at the center fire for meeting, prayers, inspirational talks and to distribute information regarding the next day's travels. When necessary, the leaders reproved people who complained or handled issues of misconduct. The leadership encouraged and directed the company in all aspects of life, including hygiene.

The Madsen family sat and visited with other Danish Saints as they waited for the meeting to commence. Jens Nielson, his wife, Elsie, and their five-year-old son Niels, shared a tent with the Madsens. Elsie had fared quite well in cooking by fire and was offering Ane advice on how to space out the embers to prevent burning.

A Swedish couple that had been living in Denmark, Olof Wickland and his pregnant wife, Ella, and their four children, settled themselves next to Johanna. They had boarded the steamship *Rhoda* with the Madsens and they had made every leg of the journey together. Johanna smiled and asked Ella what they planned on naming the baby.

"Girl," Ella smiled, "Kerstin. *Efter Olof moder.*" After Olof's mother. "Boy," Ella said, "Jacob. *Efter Olof fader.*"

Johanna smiled and nodded. She remembered how difficult her mother's pregnancy with Andrew had been. She couldn't imagine her mother having to make this trek while also pregnant. Johanna respected Ella for her courage and strength.

The sun had just set, and the pioneers were growing tired. The meeting was ready to commence and interpreters stood ready to relay the night's messages to the non-English speaking Saints.

After an invocation, Captain Willie stood to address the group. He acknowledged that although it was late in the season and they had suffered many delays, that they would, without question, continue moving forward in their journey. As Captain Willie spoke, Sub-captain Levi Savage listened with a knot in his chest.

Savage was born and reared in Ohio. He was returning from serving a mission in Burma and other areas of the Far East when he was made sub-captain of the Willie Company. He had joined the church ten years prior and enlisted in the California-bound Mormon Battalion when the U.S. government called LDS men from their westward-traveling families to fight in the war with Mexico. The battalion was mustered out in San Diego on July 16, 1847 and split into several groups. Most of them were bent on traveling from California to Utah Territory to be reunited with their families.

General Stephen W. Kearny was one of the officers who led the Battalion on its historic 2,000-mile-plus march across what became the southwestern United States. He also directed the group across the Sierra Nevada Mountains where they happened upon one of the sites where members of the Donner/Reed pioneer company had met with disaster in the previous year.

The Donner/Reed group of 87 pioneers from Missouri headed for California in May, 1846. They took some bad advice when they reached what later became Utah Territory, diverging from the usual Oregon Trail to take the Hastings Cutoff. That took them into the Wasatch Mountains and across the Great Salt Lake Desert, where they suffered serious losses of equipment and supplies. They reached the Sierra Nevadas late in the season and were trapped in deep snow. As members of the group started dying, others resorted to cannibalism to survive, ensuring the group a lasting place in pioneer history. Only 48 of the group survived. Kearny and his men buried what human remains they could find at what would later be referred to as the first cannibal camp, and attempted to burn the cabins at the site. Later, they came across the second cannibal camp where human remains lingered, but no body was found whole. Kearny and his men left the camp as it was and pressed on.

Ten weeks later Levi traveled down this same path with a group of men returning to Great Salt Lake. At sundown they came across the grisly remains of the second cannibal camp. Corpses were left in pieces and scattered in all directions around the camp. The horrifying images lingered in Savage's thoughts. He knew what harsh and untempered winter could do. With his wife having died years earlier, the only family he had left was his young son, who was being cared for by his sister. He missed his son and knew the boy needed a father. He didn't know if he wanted to risk a mountain crossing so late in the season.

He removed his hat, feeling the cool breeze of the evening tousle his thinning curly brown hair. He ran his fingers anxiously over his beard. He felt compelled to speak, but would not interrupt his captain. He would show at least that much respect, knowing what he was about to say would cut through the captain's words like a sword.

Willie finished his remarks, and Savage stood to address the congregation, his heart burning with anxiety. "Brothers and Sisters," he said, his lips trembling "I know you are eager to move forward on this trip but I urge you to stay in Florence."

A quick murmur filled the crowd. "If you stay here for the winter," Savage continued, "you have a better chance of survival and can be ready to finish the trek next spring. If not, you will face cold that will freeze you to your bones. You will wade in snow up to your knees and sleep on cold ground with nothing but a thin blanket to keep you warm, only to awake to have to dig out your handcarts in the morning and continue wading in the freezing snow." Tears fell from his eyes. "If you continue on this late in the season, I tell you that your bones will strew the way."

Ole felt the intensity and concern of Levi's words before the translation reached his ears. Members of the company were thrown into confusion and fear.

Willie knew there could be no rifts in leadership. Once Savage took his seat an eerie silence fell over the company as they awaited further instruction. The captain, clearly dissatisfied with Levi's fear-provoking words, stood and spoke again.

"The God I serve is a God who saves to the uttermost, and I want no Job's comforters with me," Willie said, admonishing Savage's failed attempt to dissuade the Saints, and in turn, making them only feel worse. "It is not wise to question that God will save his children. Surely God wishes us to reach Zion and He will take care of those of us who are faithful. Elder Savage, to hear you say otherwise brings into question your loyalty and your faith."

Savage stood, thinking back on the Donner Party. He had seen firsthand the truth of his words—*your bones will strew the way*. With echoes of these gruesome images in his mind, he could not hide his tears as he spoke again. "I have only spoken the truth. If you wish to replace me in my services," he said to Willie, "you are welcome to do so and I will not think ill of you. But you and I both know I speak the truth."

The Madsen girls listened to the translation and studied their father's reaction. Ole showed no change in countenance so as to not reveal his concern.

"Father?" Johanna murmured.

Ole glanced at his wife for direction. She held that fierce look of determination in her eyes that bolstered his strength and resolve.

"We must move forward," Ole said, addressing his family now. "We did not come this far to live in a dugout as they did at Winter Quarters and risk death. We are traveling to Zion. There is no work or food for us here. How are we to survive? We have no choice but to keep going."

Ane nodded, looking around her. Everyone looked toward the leaders for reassurance. Just then, a man by the name of William H. Kimball, the son of Heber C. Kimball, a member of the church's First Presidency, stood to speak. He was passing through on his way to Great Salt Lake by carriage and had joined their meeting. Kimball had been working since February of that year in preparing Iowa City and Florence for the handcart companies that would pass through. He had traveled back and forth along the trail several times making these arrangements. He had dark hair and a trimmed beard hiding a dimple in his chin. The red military sash he often wore for luck was wrapped around his waist. It originally belonged to the Prophet Joseph Smith, and was bestowed on Kimball, by his father, after William's first military commission in 1849.

The commotion subsided as Kimball talked. Ole understood only a few words, not enough to make sense of it, but when Kimball finished speaking, a calm fell over the crowd. Many people were smiling and others cheered.

"What did he say?" Ole asked the translator.

"He rebuked those of little faith and promised he would stuff into his mouth all the snow we would ever see on our journey to the valley." The translator smiled.

With that, Savage's concern turned to anger. He stood, biting his indignation, and addressed the company again. He thought of his four-year-old son at home and knew there was a possibility that he might never see him again. "Brethren and sisters, what I have said to you I know to be true," he paused, "but seeing as you are to go forward, I will go with you, will help you all I can, will work with you, will rest with you, will suffer with you and, if necessary, I will die with you. May God in his mercy bless and preserve us," he said flatly.

A hush fell over the crowd. A ghostly silence whispered concern as their faith balanced between two opinions.

Willie knew he had to restore their spirits. He stood before his company stating, "We will continue forward with faith. I have no doubt that God can create a safe passage for us and will do so if we have but faith in Him, and unless I receive a message from the Prophet Brigham Young urging us to stay in Florence, we shall move forward."

The crowd cheered, and the decision was made. Some of the party chose to stay, but most were anxious to get to Zion and had faith in God and their leaders that they would arrive unharmed. In the heat of August, the thought of wading in snow up to their knees seemed unlikely. They believed the words of Kimball and Captain Willie.

What they didn't know was that the Prophet Brigham Young was currently unaware of their decision to move forward. If Brigham had known, he later said, he would have, without hesitation, urged them to stay.

NOW
ဢ
April 1997

*"There is a place / I sometimes go / And certain things /
I somehow know."*
—*Tyme*

My brother KC sat comfortably on the couch next to his wife,
Nancy. KC always had a thing about finding the perfect couch,
and he was always willing to pay top dollar for it once he found it.
The couch had to have the right amount of firmness, but still be
plush and comfortable. On this particular Sunday afternoon, he
was watching the intermission program playing between sessions
of the LDS General Conference.

KC adjusted his glasses as a special program on the handcart
tragedy showed Prophet Gordon B. Hinckley speaking at Rock
Creek. Rock Creek is an empty piece of dry and windy land in
Wyoming. President Hinckley told how thirteen pioneers immigrating to Utah had died in one night and were buried together at
Rock Creek in one mass grave. A monument had been raised at
the site honoring those lost. The camera scrolled over the monument, allowing home viewers to see each name of those buried in
the common grave.

KC gazed at the screen as the names passed over it. Suddenly a name from the plaque jumped out at him as if he were seeing it in 3D. He felt a sudden rush of emotion.

The name was Ole Madsen. KC stood and pointed to the screen stating, "I'm related to that man." By this time the name was no longer on the screen, but it was indelibly printed on his brain.

"How do you know?" his wife asked.

In truth, KC didn't know. Not for sure, anyway. In that moment, all he had was a feeling in his chest and clarity in his mind that told him this was true, so all he could say to his wife was, "I just know."

THEN

ℰℭ

August 30, 1856

"What I thought I knew / I wanted to scream."
—*Requiem*

*M*arie heard gasps and heated remarks that quickly roused her. She sat up and rubbed the sleep from her eyes. The wagon had come to a dead halt. She lifted the canvas flap and peered out. Three shallow graves had been freshly made. The Willie Company was the first to arrive at the scene of the butchery near a site that later became Wood River, Nebraska. The horrible stench lingered like a haunting. Captain Willie and Sub-captain Atwood, with the help of other men, packed excess mounds of dirt onto the freshly dug graves to stifle the stench and discourage wolves. The graves belonged to the victims of an Indian raid, two teamsters and a baby. The baby's mother, a Mrs. Wilson, had been carried off by the Indians.

In the wagon, Marie held her doll close to her heart, feeling panicked. She heard hushed whispers about red faces attacking a wagon train. She didn't know the attack had not been on the Willie train, but on a company that belonged to a man named Almon Babbitt.

Babbitt, one of Utah Territory's two representatives to the U.S. Congress, had made more than 20 trips across the country to represent the territory and conduct business. This time, his westbound wagons were loaded with goods and supplies needed in the territory. Babbitt was not traveling with his cargo when the wagon train was attacked; he had left later and was behind them on the trail, but was catching up quickly traveling on a light buggy drawn by fast horses. But within a couple of weeks, the same group of Cheyenne Indians who had conducted the raid near Wood River would attack Babbitt and his small group at Ash Hollow. Most were killed quickly in a volley of arrows, Babbitt would fight fearlessly against his Indian attackers but he would not survive. His skull would be split from the thrash of a tomahawk and his head scalped.

If Marie had known that the people harmed were not in her company, she may have received some small comfort from this. But in her confused and fearful state she believed the Indians had attacked and killed people from her company. She clung tightly to her doll, tears dripping from her eyes, and pleaded with God to keep her family safe.

THEN

∽

September 3, 1856

*"The path is but a song / Just let the music /
Pull you along"*
—*Along the Path*

*T*he fire crackled and popped as the dry splinters of sagebrush smoked and caught fire. Ole added a half dozen brown buffalo chips that were dry, brittle and cracked by long hot days in the sun. A large roast hung above the fire on a string. The string attached to a cast iron tripod that usually held their heavy pot above the fire. As the string unwound, the meat turned and browned evenly on all sides.

Many of the camp were celebrating and in high spirits this evening. They were growing accustomed to life on the trail and no longer faced persecution as they traveled, having already passed through all the towns in Iowa and Nebraska Territory.

Ane joined her daughters in song and dance. They sang in broken English *Come, Come, Ye Saints,* the beloved pioneer anthem written by William Clayton as he sat on a muddy riverbank in Iowa, lonely for the young wife he had left in Nauvoo, who was soon to deliver a child. It became the soulful expression for thousands who crossed the Plains in the mid-1850s.

There was livelier music too, and the girls laughed and sang as they twirled their skirts, locking elbows and spinning each other around. Ole laughed and clapped, providing them a beat as they skipped. The spirit of the night was strong, and Ole couldn't help but join them, swinging Andrew around and lifting Marie in his arms as they danced and sang until they were sufficiently tired and the buffalo meat was cooked. They sat around the fire, still in high spirits, sharing their meal with Peter Madsen and Joseph Elder.

Peter sat next to Ole and patted him on the back, "A well deserved large chunk of buffalo for your family tonight Ole. You are quite the hunter."

Ole chuckled. They all knew his kill was sheer luck.

"Who knew my husband had such a talent for hunting," Ane jested. "I am sure it will be of much use to us when we reach the valley."

Ole laughed. "I am a man of many talents my beloved, that you often do not see," he teased.

"I see them. It is why I married you, my love." Ane retorted and Peter and Ole laughed.

Joseph Elder spoke only English, and Peter relayed the jest to him.

Joseph laughed and replied, "From where I sat, I couldn't tell who hit the large bull. All I could see were men clumsily shooting and I feared one of us might be hit instead of the buffalo. In fact, I am glad we are not having a wake," he said.

Peter laughed, "That was quite a sight. Those dumb animals walked right down the middle of the handcart train."

"And I have never seen such a barrage of ordnance," Joseph continued. "And everyone was claiming victory. Now I do not doubt this man shot, but how do you know he hit it?" he pointed to Ole.

"I was standing right there," Peter said.

Ole followed the men as they spoke, understanding only bits of English.

"You only brought in a prairie dog, Joseph," Peter said. "Could it be that perhaps you are just a little set back?"

"I have shot my share," Joseph said smugly, "and I don't want to take any glory away from this farmer; just saying that it was a sight."

"Here is the way it is," Peter said, "I am writing it down in the journal that Ole Madsen shot one buffalo and I will give credit for the other buffalo shot to an Englishman." Peter said it first in English then in Danish so Ole understood.

"Which Englishman?" Joseph asked.

"Doesn't matter." Peter said, "No Englishman will ever read this little account. I fear the Danish tongue will be gone here soon and who will ever read this thing? What I write in here is the truth. It is my charge," he quipped.

"Do you write everything down in that journal?" Ole asked.

"Not everything," Peter said, "Did you hear of Robert Caldwell?"

Ole shook his head.

"Broke his collar bone," Peter stated.

"How did he accomplish that?"

Peter smiled. "He attempted to milk a heifer."

Ole laughed. "Have you heard the story of the *Jutlander and His Stockings*?"

Peter shook his head.

Ole never missed an opportunity to share a story.

"Papa, I have heard this one before," Marie cut in.

"Well, which one would you like me to tell?"

"*The Girl Clad in Mouse Skin.*"

Ole laughed.

"Marie," Johanna stepped in, "You have heard that story more than a dozen times."

"Let Father tell his story," Kristina interjected.

Marie sighed and settled.

Ole relayed the story to Peter, who translated it for Joseph.

"A well-dressed man from Jutland once took a drop too much of drink," Ole began, "and consequently lost command of his legs and fell asleep on the high-road. While he was there, a wayfarer passed him, and upon seeing his good stockings, took them off the Jutlander's feet and replaced them with his own worn stockings."

"What any good Samaritan would do," Peter joked.

"Yes," Ole continued. "Well a man came driving along and shouted, 'Get your legs out of the road or I shall run them over!' The Jutlander awoke and looked down at his legs and saw a pair of ragged stockings, and remembering his own pretty white stockings he answered, 'Drive on! These are not my legs!'"

The men laughed.

"Quite the story-teller, Ole," Peter said.

Ole shrugged. "Just one of my many talents."

"Andrew is tired, as am I," Ane interjected. "Girls, time for bed."

The girls reluctantly followed, dragging their feet.

"Just because we are not in Denmark, does not mean the troll will not get you!" Ole called after them.

"Then you had better come to bed, Father, or the troll will be after you," Johanna called back, and the girls giggled.

"Another one of your tall tales?" Peter asked.

"One of the best," Ole smiled.

Peter and Joseph stood and bid Ole farewell.

Ole sat alone, the fire waned into the soft glow of embers. He looked up at the stars sprinkling the darkness. There was a flash of lightning, followed by a low rumble lasting a few seconds before the wind picked up. Ole secured the tie-downs on the tent before stepping in, folding over the flap and securing it. He stepped carefully past sleeping pioneers to where his family slept.

At the second clap of thunder the children stirred awake. Rain hit the tent with loud thuds as a raging wind threatened to uproot it.

Ole pulled off his boots, grateful to have them while others walked barefoot or with cloth sacks wrapped around their feet. Ole missed home, but found, as they grew closer to Zion, that he was growing more grateful for the decision they had made to emigrate. He often thought of Karen and planned to write her as soon as they arrived in the valley. He would urge her to emigrate as well.

Ole lay next to his wife. There was another flash of light followed by more crackling thunder. Now the rain poured in earnest. The water infiltrated the tent and gushed around them as the wind howled. There was nothing they could do but lie huddled together, cold and wet.

The children shivered and the family scooted closer together.

The girls kept sitting up. Surely they couldn't be expected to sleep in inches of water.

"There is nothing we can do but wait for it to pass. Try to sleep," Ole urged.

The girls attempted sleep as Ane cooed, "Sleep little child, sleep," until the storm passed.

THEN

∞

September 4, 1856

"A warm wind blows / As summer leaves."
—Someday

*M*inutes before the morning bugle blew, Ole awoke to loud talking outside the tent.

"Is it time to wake up?" Ane mumbled, her eyes adjusting to the darkness.

"No," Ole whispered. "Something must have happened. Stay with the girls." Ole slipped on his boots and left the tent. His clothes were still damp. He considered changing his shirt while it was still dark, but when he heard shouting at the edge of camp he instinctively followed it instead, pulling on his suspenders. The sub-captains and Willie were speaking heatedly with the other teamsters. Peter was with them, his face registering concern.

"Gather all the able-bodied men immediately," Willie commanded. "We will assemble teams for the search."

"Ole!" Peter exclaimed. "Something has happened. I think Indians attacked or maybe there were stampedes during the storm. Twenty-two of the draft animals are missing. Captain Willie is setting up a search party for the cattle."

"I will get my rifle."

Ole returned to camp. The bugle had sounded and Ane emerged from the tent. Her hair, disheveled by sleep, was already neatly combed and pinned in a bun. She was rubbing the crust of dirt from her eyelids when Ole returned.

"What has happened?" Ane asked. "Someone in our tent said our oxen are gone."

Ole nodded, slinging his rifle over his shoulder. "Likely a stampede, maybe Indians."

"Indians?" Marie cried. She had stuck her head outside the tent to eavesdrop.

"You and your sisters get ready and set our things out to dry while I make breakfast," Ane said. Marie nodded and disappeared under the canvas flap.

"We have to go search for the oxen. Hopefully we will be back by lunch," Ole told Ane.

The girls emerged from the tent.

"You are leaving, Father?" Johanna asked, rubbing the sleep from her eyes. "It's dark. How will you see?"

"It will be light soon," Ole reassured her.

"What if you are attacked by Indians?" Marie asked.

"It will be fine," Kristina said. She too was scared, but didn't let it show. "Father will be safe. Nothing is going to happen to us."

"Father will keep us safe," Johanna assured Marie.

But Father was leaving to help with the search. Marie looked at her mother for comfort. Mother was lost in thought. Marie looked at her father, standing tall and strong and believed her sister's reassurances. Surely nothing could harm Father.

Ane watched Ole disappear in the dark. "Where is your brother?" Ane asked.

"Still asleep," Johanna answered.

Ane nodded. "Let us take care of our duties. When the men return with the oxen, we need to be ready to leave."

Ane did not allow for idle hands even with the company fixed at camp. The storm had soaked most of their things and blown the rest around camp. They spent the morning finding and drying items. Ane made sure everything was packed and ready to go in case Ole and the men returned with a herd of oxen, as she hoped. The children did their chores, washed dishes, shook out their blankets, and carried pails of water from the river.

Soon it was noon and not a single man had returned. Ane continue to stay busy to fend off worry. She prepared lunch, washed the dishes and then repacked everything, just in case. Then she found a rock to sit on while the children played hopscotch nearby.

"Metta, will you make the board?" Marie asked. "You always make them the best."

Kristina smiled with obvious pride, and scratched the dry dirt with a stick.

Ane pulled the locket from underneath her top and began running it through her fingers. She wondered how the loss of oxen would slow their progress. Even with the heat of the day upon them, Ane remembered Levi Savage's words. She knew there was no time to waste.

She was pulled from her thoughts by laughter. She turned to see a group of English Saints looking and pointing at her and her children. Their laughter seemed cruel, but Ane smiled and waved. The women turned away. Ane turned back to her children.

"Stop playing." Ane spoke, soft but firm. The children looked alarmed. Ane stood and walked toward their wagon. "We are going to read scripture. Follow me now."

Ane read to the children for an hour. Most of them fought sleep, but when their eyes grew heavy Ane nudged them back awake. After an hour Ane's eyes drooped. The children said nothing, but waited until their mother collapsed into sleep before they sneaked from the wagon and returned to their game of hopscotch.

Marie wobbled as she balanced on one foot and hopped to the next square. Johanna looked on, while Andrew entertained himself by chasing grasshoppers and Kristina, butterflies.

"'She shaped herself to a little wild hawk, and flew to the clouds so high.'" Kristina cooed the ballad of *The Maid as a Hind and a Hawk* as she crept upon a butterfly.

"What does it mean?" Marie asked, while Johanna took her turn on the board.

"It is a story about a girl who is turned into a bird by her stepmother, and her true love rescues her by offering a piece of his own flesh."

"Why would he do that?" Marie asked.

"Because he loved her," Kristina said, scrambling after another butterfly.

In her mind, Marie saw flesh being torn from a body and cringed.

"When you love someone, you are willing to sacrifice even your own flesh for them." Johanna said, easing Marie's confusion.

Marie frowned.

"I want my cup-and-ball," Andrew said. He had not yet mastered the game but was still determined. Johanna was best at it. She had found the right flick of the wrist to send the ball high in the air and land it directly in the cup.

"It's in the trunk," Kristina said. "We cannot get it."

"Mama opened the trunk to get the *Bible*. It should still be open," Marie offered.

"Mother will just take it away from us," Kristina said.

Johanna thought of her book, locked away in the chest. She had missed being able to read it every night. The thought of having it close to her was too enticing. "I will do it."

Johanna's determination was something they didn't argue with. Besides, they all wanted their treasures. They walked quietly, feeling as if each step were a betrayal. Johanna climbed the back of the wagon. She saw her mother, her face gaunt and pale, her breathing almost inaudible, as she slept. Johanna reached into the wagon with both hands; Marie and Kristina held her legs for support. Johanna lifted the trunk's lid and pulled her book from the top of the heap. She handed it to Kristina, then found Kristina's poems, Marie's doll and Andrew's game.

Johanna's eyes stayed locked on her mother's sleeping form as she slithered down from the wagon. Each child held the coveted object as if his or her life depended on it, and keeping quiet they ran with thudding hearts, until they reached the edge of camp.

*   *   *

Ole felt the sun's harshness particularly cruel today as he strained to see. Peter strode a few feet ahead of him. The men of the company had scattered in different directions to search for the lost cattle.

Peter kept his eyes on the ground, hoping to spot a hoof-print. "I think the storm cleared away any tracks."

They walked into the desolate landscape, isolated from the other searchers. Ole squatted and picked up a handful of dirt. He dreamed for just a moment of reaching Zion and farming his own land. The daydream dissipated as quickly as the dirt slipped through his fingers. He stood and walked on. He stayed alert, rifle at the ready, in case Indians ambushed them. What if this had been a trap to lure the men away from camp? Ole looked back to where camp was set and saw rising smoke signaling its location.

"Being delayed like this is going to take its toll, especially with the food supply as it is," Peter said.

"How do you mean?"

"We have enough food for sixty days and that is if we average seventeen miles a day. It is just enough to make it to the valley."

"Why did they not pack more?"

"They wanted to have enough for ninety days, but how would we carry it? The weight would be too much for the handcarts and wagons to carry."

"How can that be?" Ole asked.

"We either re-supply at Fort Laramie, or wait for the re-supply wagons to come to us along the trail. We are wasting time looking for the cattle."

Neither of them spoke. A moment of silence passed before Ole convinced his legs to move again, dragging them as he walked farther from his family, hoping the oxen were all he would lose.

THEN

ℰ❍

September 6–7, 1856

*"Along the path / You will likely trod /
On less than solid ground."*
—*Along the Path*

𝓣 he men spent two days searching for the oxen and found noth-ing. A flurry of questions buzzed through camp. "Will we find the oxen? How will we haul the supply wagons without them? Was it a stampede? Are we in danger of an Indian attack?"

The Madsen children were all aware of the concerns, but they trusted their parents. "Everything is going to be fine. We just need to have faith," Ane assured them. Faith became the only way to Zion.

The season was fast moving toward winter and Captain Willie knew they could no longer afford to wait. He ordered that the milk and beef cows be yoked in place of the missing oxen, but with a 3,000-pound wagon to haul, the untrained cows couldn't move it, so a hundred pounds of flour was loaded onto each cart. Even so, watching a young heifer attempt to pull a wagon was a sorry sight. The company moved forward in two shifts. The first half moved forward, unyoked their cattle and cows at midday and took them back to re-yoke them to the remaining wagons. They arrived in camp well after dark, traveling only five miles.

The extra flour on the carts made the pull laborious. The carts were not built to carry so much weight. There were many break-downs, followed by complaining and bitter discontent. Not only was their progress slowed and their labor increased, but their meat supply was affected.

As discontent spread among the company, Captain Willie did what he felt was best. He urged unity, obedience, confession and forgiveness. He stated at an early morning meeting, "If any of you in your hearts would be grumblers, pilferers and so forth, I ask that you stand aside from the rest so that the brethren might better know you." Such a taunt, Willie knew, was unlikely to be answered. He did it hoping he could shake them from their com-plaining. Such attitudes would lead to broken spirits and lack of faith. If they were going to make it to Great Salt Lake, the throng had to maintain good spirits, and be willing to follow orders.

"We can no longer afford to travel in luxury," Willie continued. The harsh words fell over the assemblage. Every person knew their mode of travel was anything but luxurious, but they under-stood the meaning behind his words. They would be required to sacrifice more.

Brother Atwood addressed Ole and others who had purchased their own wagon, including an independent wagon train headed by a Captain Siler who was traveling with the Willie Company. "I ask those that have purchased independent wagons to allow them to be consecrated and given to the Lord through his servant Presi-dent Willie, to be used as the Holy Ghost should direct, that they may give up their wagon and their oxen and confer honor on themselves by their sacrifice even if they should have to leave their luggage on the plains."

All that Ole had done for his family was for naught. Their handcart could barely carry the extra hundred pounds of flour and their linen, let alone their personal items.

The children held their breaths as they watched their father pull their trunk from the wagon and discard it at the edge of the trail.

The wagon and their personal things were gone. The children knew better than to complain or feel sorry, but they couldn't help but stand befuddled. All that was left of their belongings sat in an abandoned traveling chest on an empty dusty trail somewhere in Nebraska Territory.

Johanna opened the chest's lid and grabbed the family *Bible*.

"Leave it," Ole commanded. "Everything must stay."

Johanna caught the sadness in her throat and dropped the *Bible* back in the chest.

"We shall have all we need when we reach Zion," Ane assured.

Marie didn't wish to disobey orders, but she couldn't see the harm in grabbing her doll. When her family turned away, she crept to the trunk, slid out her doll, and ran back to the handcart, hiding her most prized possession behind her back.

Once everything had been redistributed, the trek continued. Ole waited in line, ready at his handcart as those ahead of him started to move. He noticed Marie hiding something at her side.

"Marie, what do you have?"

She wanted to lie, but pulled the doll from behind the folds of her skirt and showed it to her father.

Ole motioned for her to approach and he took the doll from her, ready to discard it.

"Papa do not get rid of it. I will carry it," Marie pleaded.

Ole looked at his daughter, his eyes soft but his voice firm. "You cannot carry her," he tried to explain, "You need to focus on carrying yourself." Ole wished he could offer his children the comfort of what little possessions they had left, but he knew they would only turn into burdens as the days wore on. The path was growing more difficult as they journeyed. "You just worry about carrying yourself, and I will worry about carrying you," he insisted.

She looked at her father and with tears in her eyes she finally nodded in compliance.

Ole's jaw clenched with displeasure as he threw his daughter's final possession into the distance. He drew his hand softly over Marie's blonde locks before picking up the handcart handle and pushing forward. He didn't look up for a long time.

THEN

∞

September 8, 1856

*"And we wend our way / Through the days it seems /
Along a bank / Of forgotten dreams."*
—Sonhar

*T*he morning was occupied with adjusting the mismatched draft teams and moving freight from one wagon to another.

Ole was busy strapping a tent to the side of a wagon when Peter approached, journal in hand, looking pale. "Peter?" he said, interrupting his friend's thoughts.

"Another wagon train has been attacked by Indians."

Ole held Peter's gaze momentarily. Peter ran his hand over his beard. Ole turned back to the rope and looped it into a slipknot.

"Where?" Ole asked.

"Seventy miles ahead. A man by the name of Henry Bauichter left camp to hunt, and returned to discover the wagon was on fire, after being ransacked." Peter's throat went dry, his voice catching as he tried to speak. Peter glanced at Marie who was sitting on the wagon with Andrew, playing with some rocks they had found that morning.

Ole lifted Marie and Andrew off the wagon. "Go help your mother," he instructed, and they scampered off.

Peter continued speaking. "Bauichter first saw a child, crying, covered in blood. A man had been shot through with an arrow and the man's wife was dead sitting upright," Peter swallowed against the lump, "Her body was completely exposed. She was treated severely and without mercy by her murderers."

"And the oxen?" Ole asked.

"None to be found."

Ole sighed.

"I must record what I have learned," Peter said, holding up his journal.

"Of course," Ole said.

Peter found a rock on the edge of camp where he sat and wrote about the recent Indian attack. After scribbling a few lines, he stopped writing in mid-sentence. He stood and threw his pencil as far as he could into the distance. He walked to where Captain Ahmanson sat and handed the journal to him, "I can no longer be clerk," he said, and walked away.

NOW

﹏

Spring 1998

"Whirling past shadows /
To see what is found."
—Sonhar

I had been asked to help organize a stake trek to Martin's Cove for the following summer. Martin's Cove was chosen because it was where the Martin Company camped and weathered snowstorms during their pilgrimage to Utah Territory. Those of us appointed to organize the trek wanted the youth to have as authentic an experience as possible. We wanted them to feel what the handcart pioneers felt walking on the trail, pulling a handcart and sleeping in a large canvas tent at night. Since KC's experience during conference, when he saw Ole Madsen's name on the monument, KC had delved into our family history and learned that Ole was our great-great grandfather. At this time, I knew very little about the journey or the pioneer experience of pulling a handcart. I was looking at the stake trek as a ward assignment and was focused on just getting my part done. This included going up with a party beforehand to set up the campsite, organize the fireside program and perform. That's right. I was going to play my guitar—in front of an audience.

The days when I performed in Primary and nearly suffered a heart attack were long past. I was still extremely nervous when I played for a crowd. But I learned a trick. I let myself dissolve into the music and allowed that feeling to carry me through.

Prior to this I had joined the thousands of others who owned a guitar but rarely played it. It wasn't until I was in my mid-thirties that I decided to start playing classical guitar.

I called a guitar teacher out of the classified pages and the next thing I knew I was parked outside her orange brick house ready for my first lesson. She answered the door. We were about the same age. She led me to a basement bedroom with two folding chairs and a dresser. I sat across from her in one of the chairs.

"Why are you here?" she asked.

I presumed the answer was obvious, but I decided to give her one nonetheless. "I want to be more serious about playing the guitar and I want to know what I'm playing and why."

She nodded. "Play me something."

I remembered little about playing the guitar and began to strum some chords.

"Hand me your pick," she interrupted. I stopped strumming and handed it to her. She took the pick and threw it across the room. "Now forget everything you think you know and we will start from there."

So, with a clean slate and open mind I began my lessons.

I spent hours learning the guitar and as I played it began to feel like an extension of me. I took my guitar almost everywhere with me and practiced every chance I got. My focus veered towards classical guitar as I studied pieces by composers such as Chopin, Bach and Beethoven. I spent endless hours practicing and my family appreciated the ambiance it added to the home. They didn't, however, always enjoy my playing while they were trying to watch television or when I was hammering out a tune on repeat. To this day, *Light up the Land* is not allowed in our house because of the hours I spent practicing the song.

Emily Christensen was a casual friend in the ward and an aspiring folk singer. Even though our styles couldn't be farther apart, we had both been asked to participate in the program at Martin's Cove. Emily was already accustomed to sharing her talents at church functions. Unlike me, she wanted to do more.

I remember going out to dinner as couples, myself and Cheri and Emily and her husband. She brought her guitar along and wanted to stop at a local coffee shop's open mic night. She had a great talent and a very comfortable, earthy voice.

I once gave Emily a copy of some lyrics to a song I was writing and a couple of days later, sitting in her living room, Emily played me her version of the song. Before she started she asked, "What does the song mean?"

"It means whatever you got out of it," I replied.

She nodded.

"What did you get out of it?" I asked, with some anxious curiosity. She went into a very cosmic detailed description of God's dealings with man and the eternal nature of our relationship with Him.

"Is that correct?" she asked me once she was finished.

I didn't know what to say. I was surprised another person had gotten so into something I had written and I was quite taken aback by it.

"Yes," I finally agreed, although it wasn't entirely true. Her explanation was much more interesting than what I had written.

Then she, in her rather quiet and simple way, played her version of the song. It was amazing listening to the texture she had added. I suddenly had a vision of taking the guitar from something I did to relax to maybe writing songs I could share with others.

That experience began for me at Martin's Cove. Before this the only other time I had performed as an adult was when I'd played Beethoven's *Moonlight Sonata* for a church program at the prompting of some friends. What was I thinking, playing something so technical as a start? After that, I was quite sure my days of performing were over—until Martin's Cove.

Emily had written a song for the program and I had worked on versions of *A Poor Wayfaring Man of Grief* and *Come, Come, Ye Saints.*

I called a high school friend of mine, Rick, who had moved to Lyman, Wyoming, and told him I was coming his way and would stop by to say hello. When I told him I was doing a trek, he told me about a stake president, Scott Lorimer, who was involved in securing the land at Martin's Cove and other historic sites for the church. Lorimer, my friend said, knew everything about the hand-cart pioneers. He suggested I get in touch with President Lorimer and ask him to speak to our stake handcart participants.

I called, thinking it would fill out the program and make my job of arranging it complete.

"President Lorimer," I introduced myself, "I am from the Farmington 13th ward, and we are coming to Martin's Cove to camp. I was wondering if you could come and speak to us."

"I'm glad to hear you're coming," he said sincerely, "but I can't come to the fireside. I get asked to speak almost every night at some type of church event, and there are only so many I can say yes to. Martin's Cove is a long drive from where I live. But I know of some missionaries who are working there that would be happy to speak to you."

"That would be great," I said, "Thanks for the info. I'm looking forward to coming up there to learn more about my great-great-grandfather. He was in the Willie Company."

"Oh yeah?" President Lorimer's interest was piqued. "What was his name?"

"Ole Madsen," I said.

There was a moment of silence before Lorimer spoke. "I'll be there," he said.

I wasn't sure I had heard him right. It was quiet for what felt like a long time, but was really only a few seconds.

Finally I said, "You'll be there?"

"Yes, I wouldn't miss it."

"Great." I didn't know what to say or what had changed. President Lorimer enlightened me.

"Ole is a great hero of mine, and I need to tell you who you are."

Who was this man talking about? I wondered. A man who was virtually a stranger to me was calling the person I knew only as a simple farmer from Denmark a hero. His voice and sincerity almost made me cry.

"I don't understand," I finally said.

"Ole truly was a great man, and I think you should know about what he had to go through, so, I'll be there."

When we hung up, I sat in silence with my thoughts. This man wasn't even related to Ole, but he clearly knew more about my ancestor than I did. He spoke as though he was Ole's brother and was willing to take his time to drive a great distance to share what he knew so I could understand my ancestor's experiences better. I was humbled and a little ashamed I hadn't been really interested in learning about Ole earlier. I thought about the vivid dream I had about my grandmother Jennette the previous fall. The dream suddenly had meaning for me now, and symbolized the opportunities I had to embrace my past. I couldn't wait until summer to hear President Lorimer speak.

NOW

ഔ

Summer 1998

*"And the place I came to be /
Was a place deep inside of me"*
—Sonhar

MARTIN'S COVE

*S*unset still lighted the horizon when I started playing the guitar. As I played for the pioneer program, I escaped all those eyes, and let the song carry me elsewhere. I floated on the song, unaware of anything around me. When I finished, I opened my eyes to the campfire that was now the brightest thing in sight. It softly illuminated the shapes of the people gathered around it. Once I saw it was dark out, I wondered how long I had been playing. I anxiously worried that I had bored them to death.

I announced that we had a special guest tonight and introduced President Lorimer. He had just arrived and was going to tell us what he knew about the handcart pioneers.

He stood in front of the campfire, wearing a cowboy hat with a feather tucked into the brim, pointing out the back. We sat in silent absorption as he told us about the people who walked through this place almost 150 years earlier. He told of the faith and courage of these humble pioneers. He spoke of the sacrifices made by ordinary men and women, and how the everyday decisions we make may seem insignificant now, but will create a ripple effect for generations. He spoke for an hour and a half, and you could have heard a pin drop the entire time.

After President Lorimer finished his remarks, the meeting came to a close. I remember feeling that I wanted to go home and kiss my wife's feet for all the little things she did—and does—for our family. I wanted to call my parents and let them know how much I appreciate them. I wanted to say "yes" to any opportunity to serve any person who came my way and do the simple things, such as giving money to a homeless man on the street. I felt inspired, transformed even, and this feeling linked me to Ole and Ane Madsen. I thought about how my life is blessed today because of the sacrifices they made long ago. I marveled at the ripple effect. Because of their unbelievable sacrifices, I am a fifth generation Mormon living the good life in a free land. In Zion.

As soon as the meeting closed, I introduced myself to President Lorimer and thanked him for coming.

"I'm a little embarrassed," I said to him. "You know more about my ancestors than I do. But from today forward that's going to change."

THEN

&

September 12, 1856

"The way ahead / Far from view."
—Someday

$\mathcal{T}$he bugle sounded and the people of the company drowsily pulled themselves from their slumber and emerged from the tents. Ole pulled his suspenders over his shoulders, scratched his beard, and stretched the stiffness from his muscles. Despite his exhaustion, he moved through the morning routine. He started the fire for Ane, who emerged from the tent shortly, her hair neatly done, to prepare breakfast. The children followed, taking care of personal needs before shaking out the blankets and packing the cart.

The camp was already alive with people and the bustling sounds of preparation. They moved about their duties and spoke little, leaving the quiet to the morning air.

After breakfast the children took the dishes to the river to wash. The camp was growing livelier and more talkative as tents were brought down and put away.

A nearby commotion caught Ole's attention. He watched Sub-captain Atwood approach a tent and pull it down, exposing a group of tranquil sleepers who were ready to pull the tent back over them and continue their slumber.

Ole laughed, amused, and looked upon the sleepy group with sympathy as they were required to stand before the company and confess their wrongdoing.

Once chores were done and tents loaded, the walking commenced. The Madsens were lucky that their handcart had not suffered a broken axle or significant cracks. Ole believed it was because the shared wagon had previously carried the heavier things. Now, with the weight of extra flour, they had their first mishap. A giant crack tore through the handcart and some of the wood splintered off and fell on the trail. There was nothing to do but rearrange their things on the cart and hope it didn't break further.

The girls held hands to keep pace. At times Johanna had to pull Kristina and Marie along. Ole watched the ground for rocks or other debris that would hinder the progress of the handcart and the girls kept their gaze on the dirt as well. Ane's eyes looked forward to the horizon.

Ole's exhaustion reached a breaking point after traveling twenty miles that day pulling a heavy handcart. He saw the same fatigue in the heaviness of his wife and in the children's eyes as they approached their camp that evening.

Dusk was upon them when they served supper. The children did not have the strength to play and ate with a deafening silence Ole was not used to. He watched them scrape the last crumbs from their plates and considered sending them off to bed when cheering Saints shouting hearty "Hurrahs!" countered the camp's somberness.

Ole scanned the distance and saw grand outfits of carriages, accompanied by two wagons, arrive. Joseph Elder and Andrew Smith rode beside the carriages. They had been sent out as a last search party to look for the missing oxen. Now they returned a week later with no oxen, but in the company of carriages. One carriage held Apostle Franklin D. Richards who was returning from England with a group of missionaries and the Saints rejoiced at his arrival. Some members of the Willie Company had met him briefly aboard the *Thornton* before sailing to America. He had instructed them then to obey their Captain Collins' orders.

The Saints gathered around to greet Elder Richards. He stepped from the comfort of his carriage and removed his hat, his face beaming as the Saints cheered. He had a chin-strap beard and wore a suit. He moved into the crowd that opened to make room for him. The men extended their hands in greeting, and Richards took each hand in both of his. His piercing blue eyes sparkled as he greeted them. Ole stood on the outskirts, watching the spectacle as the church leader moved from one faithful Saint to the next, moving through the cheering crowd. When it was time, Ole extended his hand and felt the warmth of a firm grip. He said nothing, but nodded as he caught Richard's gaze. The apostle smiled, and loosed his grip as he was taken under the wing of Captain Willie, who escorted him from the crowd.

"We will gather for a meeting shortly," Captain Willie instructed, and the company dutifully finished its evening meals and gathered around the central fire, singing songs as they waited for their leaders' instructions.

Elder Richards addressed the company first, "Perhaps we can start this meeting with a song. Brother Dunbar?" The designated brother promptly stood in front of the company and sang the

Psalm, "When Israel out of Egypt came / And left the proud oppressor's land / Supported by the great I AM / Safe in the hollow of his hand."

In that moment the pioneers in camp felt God's support and protection, and, despite their fatigue, they listened intently to Brother Richards' words once he stood to address the company.

"I have learned that you have lost your cattle." He gazed sternly at the crowd then with a slight smile he added, "Congratulations."

A light laughter echoed through the group.

"I am pleased, as is God, by your efforts and faith in traveling thus far, especially with handcarts. I promise you in the name of Israel's God and by the authority of the Holy Priesthood, that you will be able, by your united faith and works and God being your helper, to overcome any obstacle. Though you may have some trials to endure as proof to God that you possess true grit, neither heat nor cold nor any other thing should have power over you to seriously harm any in the camp. And you shall arrive in the valleys of the mountains with strong and healthy bodies." The crowd cheered and then quieted as he continued to counsel them on being faithful, prayerful and obedient to leaders. Then in a great booming voice he promised, "Though it might storm on your right and on your left, the Lord will keep open a way before you to get to Zion safely."

Ole looked at Ane whose eyes held the same determination in them as the day they left Denmark. He smiled at her, grateful for her strength.

"Come children, it is time for bed," Ane instructed.

Ole watched his children gratefully follow their mother to the tent and mused upon the times when they'd had to force them off to bed. Now they followed like lambs, happy and ready to collapse into sleep.

THEN

ဆ

September 13, 1856

"Climb up that far off hill /
Keep your eyes on tomorrow."
—Legacy

Shortly after breakfast, a morning meeting was unexpectedly called. The company gathered, expecting travel instructions, but soon realized this would be a very different kind of meeting. Elder Richards had learned of Brother Levi Savage's words in Florence and felt the need to publicly rebuke him to encourage any in the camp who were lacking faith due to Levi's defiant words.

"Brother Savage's rebellious words have shown a lack of faith in God," Richards said, "And all dissensions in the company must end, as they have been allowed to creep into camp and the hand of God has been heavy upon you for this cause. Brother Savage, I ask that you step forward." Brother Savage did so. His face showed neither humility nor pride.

"Brother Savage, you will have to take back the words you spoke in Florence or be tried for your fellowship. The choice is yours."

Savage shook his head so slightly it was barely noticed. He stood alarmed that the words spoken a month earlier were coming back to haunt him.

He spoke, his words soft, and catching in his throat as he forced his lungs to push them out. "I take back what I said in Florence, and return my faith to God, and I will follow Captain Willie's orders without dissension or murmuring."

Savage returned to his seat, and a hush fell over the crowd. Elder Richards paused, looking over the pioneers with a stern gaze as the event settled in their minds. "I have found a good place for crossing the Platte River." He began to instruct the camp, his mind focused now on the duties of the day. "I will ride ahead of you to Great Salt Lake and promise to send supplies as soon as I arrive."

A soft cheer flowed through the assemblage and hope slowly crept back into their hearts as the people went about fixing their carts in preparation for crossing the river. Within the hour, Peter met Ole, pulling his handcart next to his.

"I was not expecting the reproof of Brother Savage," Ole said.

"Did you see his face? Clearly neither did he," Peter said. "Brother Cunningham shared an interesting thought. He said the whole scene reminded him of Galileo, an Italian astronomer and physicist of the Renaissance, who declared that the sun stood at the center of planets, which orbit it. He was hauled up before the Roman Inquisition for teaching heresy. It was generally believed then that the sun revolved around the Earth. He was made to swear he would never again teach contrary doctrine."

"Did he deny it?"

Peter nodded, "Only to rise to his feet and mutter under his breath that the earth does revolve around the sun."

Ole smiled faintly. "Well, I hope for our sakes that Brother Savage is wrong and Brothers Kimball and Richards are right."

Peter grew silent. His face contorted. Ole watched his features move from concern, to anger, to sadness, then nothing. Peter muttered, "May the Lord provide a way."

NOW

✘

Summer 1998

*"I stand above the Sweetwater /
On hallowed ground."*
                    —*Rock Creek Hollow*

*M*y cousin Janet Lenardson walked along the trail at Rock
Creek with her husband Mike. She too was looking for answers
about our ancestry and was taking this opportunity to walk the
same path that our great-great-grandfather, Ole, had taken 150
years earlier.

She moved along the trail slowly, deliberately taking in all that
was around her—the sage, the rocks and the creek. Mike had
moved on ahead of her, and Janet sped up to catch him when she
was suddenly forced to stop. She didn't know what had stopped
her or how, but she knew she couldn't take another step forward.
Suddenly a feeling swam over her with a mighty strength. The
feeling was both overwhelming and peaceful, linking her to some
cosmic and eternal force as the earth around her became more
vibrant and alive. It was as if heaven and earth, past and present,
were all one in an instant. With a deep sense of gratitude, beautiful sadness and spiritual recognition overwhelming her senses,

Janet began to cry, and found she was unable to speak or move for several minutes.

When she regained control, she ran to tell her husband what had happened. They talked for a while about the experience, discussing possibilities of what might have happened on this spot that could hold such a strong emotional pull for her. Mike then suggested they go back to the spot together to see if the phenomenon would occur a second time.

Janet followed her husband down the trail, back to the spot. Again, the feeling came back to her. It was not as overwhelming as it had been the first time, but it was still there in a very real way. She had a difficult time describing the feeling, and could only say that she had never felt anything like it before.

Janet later described the story in a letter she sent me. After getting home from work one night, I noticed the letter from Janet in the day's mail. I set it by the bed and thought I would read it later before going to sleep. As I got into bed, I opened the letter and the first paragraph was stunning. I just stared at it and read it over a couple of times before finally turning to Cheri, and saying, "I can't believe what I am reading."

Here is the beginning of her letter in her own words:

"My interest in the Willie's Handcart Company began with the General Conference session in April 1997 and a special video presentation that was broadcast at that time on the events that occurred at several historical sites relating to pioneer Saints. At one point, there was a shot of the monument at Rock Creek and I saw the name of Ole Madsen inscribed on the plaque. I said, 'I know that name.' I immediately dug into what little family history I had and learned that he was my great-great-grandfather."

When I read this, I immediately felt that there was something greater than myself that was trying to get my attention—something that could bring our family together and perhaps bring new meaning and understanding to our lives. I felt that things were happening for a reason, even if I didn't yet fully understand what that reason was.

NOW

⅊

September 3, 1998

*I*t took me by surprise when a younger lady answered the door and suspiciously asked my brother KC and I why we were there to talk to her mother. "What are your motives?" she asked. I think she was expecting some sort of con on the elderly.

We were in Orem, Utah. At that time, it was a nice place if they could ever get the freeway system finished. It had been torn up and under construction for as long as I could remember. Driving south through the construction zone had never been fun. It was the same, the day we came knocking on Ruth's door. She lived in a retirement community where she had a little apartment near some full-time care centers.

Ruth is a great aunt to me and was then nearly a hundred years old. KC and I stood at the door unsure, as I told the woman that we were there to meet our aunt and had no other motive, other than to ask her some questions about our ancestors.

We were invited in and saw Ruth sitting in a chair in her small living room. She had on a gray flowered dress and had short gray curly hair. Ruth was tall and didn't look sunken as you would expect of someone her age. When she spoke we could tell she was very clear of mind.

We introduced ourselves as great-grandchildren of Ane Marie through her youngest son, Leonard. Ruth was a granddaughter of Ane Marie through her son Christian. Seeing Ruth made me think about the times I visited my grandmother Jennette, and the stories she told, to which I had listened half-heartedly. Now, I was thirsty to know anything this woman might be able to tell us and I didn't want to waste any time on small talk.

We started talking and quickly learned that her memories didn't flood back to her so easily. We spent some time talking about her family and waited for the stories that slowly came out. Ruth mentioned that her sister Beatrice would be visiting from Arizona and we agreed to come back with a list of questions. The second time we went back, KC had the prepared list of questions and the sisters were waiting for us. We sat down, turned on the recorder, and dived in.

Interview conducted by KC Ericksen with Aunt Ruth and Aunt Beatrice.

KC: Give me your full name.

Ruth: Ruth Isianna Ericksen

KC: [Addressing Beatrice] Ok. And now you've got to give me your name, full name.

Beatrice: My full name? You don't want my full name [she chuckles] Beatrice Christy Annie Ericksen Justice.

KC: How did you heat your house in the winter when you were younger?

Ruth: Coal.

KC: In the stoves? Did you have more than one fireplace?

Beatrice: We had one in the living room and one in the kitchen...But we used wood, I never remember coal. Well, we did coal in later years.

KC: Was it cold in the house?

Ruth: Yes.

Beatrice: Yes.

Ruth: We had a stove upstairs, and if it was really bitter cold we could make a fire in it before we went to bed to warm up the room.

KC: Did you have tons of blankets on?

Ruth: We never had electric blankets.

KC: Well, I mean, just blankets.

Beatrice: A lot of them.

Ruth: Well, we had quilts and blankets.

KC: Did you ever feel like you couldn't move?

Ruth: [Chuckles]. You could hardly turn over.

KC: Did [your dad Christian] say why [Grandpa Hans and Grandma Ane Marie] came back [from Grand Island, Nebraska]?

Beatrice: Well, they came back because so many of their children died of diphtheria. So Grandmother [Ane Marie] said, "Enough is enough, I don't want to live here anymore!"

KC: Did [Christian] ever say why they moved from Mount Pleasant originally?

Beatrice: From Mount Pleasant?

Ruth: [Hans and Ane Marie] always lived in Mount Pleasant.

Beatrice: Well they lived in Mount Pleasant, but they went back to Grand Island because I think Grandfather [Hans] thought that the farming would be...easier and better back there. But then they lost so many of their children, they lost...

KC: I think it was six.

Beatrice: They lost six at one time from diphtheria and after that [Ane Marie] said, "no more," and then they moved west.

KC: Ok, let me ask you about Hans for a minute.

Ruth: Who?

KC: Hans.

Beatrice: Grandpa.

KC: Grandpa, how tall was he?

Beatrice: Average.

Ruth: He was close to six feet. He was taller than I was.

KC: Was he? And how tall are you?

Ruth: I'm five-foot-something. Five-foot- two I think is what I am.

KC: How about Ane Marie, how tall was she?

Beatrice: Tiny.

Ruth: She was little. She was a small person.

KC: Like small, like five feet, five two?

Ruth: Petite. I think she was about four-five, four feet and five or six inches.

Beatrice: That would be real small. She was about five one or five two.

Ruth: I'm—

Beatrice: Oh, honey, you're more than that.

KC: Yeah, I think you're probably five-six or -seven.

Beatrice: You're five-five.

Ruth: No I'm not.

Beatrice: I bet you are.

Ruth: Not according to the things.

Beatrice: I bet you are.

KC: And both of them were in good health that you remember?

Ruth: Grandma [Ane Marie], never. I never knew Grandma to be well. She never could do anything...We did everything for her. We mopped the floor, we did the dishes, we baked the cookies, we made the meals. Mother did everything. If we ever went up there to eat, mother was up there two days cooking and getting ready for the meal, you know, that we were going to have.

KC: What kind of illness? Do you know?

Beatrice: I don't think she was real ill.

Ruth: I think she just had this...feeling sorry for herself.

Beatrice: She didn't want to do anything.

KC: Was she kind of distant to everyone?

Ruth: No.

KC: Was she very loving?

Ruth: [Nods her head].

KC: She was very loving of her grandkids?

Ruth: She never did say she loved me, but she never said she hated me either.

Beatrice: She never fussed over us.

KC: Well you know how you are with your grandkids, really hugging them and stuff like that.

Ruth: Yes, but she was never that way.

Beatrice: She was never that way.

KC: Hans, was Hans that way?

Beatrice: I think he was more loving.

Ruth: He was more loving than Grandmother was.

Beatrice: He would love ya. He would give you a hug.

KC: Do you remember his big beard?

Ruth: [Nods her head]. He chewed tobacco, and there was this song that was kind of popular, and it was "I'll never marry an old man, I'll tell you the reason why, his lips is full of tobacco juice and his chin is never dry." I'd sing that and Grandma would say, "Now when Grandpa comes in you sing it to him," so of course I did, and Grandpa got kind of aggravated with me. He didn't think that was so funny.

KC: How did Hans die? Were you there in Mount Pleasant when he died?

Ruth: When Hans died? I was there when he was real sick and stayed there with him, and Grandma would holler at him to get up and skim the milk because they sold cream...They had it in the pans and they'd skim it and get the cream off of it and they sold the cream. Even when he was partially unconscious, she'd holler at him to get up and skim the milk. And I'd tell her, "Well, I'll do that Grandma, I'll do it." No, Grandpa had to get up and do that until the doctor got after her. They made her sleep in the front room...while Grandpa was in the bedroom.

KC: What was the purpose of that?

Ruth: Well, because she kept hollering at him, and there he was half unconscious.

KC: Do you think she was doing that just to get him to come back to life?

Ruth: Well, she could, or she just thought nobody could do it like him. That's what I thought. He'd get all the cream and I wouldn't, [she chuckles].

KC: I've heard stories that Ane Marie was a little on the bitter side, because of all the hardships and children?

Ruth: I think that's true.

KC: You remember that about her?

Ruth:...I don't ever remember Grandmother [Ane Marie] going to church.

KC: What about Grandpa [Hans]?

Ruth: Grandpa went...but I never remember Grandmother going anywhere but in the rocking chair with a shawl around her.

KC: Did she talk very much?

Ruth: She did, she talked quite a little bit. She told us about how it was crossing the plains.

KC: What did she tell you?

Ruth: She said that...it was just so cold...The children were so hungry that they would want to eat their fingers.

KC: Did they say how hard it was to push the handcarts?

Ruth: No, she never mentioned anything about the handcarts.

Beatrice: I don't think they had that experience because I think that their father did most of the hard labor. And in fact, the reason he died is because they came to a creek and it was so cold and he had to cross the creek. He would take them one at a time so they didn't have to go through what he was going through and he caught pneumonia and died.

KC: So he actually carried them across?

Beatrice: He carried them across, his wife and children.

KC: Do you remember some stories about Grandma...coming across the plains?

Ruth: The only one I told you about, the kids starving.

KC: Yeah. Did she say anything about her father Ole?

Ruth: Only that he froze to death with his boots on.

KC: Now why was that significant, that his boots were on?

Ruth: Well, he was frozen so hard, when he went through the creek there was ice in the water...They just left them on. There were a lot of them that froze that night.

NOW

ℬ

Fall 1998

*"From the start / She set herself /
Into my heart."*
—Eutaw

*a*s my brother KC started interviewing our aunts and uncles I found myself impressed by some of their stories. I asked my Aunt Virginia, my father Max's older sister, what she considered to be the greatest invention she witnessed in her life. I expected her to say perhaps the automobile, television, or a rocket to the moon. She simply said, "Indoor plumbing." Having remembered using her outhouse on several occasions as a youngster, I think she was right. My Aunt Virginia also told us stories about how Grandpa Leonard had to cut down his own trees at Christmas, and how their refrigerator was nothing more than a big chunk of ice in a box. I enjoyed hearing their stories and appreciated the blessings I had that I often took for granted.

One thing I had a hard time hearing was when my Aunt Ruth said my great-grandmother Marie was bitter. It is true that shortly after Marie married Hans in 1865 that together they immigrated to Nebraska and were excommunicated from the church. But the thought of her being bitter nagged at me and sent me on a quest for understanding. I thought back to my experiences with Jenny and the ordeal of saying goodbye to little Joshua. I barely wished to think of it. I never wanted to feel that way again.

I didn't blame Ane Marie, but I wanted to believe we Ericksens had something more—courage, an ability to overcome—and I needed to know why? I wanted to understand her, what she'd gone through and how that had shaped her.

KC became involved in the search for our ancestors, following any lead he could find that gave us information concerning Ole, Ane Marie and her brothers and sisters. KC was the expert and family guru on our ancestors, finding and, if necessary, correcting the history as he went. He discussed his discoveries with us and showed us the details he had meticulously found. At the same time, my younger brother Steven got involved in the search. He set himself on a quest to find Karen. His search proved largely fruitless.

During this time, KC dragged me to a distant cousin's reunion that we crashed. We arrived just as they were hearing a story about their family history. It was after everyone had stuffed themselves with barbecued chicken, salad and dessert. The adults were near-unconscious while the kids ran around in the background with sugar highs.

The patriarch read from the histories, ignoring the screaming children in the background as he retold the stories that had been passed on to him. There were many degrees of attention and my newfound interest in our family history inspired me to listen that day only to discover that what this man was saying was full of errors. One that especially caught our attention was when he mentioned that Ole and his family had come to Utah Territory with the Martin Handcart Company, when in fact the Martin Company had traveled two weeks behind the Willie Company. Naturally we felt it was our duty—and we were a little smug about it—to set the record straight and tell him the truth. We informed him that the history he was reading, which had been passed down all these generations and recited at dozens of barbecues, was wrong.

We thought we'd get a "thank you," and a nice pat on the back. Yes, historical heroes we were. What we got was almost being carried out on a rail. Fortunately, my arrogance about what I thought I knew would later be replaced with humility. I met people whose knowledge made mine pale in comparison. I was amazed to find people who knew and cared about my ancestors as much as I did.

At the time, KC was taking a genealogy class through the church and asked his teacher one Sunday what he could do to find his ancestors. He explained that his previous efforts had only led to dead ends. That's when our big break came. Through an online search, they were eventually able to locate a man by the name of Ted Schofield.

KC rang up Ted and introduced himself, "I'm KC Ericksen. I'm a great-great-grandson of Ole Madsen, and great-grandson of Ane Marie Madsen. Are you by chance related to Andrew Madsen?"

Ted replied, "I can't believe you just called. I'm a descendent of Andrew Madsen and I've been searching for months for a descendent of Ane Marie because we've written a history and the only family we can't find is yours." Ted went on to say that he had been in touch with two descendants of Johanna and Kristina, and together they'd been praying to find the descendants of Ane Marie.

Shortly after this I went to visit Louise, a descendent of Kristina, who lived in the quiet town of Mt. Pleasant. It was here that

Marie had first settled with her husband Hans. I loved visiting this quaint town as the whole world felt as if it were moving slower there. It was a place to simply be. I was happy to be in this small somnolent town, eating chicken on a park bench with Cheri and basking in the sunshine.

I was told by Louise's daughter that Louise was deaf and that when I arrived I should simply walk into her house and find her. Cheri didn't like the idea, in case we were at the wrong house. So when we arrived she refused to come in with me and instead waited in the car. As I walked into Louise's house I saw her walking out of the kitchen. She was startled to see me and went to get a piece of paper and pencil so we could communicate by writing notes to each other. When we sat down on her couch she began by writing these words, "I had a dream about you last night." To which I wrote, "I hope it was a good dream?" She then wrote, "You look just like you did in the dream, only in my dream your wife wouldn't come in with you and stayed in the car." To which I simply wrote, "Do you mean like that?" and I pointed out the window to my car parked in front of her house with Cheri sitting in the passenger seat. Louise put her hand over her mouth in astonishment and became quite emotional.

There was an underlying connection drawing family members who had previously been unknown to each other together like a fisherman drawing in his lines at the end of the day. It amazed me how, as we searched for the families of Ole and Ane's children, they were also looking for us. I couldn't help but think it was as if Patriarch Ole was trying to draw his family of today together.

KC and Ted met, and with other descendants of Ole they planned an Ole Madsen reunion for the following year at Rock Creek. Letters were sent to every descendant we could find.

The reunion was great. About two hundred close and distant cousins attended, a large awning was set up, and everyone had a tent for their own family and each brought their own family history. It was a time to exchange histories and information. We talked, read and put stories together. We spent time debating details, looking for more information and simply enjoying each others' company and the scenery. By such small degrees we were fleshing out the lives of our ancestors.

One story they kept asking for and were eager to know was Ane Marie's story of five coffins in one room. It set me off on another quest and I quickly learned that the Ericksens had lost six children to diphtheria.

Diphtheria was a disease about which I had little understanding. It was simply one of the communicable diseases that had regularly swept through communities a century or more ago, dealing death to thousands. It was called the "strangling angel" because it formed wing-like membranes in the throats of its victims, causing slow suffocation. Many remedies were tried, including nitrate of silver, iodine and sulfate of iron, but they had little effect. Parents could only hold a child and watch it struggle for its last breath. Some doctors, in an act of desperation, cut into the trachea of a sufferer, to try to open an airway, again with little positive effect.

In the light of today's medical knowledge, it is apparent that diphtheria was a natural outcome of unsanitary conditions, especially as cities grew larger but no cleaner. A community could be quickly decimated as the scourge, like the Old Testament angels of death, passed through. It would take decades of experience and a new knowledge of how disease germs spread to relegate this horrid plague to history.

Knowing that my ancestors had been deprived of their children by diphtheria helped me to better understand Great-Grandmother Marie's perceived bitterness. As I considered her sorrows, there was a return of that familiar pang in my chest. I hadn't felt it for a few years, but it resided there, nonetheless. Memories returned of our little Joshua, and that night in the hospital as Jenny held him in her arms. My loss might have seemed nothing in comparison to Marie's, but there were elements of Marie's sorrow in the song I wrote after watching Jenny say goodbye to Joshua. I played this song frequently at firesides. I titled it *Jenny's Lullaby.* With my new empathy for my great-grandmother's burden of sorrow, I added the subheading, "For Ane Marie."

As our research delved deeper into the details of these sad underpinnings of our ancestors' story, I came to better understand Ane Marie's loss. The bit-by-bit additions of these years of research had made her a genuine person to me, a person with weaknesses and strengths, blessings and disappointments, lofty dreams and nightmares that contributed to a dear whole.

Music continued to be my way of connecting with Ane Marie and a way to express the feelings that stirred inside me when I learned of her losses, faith and courage—even her bitterness. As I learned about her and her family, I started to know them, to understand them, and to love them. And every song I played for them bridged the expanse of time that divided us.

THEN

☙

November 10, 1880

"On this dark and lonely night /
Without an end in sight."
    —Jenny's Lullaby:For Ane Marie

"*M*arie," her faithful husband of fifteen years, Hans, said softly. There was no response. "Marie," he touched her shoulder. She held her fourteen-year-old daughter, Hanna, in her arms as the girl slept. Sweat poured down both of them. Moments ago Hanna was waving her hands wildly into the air as she struggled to get air into her lungs. Then she coughed violently until her airway cleared and she fell asleep, exhausted from the struggle. Hanna hadn't been able to swallow food for two days and was growing weaker. It started with a sore throat and fever followed by delirium, the same as Marie's other children, now lost.

Marie was past the point of breakdown. She was no longer trying to survive; she was simply trying to hold on. To anything. In this moment that was her darling Hanna. If Hanna left her, what would be left to hold on to? She felt the depth of her losses before they were realized, and she wondered, *Is there still hope?* Did she even dare hold on to such a tenuous thing as hope? Hope that her daughter would live, and that she wouldn't have to suffer the loss of another child.

The doctor left minutes ago after forcing turpentine down Hanna's throat. He promised to check on Hanna in the morning. He would not be able to visit again tonight. A storm had blown in and it was very late already. The doctor gave Hans and Marie some hope of recovery in that Hanna was older and diphtheria mostly killed younger children. This, Marie knew all too well.

It had been difficult to lose her other three children in such a short amount of time, but not her Hanna too. Marie could see Hanna's life ahead of her. She was bright, doing well in school, and learning to read and write English, something Marie would never accomplish in her life.

Marie looked to Hans' eyes. She could barely make out his worried expression in the dim light provided by a single oil lamp resting on a side table.

"She is resting now," Hans said. "You need to rest too. I will sit with her." He opened the lid of a decorative music box by the bed. The room filled with the metal clang of notes from the music box's slowly turning cylinder. The once-light and comforting tones of *Amaryllis* now felt heavy with punition, guilt and destitution.

When Hans had persuaded Marie to leave Utah Territory for Nebraska Territory it had made so much sense. Hans was so convincing Marie was sure she had thought of the idea herself.

The Sanpete pioneers learned early that Zion meant hard work. When the Madsens arrived in the valley, they joined others in wresting a living from a land that, at first, seemed to defy all their efforts. In the mid-1860s, Zion in Sanpete also meant conflicts with the local Indians. The Native Americans of the area had watched in growing bitterness as their way of living disappeared under fenced farms and settled communities. Brigham Young's efforts to "tame" the Indians into the whites' accepted norm of agricultural life failed, but the natives' nomadic ways left them increasingly hungry as the white men competed more success-fully for land, fish and game.

In April 1865, open hostility rose out of a dispute over some cattle killed and consumed by starving Indians. Led by an aspir-ing young warrior named Black Hawk, the Indians escalated their depredations on livestock. They killed vulnerable whites who were unfortunate enough to be found away from the fortified communities and raided the far-flung forts as well. There were losses on both sides. The whites retaliated in kind, abandoning some communities, fortifying others and killing Indians indis-criminately. It was the longest and most destructive conflict between Indians and settlers in pioneer annals. From 1865 to 1867, the warfare kept settlers tense.

Marie was expecting her first child in 1866 when Hans pro-posed that they move to Nebraska, where rapid homesteading and rail-building had created a new prosperity. He had joined others in Sanpete as a Minute Man during the Indian unrest, but had lis-tened to rumors that life was better in the Midwest.

"You are asking me to leave my family behind?" Marie asked, bewildered. But it was 1866, the time of greatest danger during the Indian conflict. Marie thought of the growing life in her womb and wondered if the random raids would ever end.

"I think we can do better there. There is homestead land to be had, and the railroads are begging for workers," Hans replied stubbornly.

Marie was torn between the possibilities—life, maybe a more comfortable life—away from the threat of destruction at the hands of red men or life away from the family she so desperately wanted always in close proximity. She was tired of the struggle with the Indians, the rattlesnakes that emerged by the hundreds from their hibernation each spring. She was tired of the poverty. Which would be better for this infant who knocked little arms and legs against her extended abdomen?

She weighed the relative possibilities. "Maybe I could send new dresses to Johanna and Kristina," she ventured. "Maybe we could save enough to come back to visit. Perhaps I could wear a silk dress and have a ruffled parasol. Maybe we could even save enough to buy our own land here." Thoughts of the railroads that were even then racing from the Midwest and the Pacific, to meet at Utah's Promontory Point on May 10, 1869, seemed somehow to shrink the distances that she remembered plodding over on foot. The rails became a metal ribbon tying the nation together from coast to coast. Endlessly, she weighed the options. In the end, there was really little choice.

Hans was her husband. Wives went where their husbands decided to go. Ane without Ole? It was not to be thought of. In the spring of 1866, the Ericksens climbed into a covered wagon and set their heads east to reverse the course that had brought them to the Sanpete.

"We will not stay long," Marie promised her weeping siblings, through tears that coursed down her own cheeks. Then she watched through the gap in the canvas that covered the back of the wagon as her beloved family became dots on a sage-laced valley, then disappeared.

The rocking of the wagon as it bumped over the rudimentary roads headed east reminded Marie of how desperately she had yearned, as a 10-year-old, to be allowed to rest her weary legs in a wagon. She was thankful now for the blessing of a "modern" wagon with springs, even as she mourned each mile that separated her from what had become familiar.

The plan was to travel to Salt Lake Valley and await the birth of their baby before continuing their journey. But they were still several days from the capital, near the little community of Goshen, at the south end of Utah Lake, when Marie told Hans that he was about to become a father.

"Are you sure?" he asked, echoing the question asked, most likely, by every father since Adam. She was sure. The gripping contractions that she had tried to ignore had become insistent.

"I will find help for you," Hans said. He asked among members of the community, who recommended a Goshen woman skilled in the arts of midwifery. The frightened soon-to-be-father silently thanked Brigham Young, who had sent women back East to become physicians and then charged them with training women in the burgeoning territory to tend to the needs of childbirth. While Hans paced a groove around their wagon, Marie delivered their firstborn, a girl that they named Hanna. The date was April 26, 1866.

In 1866, the population of Grand Island, Nebraska, was 500, but the town was growing, spurred by the settlement of central Nebraska and by the demands of railroads that were relentlessly heading west. In 1868, Union Pacific came to the town and in 1872, the thriving community incorporated.

Hans was determined to have a share in the prosperity. Immediately he filed for a homestead grant under the Homestead Act of

1862 and the little family settled onto an 80-acre farm. "It doesn't look like much," Marie groaned, "We could have done better in Utah."

"But we didn't, did we?" Hans reminded her. "At least we don't have Indians breathing down our necks all the time."

"Oh, we have plenty of Indians. They just happen to be too busy fighting each other out on that island in the middle of the river to pay any attention to us." She was right about the internecine warfare among the local tribes, but she remained nervous, a legacy of the Black Hawk War. Gradually they made a nice frontier home in which they lived for 12 years. The ambitious Hans farmed and also became a railroad supplier. He soon had 34 men under his direction, cutting cord wood from the banks of the Platte River to furnish fuel for the "Iron Horses" that continued their relentless march into the west.

Hans gained his citizenship on April 13, 1874. Marie was busily producing little natural-born citizens. But in the late 1870s and early 1880s, death appeared in Grand Island in a particularly virulent form of diphtheria that threatened not only the Ericksen children, but nearly robbed their mother of her will to survive them.

By the summer of 1880, Marie had borne seven children, five of whom survived. They ranged in age from fourteen to one. Andrew and Hansine had passed earlier of the effects of diphtheria. Now, the dreaded disease struck again in earnest in the fall of that year. In just two days in October, three of Marie's children died—Willie, Anker and Hans—leaving Hanna and Christian. But now with Hanna sick too Marie quickly reached a breaking point.

Hanna was a companion to Marie and helped with the brood of younger children. The parents hoped against hope for their teenaged daughter. Hanna struggled to live and Marie struggled to have a reason for living. Hans watched anxiously from his own depths of grief.

"You need to rest, Marie," Hans pleaded again. "You will be of no help to her when she starts to recover if you have not slept."

"No, I will not leave her," Marie said, rejoicing in each labored breath Hanna took.

Hans sat on a chair by the bed and put his head in his hands. "I know this is hard, but the doctor said there was a chance..." His voice faded as he looked at his daughter, pale and haggard, gasping for air with every breath. "He told me before he left, that when he comes again he will treat her with some ice; he said it might help to bring down the fever." Hans paused, then spoke slowly, "He also said he might have to cut her, like he did Willie." The music box Marie had set by the bed to soothe Hanna wound down and Hans reset it.

Marie looked up into the dark room and said, "I am not going to let them cut her. I cannot witness such a futile monstrosity again."

Hans sighed, "Marie, we may have no other choice. If it is what the doctor thinks is best."

Marie started to cry, "Hans, do not let them cut my beautiful Hanna." It was quiet except for the tinkle of the music box. "Hans, promise me." There was no response. "Hans," the panic rose in her voice.

"I promise," he finally assured her.

Marie looked at his eyes this time and said desperately, "Hans, please go see if you can find a Mormon Elder to give Hanna a blessing." Hans shook his head as a gust of wind howled around their home. "It's too late, and in the snow..." She looked at him for a very long time before she nodded. Even though she desperately wanted her daughter to receive a Priesthood blessing, would she risk Hans catching pneumonia and possibly dying himself to accomplish that? She might. She cried at the mere thought of it. Were there no other options?

"Hans," she reached out to him. He stepped near her and clasped her hand with both of his. "Pray with me," she said.

He sat on the bed and held his wife, who held their dying daughter and together they wept as they pleaded with God for the miracle that was needed to save their darling.

They prayed until Hanna took her last breath. Then the only supplications they had left were mixed feelings of acute rage and heartbreaking surrender. Marie wondered if God was punishing them for leaving Zion. Would a kind and caring God do such a thing? Why had He prospered them in this new home if it had been such a sin? She hardly knew. When the doctor arrived the next morning he looked upon the grief-stricken faces of Hans and Marie and knew there was no recovering from the horrors they had endured. "Move back to Utah," he urged them, "There is nothing here but ghosts."

Bereft, Marie and Hans took the doctor's advice. Though Hans felt they were leaving a place where they had succeeded, he feared Marie would be irretrievably broken if she could not return to the solicitude of her family in Utah Territory. Her grief was eating her away. In early 1881, Hans, Marie and Christian boarded a Union Pacific train and retraced the route to their old home.

The inevitable smoke crusted their skin, and they ate and slept in the close quarters of the car as it rattled inexorably west. Christian slept under a bench amid the bundles that held all they had salvaged from their dozen years in Grand Island. Tucked into a bundle was the little music box that had helped ease Hanna's passage into eternity. There was no silk dress, no fringed parasol, no triumphal return with gifts, only the desperate flight from a long nightmare back to the arms of those who loved them.

Three more sons were born after their return to Mt. Pleasant: William, on November 16, 1881. He lived only three months before succumbing to pneumonia; Olof, on November 22. 1884. Again tragedy stalked the Ericksens' offspring. He died February 20, 1886. Leonard, the last of their children, was born on April 20, 1888. With Christian, he became the only other to survive into adulthood and perpetuate the family name into future generations.

NOW

๛

Fall 1998

"Mother's womb / Was the ground /
A stepping stone / 'Til wings are found."
—*Aspects*

J fit the microfilm into the slot of the large reader and whirled the spinner handle until the dull, semi-focused words came into view. I was the only one then spinning the film around the reels. The line of microfilm readers in the Church History Library was empty except for the one where I sat. At a nearby table, a woman sat quietly writing on lined note paper.

I had filled out small forms noting the file numbers and descriptions of the films I wanted to peruse and had seven reels waiting for me. I had started with the ward congregation records of Mount Pleasant, where my great-grandmother settled after returning to Utah from Nebraska, where she and Hans lived for some 12 years. I hoped to find information about the church attendance of Marie and her family. I wanted to know if she attended church, and looked to God for answers in her life after the trials she had been through. I wanted badly to see her name on a Sunday School or Relief Society roll, indications that she had taught a class; anything that would vindicate my feeling that her trials had led her toward faith and not away from it. I wanted to believe that despite everything she suffered, she'd found meaning in it all or at least some peace of mind. I wanted to know if she had been happy. It may seem silly to care about the happiness of someone who was already dead and whom I had never known. But I'd been learning so much about her that I felt connected to her. I wanted to be sure she had made it out of this life spiritually intact.

I was happy when I learned that Marie and Hans had been welcomed back into the church after being excommunicated. Excommunication was a standard practice for that time when members left the heart of the church. It did not particularly denote a loss of faith. I noted with joy that in 1899 they were sealed in the Manti Temple and that later all ten of their children were also sealed to them for time and eternity. This brought me some peace as to her faith. I felt perhaps she had found something to hold on to. But I was still concerned about her being bitter. I wanted to check church records to see if I could deduce her state of mind by her level of activity in the church.

I spent a lot of time looking at her eyes in the few pictures that we found of her. They seemed deep, sad and longing. They seemed to be looking past whoever was taking the picture into the distance, searching. Perhaps in her mind she was looking for the eyes of her father, her mother, her lost children, her sisters or brother. Perhaps the look lingered simply from the endless miles of her journeying.

In many of the pictures she had her arm across her belly as if she were trying to hold feelings inside. I wondered if I'd ever find any assurance that she had cared about life, that she had maintained hope for this life and perhaps beyond. Did she think that her family would be there down the shadowy path at the end? The assurance of the sealing that united her family forever helped put my concerns to rest, but I continued to wonder about the quality of her life.

I knew that I might just find despair, and I was preparing myself for that. I held my arm against my stomach as the micro-film records moved on, spewing endless names, dates and minutia across the screen.

All I had for sure were the impressions of those who had known her. Our old aunts had mentioned that Marie had been sick a lot. We had learned that she kept her house tidy and seemed to be pleasant. But to the question "Do you remember her going to church?" the answer was always "no." So my assumption was that she didn't want to go or that she was bitter. I even talked to the great-grandson of Johanna on the phone, and he could only remember that he had heard that she was bitter about the loss of her children.

I decided I had to accept that likelihood, but not until I had exhausted every possible source of information. I wished her to tell me herself, but how could I do that? I searched, hoping for something positive in the records.

I stared at the film ending. I had found nothing on that roll. But microfilm was not easy researching. It was very possible that I moved right past the answers that I sought as my mind wandered.

I quickly reeled the film back to the original roll, put it back into the labeled box and took it to the archive worker. She looked at me and said, "That was quick. What's next?"

I said, "Any one that you have will do. Answers are hard to come by today."

I took a new roll to the screen and started winding the reel, at the same time looking at the woman quietly reading. The desk where she sat was cluttered with papers. She wore a blouse with a blue cardigan sweater. Her brown hair was long, with streaks of gray. I sat down and without looking at her said, "Hope you're having better luck."

She spoke quietly, "It's never luck, just hard, determined work."

"I thought the early Mormons were meticulous record keepers?"

"They were, compared to others," she said, "But they were trying to get by, just like you. Do you keep a journal?"

"No," I replied.

"How will they find you someday?" she asked.

"Who?" I said.

"The ones that will most surely look, the ones who will care," she said quietly.

I considered this as I turned back to the viewer. It had never entered my mind that someday someone might be looking for Michael Ericksen.

I found nothing in the next reel. I went back to the desk to retrieve another and thought to ask the lady who was checking out my reels whether she knew anything about the Willie Company. She said she didn't, but told me I was in luck. A historian happened to be there who could help me with my questions. Great, I thought. She pointed me to the woman sitting at the desk to whom I had talked earlier. She didn't look like a historian to me. I thought historians were men who wore plaid button-up shirts and glasses.

I grabbed the next reel and headed back to the viewer, pausing for a moment at the desk where the woman was working. She didn't look up from her papers. I cleared my throat, "The lady at the front desk told me you are a historian and that you know a lot about the Willie Handcart Company and that maybe you could answer a few of my questions?"

The woman locked eyes with me, "Yes."

"Right," I sat down, "I'm looking for my great-grandmother Marie." I found myself saying. "She came across in the Willie Company and it turns out was later excommunicated from the church and then re-baptized."

"What exactly are you looking for?"

I glanced to the reel. "I just wanted to know if she went to church." *If she had faith, if she was ever happy.* "Or if she was...bitter, as some people say."

"Well, you're not going to find an answer in church attendance records." She looked directly at me.

"Why do you say that?"

"Because it wasn't like that back then. A person's faith wasn't based on whether they went to church or not, which, by the way, could be a very laborious process back then. Church wasn't set up in some easy three-hour block and the church house wasn't just around the corner. For some, attending church, including the distance they had to travel, would take up the whole day, and these people were settling a new land!"

"So church wasn't important?"

"It was important, but people during that time didn't look at church attendance like we do. People looked instead at how people supported and cared for their families. How they kept their farm and treated their neighbors."

I nodded and laughed. I had planned on spending the rest of the day poring over these reels for some peace of mind, and discovered that peace in a few minutes through the mouth of this history-steeped angel. I had been basing my perception of Marie's faith on what mine looked like today, and falsely trying to understand her from my limited perspective on what I thought life should be like.

The historian and I continued talking and she helped me realize many things. Today, you have depression, you take a pill. You have stomach problems, you take a pill. Major illnesses (including diphtheria) are staved off at birth by vaccines. None of that applied when Marie lost her children to a fatal disease. She didn't have a pill she could take when she was feeling depressed or ill, nor did she have a professional counselor she could talk to when her faith was challenged by the enormity of the events in her life.

That's when I realized I would never truly understand Marie the way I wanted to. Her faith was going to look much different from mine. It wasn't something I could measure, catalog and put in a box marked "church attendance = proof Marie had faith and was happy." I was foolish to think I could do that in the first place. That I could find her name on attendance rolls and declare to my aunts: "You see! She wasn't bitter! She attended Church! That means she was happy! You must have been mistaken!" At this phase in my own life I hadn't yet learned that happiness and faithfulness don't always coexist.

I realized my pride wanted to have the ancestor with perfect faith. Instead, I accepted the ancestor I had; the woman who suffered and overcame many losses. I understood that researching Marie's life and doing the firesides was a way for me to get through the hard things happening in my life. When I compared my struggles to Marie's it always helped me put things into perspective.

Some time later I came across a document my grandfather Leonard had written about his mother Marie. He wrote it in 1925 when he was living in Hamer, Idaho, several years before she died. He entitled it, *What I Owe My Mother.* Not until I read this dedication to Marie from her youngest son, did I truly understand my great-grandmother. It gave me all the resolution I needed, and taught me what faith truly looks like.

What I Owe My Mother
By Leonard Ericksen

The first conscious remembrance I have of my mother, is of a wonderful smile hovering over me...As life went by and perplexities, vexations, and tribulations appeared it became my habit to look to this smile for strength when courage was low and results uncertain.

I well remember its stimulus as I lisped my first effort from the school stage, and timidly sought her face in the audience; its consolation when I was sick.

When the time came that issues of life must be met without my mother at hand, I found that such smiles as hers were rare and were not reflex...I found that her smile was born of the spirit. It was the expression of her interpretation of life. My mother's courage was not the sink or swim, live or die variety. Life to her was not a struggle or an affliction, but a beautiful privilege to live and act. She loved the world and everything in it, and the Great Giver for allow-

ing her to be part of His creation. This was the secret to her smile.

THEN

&

October 1, 1856

"If we just stay together /
We will surely make it home."
—*Tyme*

FORT LARAMIE, WYOMING

*W*illie, Atwood and Savage approached the outskirts of Fort Laramie. The fort consisted of a fifteen-foot high adobe wall that encompassed a square. Two blockhouses stood on opposing corners, which allowed the soldiers to sweep the perimeter in case of attack. Above the entrance was a large blockhouse with a cannon poking out. The first gate was opened and the men stepped under the archway approaching the second gate, which remained closed.

"What can I do for you?" The men looked up. A soldier's head peeked out of a small square window high above the ground.

"We are a handcart company traveling to Great Salt Lake. We are in need of food and supplies," Willie answered.

"Our supplies are limited," the soldier answered.

"I believe a man by the name of Franklin Richards stopped by here, likely three weeks ago, to purchase supplies for us," Willie said.

The man slid the window shut and pulled the gate open. Another soldier greeted them. He was dressed traditionally in a navy blue frock and pants with gold-plated buttons and a matching hat and gloves.

"We are looking to re-supply our provisions," Willie said, and the soldier directed them across the 150-foot square to a small cabin. A number of cabins including housing, offices and shops surrounded the interior of the fort and the roofs reached within three feet of the top of the palisades against which they sat.

The men followed Willie across the partitioned square and into the building. A man in civilian clothes sat making notes in a leather-bound book. He wore a yellowing shirt and suspenders.

"What can I help you with?"

Willie removed his hat and extended his hand, "I am Captain James Willie." The shopkeeper shook his hand. "I am bringing a handcart company across the plains. These are my sub-captains, Millen Atwood and Levi Savage and we need to re-supply."

"I am afraid we have little to offer."

"I believe a man by the name of Franklin Richards passed by here a few weeks ago."

The man nodded and stepped into a back room. He returned with a folded piece of paper and handed it to Willie.

Confused, Willie opened the letter and read in silence.

After a few moments, Atwood inquired, "What does it say?"

"He was unable to purchase supplies for us," Willie said.

"I told you we have little available." The shopkeeper frowned.

Atwood rubbed his beard in frustration.

"Sir, do you have anything at all we can purchase?" Savage asked.

"The only thing we have is some hard bread."

"How much are you selling it for?" Atwood asked.

Willie stayed quiet. His mind rolled over this bad news and the choices he would soon have to make.

"Twenty cents a pound," the man replied.

Savage's eyebrows rose in surprise, "Sir, we paid three cents for flour in Iowa."

"That is the cost, sir." The man spoke without apology.

"Buy what you can." Willie looked at Savage. "Put it on the church fund." Willie donned his hat and left. Atwood quickly followed.

"What else did the letter say?" Atwood asked, sensing something.

"Elder Richards said the re-supply wagons will meet us at South Pass."

"That is too far away," Atwood noted.

Willie nodded, but said nothing.

"What are our options?"

Willie stopped, "At the rate we are traveling, we will likely run out of food in a couple of weeks, and it is going to take us at least three weeks to get there.

"So we will ration the food."

"We will have to, but it will be scarcely enough even then. We will have to move at a faster pace to keep ahead of any storms and we are in mountain territory. We will be expending more energy with less food."

They both knew it was their only option, though it did not look good.

"We will reduce from a pound of flour per day for adults to three-quarters. I dare not lower it any more than that or we will have Saints dropping dead on the trail," Willie sighed.

Savage approached, "I managed to purchase the bread, but there is only enough to last the company a day."

Willie shook his head. Giving up was not an option. He took a deep breath and with it, strength. "Elder Richards promised us deliverance so long as we have faith. We will do what we must and trust in the Lord."

THEN

෨

October 19, 1856

$\mathcal{T}$ he flat prairie trail ended and rolled into hills that turned into desolate mountains, sparse in foliage, sharp with rocks and only welcoming to the eyes. Ole remembered the plush grass of the plains and compared it to the dusty foothills of Wyoming, overrun with sagebrush, cacti and bedrock. He dared not think this was the road leading them to Zion as he surveyed the rocky high desert terrain looming ahead.

The cold had been creeping up on them for weeks, beginning with frost on the ground in the morning, followed by cool evenings. Harsh and unrelenting winds and blustering snow came next. Temperatures quickly dropped from 60 degrees Fahrenheit to below 40 degrees during the day and near 20 degrees at night. In the two and a half weeks since they started rationing food, the trail had also become increasingly more difficult and jagged. They had rolled on each morning, fighting the cold as they labored to move. Then one day after lunch, a blizzard came.

Kristina carried a chalky white rock small enough to disappear into her palm when she closed her fist. When the walking grew exhausting and her body seemed about to freeze she squeezed the rock to regain her strength. Johanna had a similar ritual, except for her it was humming. When the company sang to ignite spirits and faith, Johanna softly hummed, and let the soothing vibration in the back of her throat carry her along the trail.

Marie and Andrew gathered their strength from their mother or sisters by grasping their hands firmly and trying to keep in step. Ole plodded forward, pulling the cart and thinking of his family when his determination wavered. Luckily, Ane had enough determination for both of them. She encouraged the family when she spoke, "We can survive on less food," and "What we lack in our belly, we gain in our faith."

The labor of walking on less sustenance was exhausting. The rations had dropped to only ten ounces of flour a day for men, nine ounces for women and three to six ounces for children. This was the equivalent of six slices of bread per day for an adult male. The hunger had become so overpowering that some in the party began to steal. To prevent the theft, the leaders packed all the flour onto three wagons at night and posted a guard.

The harsh trail, hunger and the bitter cold began to take its toll. Many were growing ill. They were loaded onto the wagons and soon there was barely enough room to fit them in.

Thick snowflakes fell around them as they walked. Moving helped them stay warm. But at night, blankets were few, and this night would be a cold one. The storm grew heavier as the Madsens labored to walk. Babies and toddlers wailed from the extreme cold and there was no way to pacify them. They became the voice of the trail.

"This will pass." Ane wanted desperately to believe in her own words. Was she not the one who had asked Ole to bring the missionaries by? Who had insisted they emigrate? Now she wondered if it would all be for naught. She had put her children in danger. But surely this is what God wanted for them. As the thick flakes fell on her, she willed herself to maintain faith amidst growing doubts.

Ane held Marie's limp and cold hand. She squeezed that little hand, willing life back into her daughter. Marie squeezed back, and they grasped each other tightly as they moved forward.

Men began to collapse on the trail mid-step. Their bodies were lifted by their leaders and laid into one of the wagons. The bodies of the sick and weak were piling up in the wagons. Ole prayed to God he wouldn't be next. He, too, was beginning to question his decisions.

Why had they not listened to Savage, who knew more about the dangers of winter on such a trail than the others? Ole felt like a fool who had misplaced his faith, begging for a miracle now rather than having listened to the voice of reason earlier.

A shaft of light appeared ahead of them, shining through the clouds and resting comfortably on the ground. The family looked upon it transfixed. It lingered just ahead of them, offering a moment of warmth and what would be their last reprieve from the storm. They inexorably marched onward, gazing at the beauty of the moment and aching for the clouds to thin and the storm to stop.

While the pioneers labored on, four figures appeared on the trail. They rode horses and wore thick coats and hats.

The men looked upon the dreary company with painful awareness. When Franklin Richards had arrived in the valley, he had informed Brigham Young that there were pioneers traveling late in the season and in need of help. President Young immediately sent out a rescue party, but the rescuers were not expecting this. The hollowness and lack of life in the eyes of the travelers was difficult to look upon.

"Brothers and sisters!" One of the men shouted, "Supply wagons are within one day's ride from you! With all the food and supplies you could need!"

It took a moment for the words to sink in. The Madsens looked at each other, exhausted, and managed weary smiles. They needed only to make it one more day. One more day! Surely they could do that. If they could just make it through that day, they would be provided food and warmth, and maybe even a decent moment of restorative rest.

They plodded on with renewed strength. Many shouted "hurrahs!" and sang.

Ole watched one of the rescuers, with tears in his eyes, lift an onion from his satchel and toss it to a woman. Ole realized the rescuer saw in them what had been creeping upon them for some time—gaunt faces and thinned bodies hidden beneath baggy clothes. But now, there was hope. The wagons would be there to rescue them soon. They would survive.

THEN

ᔕ

October 20, 1856

*"She looks past her sorrow /
And prays his soul to keep."*
—*Legacy*

*T*he Madsen family woke the next day to twelve inches of fresh snowfall and a continuing snowstorm. Although there had been deaths along the trail they had been sporadic, nothing like this. Five had died the day before, and in the coming days, there would be seven more deaths. Even movement could not allay the piercing cold of winter. It became the only feeling they knew; warmth was but a distant memory impossible to recover. The pang of hunger was a constant companion as the last of the provisions had been issued the night before in anticipation of the rescue wagons. The rescuers had ridden back on the trail to find the Martin Handcart Company, which was also in dire need.

The Willie Company was camped near the Sweetwater River exposed to harsh winds with limited wood available. With no food left, Willie had decided the group should rest and wait while he and Joseph Elder left camp, riding mules, in search of their rescuers. The remembrance of Levi Savage's words that had been so easily rejected now hung in the thoughts of the pioneers: "Your bones will strew the way."

The Madsens lay huddled together in the tent. It seemed a long time ago that they were able to lie comfortably together and be lulled to sleep by the humming of crickets and awakened in the morning by the racket of birds. The only sounds now were the howling winds, and, if they were lucky to find sage dry enough, they were blessed with the popping of fire.

Marie's eyes opened to dark gray shapes stirring inside the tent. Her stomach ached with hunger and she was growing weak with despair. She didn't move, as movement let the cold dive into the gaps. She was pressed between her mother and Kristina, whose arms held her close. Kristina's face was buried in the back of her neck. The steady rhythm of Kristina's breathing at night was the only thing that lulled Marie to sleep.

Outside their tent, the sound of wailing could be heard. It sent cold chills up their spines, even colder than the wintry air. In the whole trip they had only heard it a few times, usually when someone's loved one died. But the last couple of days the sounds of mourning had grown more constant and desperate.

The family wanted to stay huddled together and rest until food arrived. They ignored the call of nature as long as they could, until Andrew could hold it no longer and began to stir.

Ole was summoned to help find game. He left with the other brothers at first light. With no food in the camp and the cattle dropping dead on the trail, it was ordered that a couple of cows be slaughtered. It was something at least, but didn't satisfy the hunger of the sheer numbers who needed sustenance. In desperation, many ate leaves and boiled animal bones, leather or rawhide to make soup. It was the only meal available to the women and children that day. The men would go hungry.

Ole trudged along. It was getting easier to be in the cold, perhaps because he could no longer feel it. His body was going numb from frost. He looked upon the vast rocky landscape covered in snow. His doubts overwhelmed him. He had nothing left. He couldn't think about what could have been had he made a different choice. It drove him mad to think that one decision had changed everything for his family. How could he not have foreseen this? Was it his pride that got in the way of reason? Or was it his fear of ridicule and being accused of lack of faith that had made him ignore the warnings of Brother Savage?

The decisions he had made that brought him and his family to this point replayed in his mind: bringing the missionaries home, baptism, choosing to emigrate, not staying in Florence despite the warnings. These thoughts looped in his mind in an endless rotation, and no matter how many times he tried to rewrite it in his head, it didn't change the fact that he was standing in several inches of snow while his family lay huddled together on cold ground freezing to death.

He fell to his knees, tears wetting his face as he looked up to the gray sky.

"Father," he whimpered and repeated himself until the word turned to a cry. "Father! I have nothing left except my family. Please spare my family. Please," he pleaded. He had given up so much already. He had lost his wagon, his possessions, his farm, and Karen. The last thing to go was his pride. Now it could be his family lost to the trail and to the wolves. He could not bear the thought.

About noon Ole returned with the rest of the hunters, empty-handed. He walked somberly to his family's tent and saw they were huddled by a small fire. They were ragged with the look of death. Ole yearned to say something to give them hope when he now felt there was none. The moment of hope they had found on the trail the day before now only taunted them. The snow was too deep even if they were strong enough to travel and above them the skies were threatening more snow. Most likely this snow-covered bottomland against the Sweetwater River was going to be the place where they all were going die. They did not have the power to do anything about it.

He approached his family and smiled. "Perhaps this is a one-buffalo gun," he said, displaying his rifle.

Ane managed a faint smile. "Captain Willie and Joseph Elder have gone out to find the wagons from Great Salt Lake."

Ole nodded.

"Will they find them?" Johanna asked, wishing to hear the truth, not wanting to hope if hope was lost.

Ole paused, tears forming in the creases of his eyes. "I made a mistake," he began to say. Ane touched his arm reassuringly. The children stayed quiet, not knowing what to think.

"We should never have left Nebraska. We should have stayed like some of the others."

Ane wanted to protest. Her lips began to move, but she stopped and listened as he went on, "I know now that it was my pride. Wanting to keep our possessions. And that damned wagon! I bought it for us, for our protection, for our things, to make it easier and now it all means nothing."

The girls didn't understand. They held each other. Johanna and Kristina cried. Andrew clung to Ane, his face browned from sun and dirt. Even amidst all the commotion, he began nodding off in a state of exhaustion.

"I saw this opportunity, and I let my impatience and desires cloud my judgment." Ole was talking more to himself than to his family. No one knew what to say. With lack of food, warmth, and hope, the family was breaking down as emotions engulfed them. The girls cried and looked at their father, the man they deemed invulnerable, as he questioned everything.

"We cannot say that Nebraska would have been better for us," Ane said, "You remember hearing of Winter Quarters, and all those who died in such an ugly winter," her voice quavered. She was exhausted and tired. She wanted to comfort her family. She wanted to have hope, but how? Beneath her show of bravado, she too blamed herself for the position they were in.

Ole looked at his family, and that stern gaze they remembered returned to his features and provided some comfort. "This does not change what I believe, you hear me?" he said, looking at each one of them. The children nodded. "There is no one to blame but myself." He looked to Ane, who had always been so sure and determined. He saw the doubt in her eyes mirror his own.

Still, she looked at him sternly, "The wagons will be here," she said. "I do not regret the choices I have made."

This would be one of the darkest nights for the Madsen family as the hunger in them burned so hot that it felt like no amount of food would satisfy it. Without food, adequate shelter or hope, all they had left to cling to was each other.

THEN

ℰ

October 21, 1856

*"...she searches her soul to find /
A simple peace of mind."*
—*Jenny's Lullaby*

SWEETWATER

*C*old. Hungry. Desperate.

The rescue wagons had not arrived after a day and half of waiting. Captain Willie and Joseph Elder had not returned, and the company grew concerned. The Madsen family, like many others, existed in a place beyond despair. The landscape was pale with snow and haunting gray clouds hovered in the sky above.

The company knew for certain that there was no way they could get out of this hardship on their own. They needed the rescue they had thought would arrive. But it, too, had failed them. They had to look to another source for physical salvation that they could not provide for themselves. They had to put their faith in others and believe, even when they lacked hope that the rescuers were on their way. Just as they once had looked to Christ and his Atonement for a spiritual rescue, they now looked to the horizon for a mortal rescue.

They waited.

Cold. Hungry. Desperate.

The Madsens lay side by side. Blankets were meager and provided little warmth. Andrew slept between Ole and Ane. Marie, Johanna and Kristina lay on the other side of Ane, spooned together and holding each other as they drifted in and out of sleep. Ane had heated rocks for them by last night's fire and placed them next to the children for warmth.

Ane gazed upon Andrew, watching his chest rise and fall with each breath. Her heart twisted in knots at the thought of losing any of her children, as so many others had. Susannah Osborne had buried her seven-year-old son only days earlier. Ane worried that tomorrow she would be burying one of her own children. Or more.

She held Andrew tight and tears formed in her eyes.

Ole watched his wife clench her teeth as she fought back the multitude of emotions threatening to overwhelm her. He brushed his hand across her cheek. Ane pulled away, wiping away tears. Ole placed his hand over hers.

"What if..." Ane began.

"Shhhh." Ole squeezed her hand, "You will make yourself sick with worry."

"I already am sick," Ane whispered, tears still flowing.

"Even if we..." she couldn't bring herself to say the word *survive*. "What kind of life are we to have here?"

"The life we want to have."

"They are supposed to be men of God," Ane's voice rose. She took a quick breath and whispered, "They led us into a storm without provisions." Ane smoothed Andrew's hair, her lip quivering. "I had faith."

Ole didn't know what to say, as his thoughts had been much the same. Still, he blamed himself more than he blamed anyone else.

"All is not lost, Ane." He scarcely believed his own words, but he wanted to have hope. "We are all as well as we can be, considering. We are still here. We have each other."

"We are on death's door," Ane whispered, "because of them."

Ole sighed, "Was I not ordained an Elder myself? Am I not fallible?"

Ane rubbed her lips together as she cried. The day Ole had been ordained an Elder in the Priesthood had been one of the happiest of her life. Comparing that joyous moment to this bitter hell was a cruel reminder of her dreams of Zion.

"Our leaders are doing all they can and so must we." Ole hated having to be the one to say it. Ane had always been the strong one. To see her so unsure weakened his resolve.

Ane nodded and managed a slight smile, "You will always be my imperfect and incorrigible Ole."

Ole's fear melted just enough to allow a small place for faith. He grabbed her face and kissed her tears.

"I will not let anything happen to our children. I will make sure—"

"You cannot control this. No more than our leaders can control the weather."

"Listen to me," Ole said, holding her face in his hands. "I will do everything I can to deliver my family safely to Zion. I promise. God has done enough. He can at least give me this."

Ane shook her head, "Do not talk like that."

"Like what?"

"Do not tempt God," she said sternly.

Ole sighed, "Ane my dear, my family is starving. God should be the one worried about tempting me."

Ane said nothing, but looked at her husband, his eyes wild with a stubborn determination.

They sat in silence, holding each other's gaze. Suddenly they heard shouting outside their tent.

"Wagons! Wagons!"

Ane finally wept. Ole leaped from the tent and spotted the wagons pulling in. He sprinted toward them, finding a sudden burst of energy. He would get food for his family. Many around the camp were yelling, some were crying. Ole ran past them and met the wagons with a throng of others, weak and ragged, waiting for food.

"Please," Ole cried in English to his rescuers, his hand extended. One of the rescuers held out a blanket that Ole received, but he was not in want of warmth at this moment. He extended his hand again as the mass of people grew around him. "Bread," Ole cried.

"You have to wait, we will distribute it in divisions."

Ole shook his head, and cried again, "Bread!" He followed alongside the rolling wagon, careful not to push others who also cried out for food.

The rescuer looked upon Ole's gaunt face and upon the throng of others descending upon them. He reached into his sack and discretely handed Ole an onion. Ole, grateful beyond words, found himself kissing the hand of the rescuer. He ran back to the tent, onion and blanket in hand. Inside, his family still huddled together, but all the children were awake and crying. Ole burst through the tent flap and placed the blanket over them. Then he gave each a bite of onion. Nothing had ever tasted so good.

As they ate, their empty stomachs burned. Ole took a few bites, relishing the burst of flavor and juices in his mouth. How good it felt to swallow. He then settled in with his family to find warmth. After several minutes, he hurtled toward the tent's entrance, lifted the flap and vomited.

THEN

⅗

October 23, 1856

"Hell's fury fell."
—*Rock Creek Hollow*

ROCKY RIDGE
7 A.M.

*W*illiam H. Kimball reached down and grabbed a handful of snow. His hands, nearly frozen, were barely able to feel the soft flakes coalescing into a ball in his hand. He thought back to his words, when he had promised blithely that he would stuff in his mouth all the snow they would see. He gazed upon the white landscape, ashamed. He had come back with the rescuers to do his part in making sure the company, who had trusted in him, would be delivered to Zion. He thought upon the words his father Heber C. Kimball had spoken to him before he left, "If you die during this trip, you will die endeavoring to save the people, and who has greater love than he who lays down his life for his friends."

Somewhat fortified by the food that Kimball and the rest of the rescuers brought, the Willie Company now faced the worst challenge of the trail, the ascent up Rocky Ridge, a five-mile climb from where they were, to the summit, through rocky terrain, wading in snow up to their knees. Temperatures had dropped way below freezing. Kimball knew he would have to push them, whip them if necessary. If they did not move, they would die. This would be the hardest part of their journey, and they would have to do it when at their weakest. But they had no choice. They had to move.

Most of the relief wagons moved on to the Martin Company, which was two weeks behind them and also in dire need. It was a decision the Willie Company had made together. When the situation was explained and voted on, the company unanimously raised their hands in support. They had faith that other wagons would be along for them. They knew the Martin Company was likely worse off than they. Kimball had sent a messenger ahead to South Pass the day before with a note relating the deplorable conditions of the company and informing them of their arrival. The provisions the Willie Company had now would last them until the next relief train arrived, but they would have to move forward to meet it, and that meant climbing the ridge.

A man limped by Kimball, stopping only a moment to rest at the fire before moving on and finding a place to relieve himself. *He could be dead by morning,* Kimball thought, shaking from his mind the horrific image of the frozen bodies they had buried the night before.

Kimball gazed at the fire. He couldn't imagine anyone surviving this if the approaching storm were to lay down another foot of snow. The hard winds began to blow, presaging more snowfall.

Kimball looked Captain Willie in the eyes, but Willie could feel he wasn't looking at him, rather beyond him to the ridge, to the climb ahead. "Captain," Kimball spoke, "Get your leaders assembled immediately."

Willie nodded, walked to the center of camp and rounded up his sub-captains who were busy helping those who were ill by packing up their tents. Many were sick, and when they ate they would not feel satisfied, and upon eating would vomit, or lose their bowels. Dysentery was rampant.

As the sub-captains grouped around the fire, Kimball looked at them and without emotion or inflection in his voice said, "I am taking command of the company. I know you want to stay a couple of days, but we do not have days or even hours. I don't know if we can make it without losing half of them, but those who can make it will only live if we go now. We will have to drive them, we will have to push them and we will have to put the strap to them if necessary. Their lives—and yours, depend on your resolve. We leave in two hours. Find if there are any dead before we go, and get them in the ground."

There was no discussion, not even a question. They all knew what had to be done and what it meant if they failed.

8 A.M.

Marie hugged Kristina for warmth as she slept. Marie dreamed of walking by her old church in Jyderup in the summer and looking up at the large white bird as it sat in the belfry. Some boys were throwing rocks at the bird. She looked around, intending to scold them and noticed dark figures in large numbers slowly moving up behind them. She tried to call to them, but no words came out.

One of the boys picked up a palm-sized rock and threw it at the bird. It jumped as the rock passed it and hit the bell. The dream ended as she awoke.

"Time to get up, my little lambs," Ane greeted them. The children stirred. Despite the extra rest and some food, they awoke with the same lack of energy. "The snow is coming down, and we are moving today. We must pack up the tent and our things. I already have food prepared for you."

The children rubbed the sleep from their eyes, wrapped themselves in thin blankets and braved the severe cold. They ate while Ole and others collapsed the tent and packed it.

"The climb today will be brutal," Ole muttered to Ane as he used a tin plate to dig out the handcart, making sure the children didn't overhear. "The wagons will be used to carry the sick and dying. I have been assured that Andrew and Marie will be able to ride, but Kristina and Johanna—"

"They can manage," Ane said coolly. She did not lack compassion for her young girls, Ole knew. She just had to find the strength and faith that their family was struggling to maintain. She would be the one to carry them through, and any sign of fear, any weakness would infect her whole family. She would not allow it.

It was a gift Ole did not have, but he loved it in Ane. He finished tying down their things and joined the children bunched around the fire.

"Finish up and wash your dishes," Ole said, "Johanna and Kristina, you are going to be with us pushing the cart. You are strong girls and I know you can do it." He spoke as if it were any other day. "Marie and Andrew, you will be in the wagon. Your job is to take care of the sick. The sick will be frozen. You must rub their limbs to restore warmth."

The children looked at him puzzled. Was he serious?

"Did you hear me?" Ole spat. The children all nodded. "Yes, Father."

"Good." Ole walked behind the wagon so his children could not see his grief. His children's faces were excruciating to look upon. They had beheld the very face of death, and now they were being asked to arise and climb. He bit his fist until the grief passed, and then pulled away his hand and saw teeth marks in his knuckles. He felt nothing.

9 A.M.

The sick were being loaded back into the wagons. Ole lifted Andrew and Marie up and put them beside the ill and dying. "I will see you tonight for dinner. Remember your duty." He knew they needed something to do, to keep them awake and active, lest they close their eyes to rest and freeze.

Marie nodded, her mouth agape, her features gaunt. Ole turned away from her as the wagon moved off. He looked at Kristina and Johanna hugging each other. Ane was ready to pull the cart. Ole climbed between the handles with her and grabbed the bar, gently placing his hand over hers. He looked at her and squeezed her hand. Any strength they had left they would find in each other. They had to look past the sadness in each other's eyes to find their Zion.

"Whatever happens, do not stop to rest," Ole instructed his family. "We have to keep moving, no matter what." The girls nodded in understanding and looked up at the steep ridge. This mountain appeared to be the only thing standing between them and deliverance.

Many in the company would have preferred to stay at camp. Their spirits had given up long ago. The flame that had once burned so bright in their hearts and longed for Zion had burned out and turned cold. Their will for living was fading, but they moved on like the walking dead.

They could have fought against it, begged for another way or gone off the path in hopes of finding an easier passage. Instead, they looked upon the trail ahead, the rough ridge, now bound by thick snow, and they accepted the path they had chosen. The men, women and children of the company latched onto their handcarts, which carried the only things they had left on this earth besides each other, and they climbed.

They moved slowly and laboriously. The Madsens didn't know which was worse, waiting and anticipating the trek ahead, standing still in the cold, dark and uninviting morning, or having the feeling of pins and needles rush over their bodies every time they moved.

They looked to each other for support, for strength, and at times, motivation, to remember why and for whom they lived.

11 A.M.

The ascent was brutal, the scene around them horrific. Men and women who barely had the strength to get up this morning, collapsed the first mile of the climb. Two men had already collapsed dead and were buried at the base. The punishing wind beat down upon them. The snow hit them like bits of ice as it fell. The same blustering wind that had been such a sweet relief in the blazing heat of the summer now slashed their frostbitten faces. The cross-wind whipped the women's skirts and loosed their hair from under their bonnets. The strands of hair mingled with the snow and became tiny icicles that whipped against their skin.

The snow absorbed all sound except the unrelenting howling of the wind, so strong that it haunted their ears with its cries. The wind was a demon telling them to give up, to surrender and to die. But they ignored the wind's cries and pushed on. They moved, barely able to hear the creak of the wheels or crunch of the snow. Not even the sound of their own labored breathing was audible.

With their limbs unfeeling, they struggled to wade through heavy thick snow. Perhaps it was better that their feet were numb so they couldn't feel the rough terrain beneath them.

At one point, the steepness of the climb and their failing strength made it impossible for Ole, or anyone, to move forward without assistance. They attempted to move by grasping the cart's handle and falling forward with their weight, only to be pushed back by the wind. The cart fell backward too, as the handle flew up towards their necks. With all their strength, they gripped the handle and pulled it down, securing it just beneath their ribs as they leaned forward and pushed. Still, the carts did not move. The sub-captains, along with other men who still had strength, stood behind the foundered carts and as a group, pushed, helping the handcarts move individually and slowly up the steep ridge. Ole waited his turn. He looked at Ane, who stood next to him. Her determination was slipping. He looked at his daughters, Johanna and Kristina, shivering; their eyes closed as the cold pierced them like ice, making them freeze and dry before every blink.

Peter Madsen approached from behind, "You must keep moving or you will freeze."

"We cannot move the cart without more help," Ole said.

"Keep trying. We are instructed to keep moving."

Ole nodded and turned to his daughters, "Keep walking, keep moving ahead of us if you need to. We will be right behind you." They nodded. Hands held tight, eyes shut, the girls waded through the snow, at times placing their hands on the ground and crawling. Ole and Ane pushed their handcart. Others helped, but made little progress. Soon the men who had pushed the other carts forward returned. Ole and Peter's carts were pushed through the worst of the climb. Ole and Ane managed to push the cart forward at a steadier pace as they caught up with their girls. Ole waded through the deep snowdrifts with his sturdy boots, providing footprints for Johanna and Kristina to step into as they followed behind him.

2 P.M.

There was no stop for lunch. They ate as they moved. Many walked barefoot as their shoes unraveled and fell from their feet. Some gathered the leather from their boots and chewed it, while others ate leaves and bark. Many ate snow to quench their thirst.

Kristina heard a cry nearby and opened her eyes peering over the blanket wrapped around her face. She saw a young boy no older than four years old, crying, as he lay barefoot on the snow-covered trail. Another boy, near Kristina's age, picked up the crying child. His arms shook as he held the little one. The older boy marched on with his sobbing brother in his arms. Kristina closed her eyes and held to the handcart, letting it lead her.

A man collapsed beside Ole, losing his bowels. His wife rushed to his side, crying. He was not dead, but could not move. One of her sons lifted the man onto a nearby wagon, on top of another man who was either sick or dead. They walked on.

A woman, carrying a child, collapsed. The child fell to the ground and wailed. The mother only half-conscious, stared at the baby in despair, wanting to hold it, but unable to move her arms. Another sister swooped the baby into her arms. They waited for the relief wagon to come near. From inside, willing hands lifted the woman onto the wagon with others who were near death's door. There was barely enough room for her. They stacked the bodies, one on top of another, despite the risk of suffocating.

The tips of toes and fingers grew black or swollen from frostbite. Men and women vomited or lost their bowels along the trail, but never stopped to rest, because rest meant freezing and freezing meant death. Some had come to look upon death as a mercy. Death meant warmth. Death was light.

Life was cruel, cold, heavy and dark. Life was pain. Death was deliverance, and many would welcome it. Others doggedly clung to life and willed themselves to walk on.

Marie watched as one after another of the company was loaded onto the wagon. There was not enough room to fit them all. Marie did as her father instructed, and when she could, she rubbed the limbs of those who lie dying. She rubbed the black fingertips of a woman who lay next to her, moaning. Marie scooted closer to the woman to share her warmth. The woman's skirt was tattered and hung just below her knees. Marie began massaging her legs as Father had instructed when she realized the woman's skirt had been previously soiled. She recoiled, wiping her hands, and scooted back as another person was loaded onto the cart.

The woman being loaded gripped her eye as she cried. The skin around the woman's eye was red and swollen, her eyeball pale and frozen, "I cannot see!" she wailed as she rubbed her eye trying to restore its warmth.

Marie hugged her arms around Andrew as he sat sobbing next to her. "My foot," Andrew cried. It was stuck contorted under a body. Marie struggled to lift a body off her brother. Andrew pushed and wriggled until his leather boot slipped off and his foot came free. Marie pushed him into the corner, sitting him on top of the feet of someone who looked to have already expired. She silently repeated a prayer, *Please God, let my family live.*

Soon, the cart began to overflow with bodies of the dying and sick. Marie found herself sitting next to and on top of those that were fouled by diarrhea and others by death. The smell in the wagon, the feces and stench of death, was revolting. The freezing temperatures provided some relief, in that it slowed the decomposition of flesh. Marie watched as a girl was loaded on the wagon. She was conscious, but her fingers were black with frostbite. Marie watched, horrified, as the young girl bit viciously into her fingers, tearing and eating the flesh from her own bones. The girl looked at Marie's fingers, purple, but not frostbitten. Marie, afraid the girl would eat her fingers too, quickly hid them under the blanket.

4 P.M.

The assault on Rocky Ridge was slow. Every ounce of will was needed to move forward. More fell, many were lying down in the snow in hopes of rest, others hoping to die. The Madsens passed the Nielsons, and heard Jens pleading with his wife, Elsie, "Leave me by the trail in the snow to die, and you go ahead and try to keep up with the company and save your life." Jens' feet, frozen and frostbitten, could not feel the ground he trod on. Unable to feel the angle of his feet as he plodded on, had caused the right foot to curve under and deform. He could not take another step.

Elsie shook her head and pleaded with him, "Ride. I cannot leave you. I can pull the cart."

The Madsens passed. They wanted to help, but they had barely enough life left to keep moving forward. All they could do was send out a silent prayer.

6 P.M.

The dark storm clouds overhead would not relent. The worst of the climb was over, but the pioneers still had several miles to go before they would be at the Rock Creek campsite. The campsite was ideal as it had water, sufficient grazing for the animals, and fuel to make fires. Desperate leaders were literally whipping or slapping stragglers to force them forward. Their only hope was to keep moving.

Anders Jensen had his handcart tied to one of the wagons and he held to the wagon for support. He slipped and fell and the handcart ran over him. He was quickly loaded onto the cart, but died soon after. His wife, Anne, distraught over the loss of her husband sat on a large overturned kettle and wept. Her eleven-year-old son, Michael, watched, helpless to console her as she heaved deep sobs. A man helping to manage the company approached them. He carried a walking stick and struck Anne harshly on the back. "Get up and go on," he demanded, yelling over the wind. "You cannot sit here crying. We have to go at once or we will all die." Michael's face flushed with anger, he wanted to lunge at the man for his insolence, but what could he really do? He was just a boy.

The message the man sent when he thwacked the widow on the back was repeated along the trail. There was no time to grieve. Only this: Keep moving or you too will die.

When a wagon carrying the sick was not in sight, men carried on their back those unable to walk.

Ane looked upon Ella Wickland, who had finally given birth on October sixteenth on the winter-bound banks of the Sweetwater. The hem of the mother's skirt was dirty with dried blood. Ane saw her nursing her infant boy, Jacob, as she walked, only for the baby to turn away crying, its mouth coated with blood. The woman didn't have the vital nutrients her body needed to create breast milk for her child. It reminded Ane of the child that had been born on the *Thornton,* James Moulton. The boy's skeletal frame was now all that remained of him, and through his flesh could be seen the steady beat of his indomitable heart. Ane thanked God that at least her children were not infants.

Johanna and Kristina each held to their cart with one hand, the other hand being used to grip a blanket together around their shoulders. Kristina slipped, her face hitting snow. Johanna rushed to her side and Ane stopped the cart, climbed over the bar and hurried to her daughters. They tried to help her stand, but she could not. She was no longer able to feel her legs beneath her. Ole knelt down beside her and held his daughter's frozen hand.

"I will wait here for a wagon to pass and load her in."

Ane considered, "No. Even if one is to come by soon, you will grow cold and tired waiting. Besides they are too full."

"Then I will carry her," Ole insisted.

Ane prayed for strength, and began, almost without thought, to rub Kristina's legs. Johanna did the same, and Ole held Kristina to his chest, rubbing her arms and shoulders.

They did so vigorously and repeatedly, whispering prayers, until Kristina sat up and said, "I can walk."

They helped her to rise and continued the relentless march forward.

They tried to keep single-minded to the trail, focusing on each step forward instead of the horrors around them lest their resolve should weaken.

Determination kept the Madsens moving forward. They would not sacrifice everything to die only a few hundred miles from Zion.

10 P.M.

Ole looked down at the handcart to make sure his hands were still grasping the bar. He could barely see in the dark and wondered what time it was and how much longer until they reached camp. He guessed that Rock Creek couldn't be more than four miles away. He gazed upon the hands he no longer felt and noticed they were turning black. They reached a stream and the girls were about to tie up their skirts and wade across when Ole stopped them.

"No. Wait for me." He stepped into the creek's freezing water, which made the river they had been baptized in back home seem warm. Dodging slabs of ice floating along the creek, Ole pulled the handcart across and up on the other side. His hands had frozen to the handle; the flesh tore as he pulled them off. He walked back across the creek, water to his waist in some places. Ane and the girls waited his return.

"Come," he shouted above the wind. His arms were opened. Ane nudged Johanna forward. Johanna stumbled a bit as she walked to the edge of the creek. She wrapped her arms around her father's neck and he scooped her up in his arms. Neither said a word as he cradled her carefully and crossed the stream. He set her down gently on the other side. Then he walked back across to gather up Kristina. He was not being courageous as he bore the freezing stream for his wife and children. He simply chose between the lesser of two evils—the pain and suffering he would endure in the river, a physical pain that he could stand to bear, or the pain and suffering he would feel if he had to watch his family wade across and freeze. It was not a decision. The choice had already been made the moment Ole proposed marriage to his wife and welcomed these beautiful daughters into the world.

Tears wet Kristina's cheeks, "Father, I am scared," she muttered.

"There is nothing to be afraid of. I am going to take care of you." He set her down and quickly returned for Ane, carrying her safely across.

Within minutes, Ole's pants and boots froze to his body. He ignored the rigidity of his clothes and the stiffness of his legs and told himself to keep moving.

1 A.M.

The light glow of fires in the distance a couple miles ahead alerted the Madsens that they were nearing the campsite. "We are almost there," Ole called to his girls. They followed blindly, holding onto the cart, their eyes closed to keep from freezing. *Soon we can rest,* Ole thought. *We can kneel by a warm fire and pray.*

Ole heard shouting just ahead of them. Two dark silhouettes appeared, one sitting in a stupor refusing to move forward, the other standing over him trying to reason with him. "Well, if you are not going," the brother yelled to the man who was ready to die, "then I am to give you a whipping before I go." He slapped the man hard on the cheek and hastened forward. The assaulted man was so flush with indignation he rose up and angrily chased after the man who had landed the blow, ready to land his own retribution upon him. They reached camp, alive.

When the Madsens reached camp they found it in disarray. With not enough able men to do the work, only a few fires were built and tents were not pitched. Many of the company leaders had been busy unloading the ill from handcarts or wagons, and wrapping them in blankets and setting them next to the fire. The animals had been unhitched from the wagons to find water, grazing and rest. When the rear wagons that were picking up stragglers did not reach camp, Willie went on foot in search of them. They had stalled at Strawberry Creek. Once this was learned wagons were re-hitched and sent back for them.

Ole dropped the tongue of the handcart and fell to his knees. His arms pushed against the earth as if he were fighting it like a mad man, and with all his strength he brushed the snow aside to form a small clearing. Then moving his arms in a circular motion, he cleared a circle about four feet across to build a fire.

Ane, seeing the wagons overflowing with the sick and dead began yelling for Marie and Andrew.

"Marie!" she cried, tears wetting her cheeks. "Andrew!" her cry turned to a scream, and she repeated the call, rushing from one wagon to the next, looking for her children.

"Marie! Andrew!"

"Mama!" Ane heard Marie cry. She rushed to a wagon and saw her little girl amongst the dying and dead.

"Marie!" Ane pulled her daughter from the wagon and collapsed to the ground, weeping as she held her.

Ole grabbed Andrew from the wagon and his weak arms nearly dropped the boy. He quickly handed Andrew to Johanna, who folded him into a blanket. Andrew cried with Marie, yelling for his mother as he sobbed. They were all safe, alive. Kristina and Johanna cried too, grateful, yet deathly afraid. They wailed, inconsolable.

Marie hung on her mother and cried. To see her family still alive overwhelmed her with gratitude and also with fear. One of them could be next. She had become familiar with death. She watched depleted pioneers take their last breaths. The dead's glassy frozen eyes had mocked her, making her feel guilty for living. "Papa," Marie wailed.

Ole wanted to go to her. He wished to comfort all his children, but more than that he wanted them to stay alive. He leaned down to Johanna and Kristina, ran his black fingers through their wet hair. "Grab some sage," he told them. They nodded through their tears. They left the blanket wrapped around Andrew and went to find fuel for a fire. The snow was so deep they had to gather twigs sticking above the snowdrifts.

Ole turned to Ane and said in quiet desperation, "Pull the canvas off, set it here, I will get the fire started." Then he stumbled off toward the girls to help them gather kindling. Ane left Marie and crawled over to the handcart, untying the hemp cord that held the canvas to the cart.

A few minutes later, Ole and the girls returned. He had some willows under his arm and a piece of burning sagebrush that he had lit from a nearby fire. He carefully set the burning sagebrush down, put some of the willows on top and blew, nursing the flame into a fire.

He looked to Kristina, "Metta." His arms reached for her kindling. She unraveled her tattered skirt and handed him some sagebrush. She looked into her father's eyes. Eyes that used to smile, that had relayed strength this morning, now showed exhaustion.

Assured that the fire was going, Ole turned his attention to the handcart where Ane was taking their belongings and setting them on the ground. Marie and Andrew helped dig out a place for their tent with a tin pan. Ole took a few steps to the cart, grabbed hold of the canvas and ripped it from the cart, spilling the few remaining articles onto the ground. "That is enough," he told Marie and Andrew. He laid the canvas next to the fire, "Get on." He told his children. He would have happily lifted them on had he the strength.

Ole saw that Ane had fallen to her knees, sobbing. Ole did not go to her, but lifted the items that had fallen to the ground and placed them back on the cart. He pulled the cart to their campsite to shelter his children from the snow that was now lightly falling. Only then did Ole take Ane in his arms as they knelt in the snow. The camp was consumed with sorrow, sobbing and weeping in all directions. The Madsens listened to the hiss of the sagebrush as it smoked and burned, the fire drawing the liquid out. The fire would eventually be lost to the cold night, but not before they felt it. The warmth it provided was welcomed but painful. As their bodies slowly thawed, muscles and joints began to ache and nerves screamed with pain. Ole lay down next to Ane, farthest from the fire. He could no longer feel his legs and could scarcely move them. Ane saw the light in his eyes begin to fade.

"Ole." Her voice was harsh and barely audible. "Ole!" she said more forcefully. She clasped his black fingers, "Dear God, let him stay."

He whispered in Danish, *"Jeg er altid her."* I am always here.

She kissed him and held him tight, providing some warmth for his dying moments. His eyes darted and looked beyond her. The muscles in his flexed face softened. The last of the warmth was consumed by the cold. He was dead. She said nothing. She lay next to him, eyes shut, and begged for rest.

THEN

∽

October 24, 1856

*"Fierce cold wrapped around her /
As she stared blankly on."*
—*Rock Creek Hollow*

ROCK CREEK HOLLOW

*D*arkness was in the clouds and in the hearts of the surviving Madsens. Ane stood with the children, staring into the vast distance of the high plateau near South Pass. The wind shifted, sending waves of white powder across the distant slant of the draw. She had been unaware of anything that was said at the service for her husband and for twelve others who had died on the Gethsemane of Rocky Ridge. She could not organize a thought in her mind.

"Sister Madsen," a hand touched her shoulder. She was lost in her grief. "Sister Madsen," she turned her head toward the voice long before her eyes looked into his. "Sister Madsen," Elder Christensen said softly, "Stay as long as you like. No one will start the burial until you are ready."

Ane looked around and noticed no adults were near. She felt a tug on her dress. Andrew had his face buried in her skirt while the girls huddled around her, their eyes on the ground, the scene before them too difficult to look upon. They did not want to see the thirteen corpses that lay in a circular formation, very much like the spokes of a wheel.

Marie recognized the little girl from the night before, who sat across from her in the wagon and gnawed on her own flesh. She lay dead next to Niels Nielson with whom Marie's family had shared a tent. She remembered hearing that Niels' father's foot had been badly deformed by the trek up the ridge.

Early that morning, Ane had heard the wagon approach and the call for the dead. She quietly got up and directed the workers to Ole's body. They loaded him on a cart as the children watched, confused and scared.

Marie wanted to cry out, "Mother, what are you doing?! He is tired! He is only sleeping!" But deep down she knew it wasn't true. Their father was dead. The girls cried. Johanna comforted them, saying their father was in Heaven and they would see him again. Ane felt a pang of guilt for not being the one to offer comfort to her young ones. But she couldn't turn away from Ole. Not yet.

She watched as the men tried removing his boots with the thought that they might be of use to someone else, as many in camp were walking barefoot. But they were frozen stiff. A layer of ice secured them to his feet forever. The men gave up and rode on, collecting the dead. Ane looked on, not with interest, but with a heavy heart that needed a distraction. She saw Sister Lolly Nielsen, who had been traveling with the Wickland family, frozen stiff. Eight-year-old Christina Wickland had lain by Lolly's side through the night to provide her warmth, but it had not been enough. Ane watched as the men attempted to lift Lolly, only to discover that her hair was frozen to the ground. They scrambled to find something they could use to cut the dead woman's hair.

Ane thought of how she would have found such a scene amusing if it had been one of Ole's tall tales, something he told his girls to ensure they never went out in a storm without their capes and bonnets. But this was real. Horrific was the only word that came to Ane's mind, but even such a word felt like an understatement.

A bonfire blazed to help thaw the ground for grave digging. Once the bodies were gathered, the men used oxen to break the ground, and then a couple of men dug the graves as deep as they could get them. The bodies were placed in a circular formation with their feet at the center and their heads out. Once the bodies were placed a brief prayer was conducted. Ane had seen it before. She knew they would cover the bodies with rocks and dirt and then throw burnt coals over the area to try to keep wolves away.

A Scottish woman by the name of Ann Stewart, convinced that her husband was still breathing despite his rigid frozen body, had the gravediggers drag him from the grave and to a fire where she was able to revive him. Ane knew by the way Ole's blood pooled on the side of his pale face that a similar fate did not exist for him. He would not be revived.

She looked up from the bodies into the eyes of Elder Christensen. He had taken over for Peter Madsen as Danish company clerk. Peter had attended Ole's service, but had not stayed. Some families of the dead were too despondent or physically unable to attend the service. Most everyone who remained at the gravesite stared blankly ahead.

The children could hardly feel the loss of their father. They added grief to the only other two feelings they were aware of—cold and hungry.

THEN

❧

October 26, 1856

*"She tries to see tomorrow / Not knowing
where to start / Silent and alone now."*
—*Legacy*

*T*he morning light shone around their encampment, and spread to the distant hills. The stillness beckoned a loneliness that was accentuated by the numbing cold. What was left of the Madsen family lay huddled in a wagon, pressed tightly together. As Ane opened her eyes, her first thoughts were not how hard the wagon's planed boards felt under her, but that she could not remember the last time she had awakened in a different position. She had learned to confine herself to sleeping in a tent with twenty people. The cold prevented their moving until morning once they were bedded down. They did not move to relieve themselves, nor if they were sick, nor even if they feared the person next to them was not contributing to the general heat because he or she had expired.

With the burial complete, Ane's mind was bombarded with the reality of her husband's death. She wondered who would join him today. She knew it couldn't be her. She would not leave her children orphans.

When the snow arrived and the food had run out, the resolution of her fate had settled upon her. She had prayed for relief, for help to get her family to Zion. Now she found a resolve known only to a few. She had walked to the brink, abandoning all belief, and just before the bitter end, she was pulled from the abyss by faith.

Ane said a silent prayer. *Let me have the strength to get through what you have deemed that I must. Let my children see my unwavering faith.*

Ane touched each of her children as she had done several times in the middle of the night to feel the air moving their bodies, making sure none had died.

She could hear the indistinguishable words of men talking low and then the crackle of fire as pine tar expanded and popped. She carefully slid out of the wagon, walked a little way from the group and relieved herself. They had learned early in their travels that privacy must be sacrificed as a cost of safety.

Ane returned to the wagon and woke her children. They looked like four little puppies wrapped together. Andrew was first to open his eyes and speak.

"I saw Father last night," Andrew said using the Danish word *mareridt,* which meant, "bad dream."

"We were trying to get his boots off because Captain Ahmanson wanted to wear them and then the wolves came," Andrew said. "We wanted to run, but Father got up and backed them away from us with his gun, and then he yelled that he would show them the leather of his boot; and he chased them into the night, leaving us alone. More came and chased after him."

"We must not fear." Ane held her son. One hand rubbed his hair and the other hand ran across the gun they had laid along the side of the wagon. She would not let it out of her sight. She looked into the eyes of the other three children. Marie was quietly weeping in the arms of Johanna.

Ane pulled herself out of the recesses of her personal hell and looked for the right words to keep her family afloat. Their goal of Zion had not been reached yet, and she was not one to give up. She would move on and so must her children

She thought of Ole's words spoken just a few days earlier. It was strange how she had been in his arms when he spoke them. Never again. She was still adjusting to the reality of the loss. But she remembered his words, "I will do everything I can to deliver my family safely to Zion." He had delivered on his promise to his death, and Ane took comfort in believing he was doing that still, from the other side.

"Let us move." Ane addressed the children. "There will be food today." Suddenly there was a great shout, and they all looked to see a broken handcart burst into flames as it had been dragged into the fire at the center of the camp. Three more unusable handcarts were burned that morning, as wagons arrived with food and clothing.

Ane gazed upon the blazing handcarts and thought of Ole. *What clever remark might he make if he were here?* She wondered. Perhaps, "Happy to see the handcart finally being put to good use." She managed a slight smile and hoped he was somewhere thinking just that. The belief that he was still with her somewhere, somehow, gave her strength.

After breakfast the family returned to their assigned wagon and waited while the horses were hitched. The relief a wagon provided was immensely felt. Ane pulled a comb from the silk pouch she carried around her neck and gave it to Johanna. "Do your best with your sisters and I will comb your hair while we ride. Today we will hold our heads up and be strong. We will make your father proud. He will be with us, watching over us, while we travel to Zion." She knelt and they held each other as she said their morning prayer.

The morning sun glistened on the comb as Johanna ran it through Marie's hair. Ane noticed the rescuers were eating breakfast. To Ane and the others of the Willie Company, they were angels sent from a prophet of God. They brought food, dragged in firewood and cared for the battered pioneers night and day. They stood guard. They were the last to sleep and would only eat after all in the handcart group were fed.

Ane watched them prepare flapjacks. They were not used to cooking over a fire, and after burning a few, they decided to give up on salvaging them and instead tossed them in the bushes and started over. Ane walked to the bushes behind the rescuer's fire and picked up their burnt flapjacks. She ate several ravenously and tucked the rest into her silk pouch.

One of the rescuers saw Ane and went to her, asking, "Are you hungry? Did you get some food?"

Ane was unable to interpret his English. She picked up the last flapjack from the bushes as sub-captain Ahmanson approached.

"She cannot understand you," Ahmanson explained.

The rescuer touched her arm and said, "You will never be hungry again, we have plenty and more wagons are coming." Ahmanson translated his words into Danish.

Ane looked into the rescuers' eyes, tears forming in her own. She wiped them away with her hand and spoke to the rescuer in Danish. When she was finished, she turned and walked toward her wagon, stuffing the last flapjack in her pouch.

"What did she say?" The rescuer asked Ahmanson.

Ahmanson smiled. "As with Ole, you will not always be with me, and these flapjacks did not come to me through your hand."

NOW

✢

February 2006

"White are the far-off plains... /
And denser still the snow."
— *Archibald Lampman, Snow*

"She's more famous than you'll ever be." I looked in the direction of the words that were coming out of the mouth between the rough beard and mustache of the wrangler who was saddling up the gray mule next to the deep reddish one I sat on.

We were on the set of *Sweetwater Rescue,* a film depiction of the rescue of the Willie and Martin handcart companies. Footage from the production would also later be used for another documentary about Ole Madsen and his family entitled *Walking in Obedience: The Ole Madsen Story.* For a month I had trained for this part on a horse so I wouldn't look lame on camera. Now I sat in the freezing cold on a mule, looking lame.

I had been riding the large mule for about an hour in sub-zero temperatures at Rock Creek Hollow, Wyoming. The snowy dirt roads and the area around the gravel parking lot were filled with film equipment trailers, a couple of large cafeteria tents and a larger trailer for wardrobe fitting. The film crew was busy setting up.

The filmmaker, Lee Groberg, was in the final days of shooting his newest film. Lee's company, Groberg Films, specializes in documentaries. Lee was being very professional, determined that everything be authentic. I wondered, as I sat freezing on the mule, if he had gone too far.

The day before I had barely survived being caught in a massive snowdrift. Granted, I was in my brother KC's 4-wheel-drive Tahoe at the time, but that didn't make the blizzard any less treacherous.

KC had been driving, while I sat shotgun. The morning shoot had been cancelled and we were unaware at the time that weather conditions would shut us down for the whole day. Road graders had given up as the storm dumped snow so deep the drivers couldn't tell where the road was. Unaware, we continued our drive to the film site. We approached a slight bend in the road that KC took quite cautiously. Suddenly I spotted a figure crawling out from under an old broken-down truck. As soon as the man spotted us he began to wave and KC pulled over. The young man was shivering and obviously frightened. He was cold, wet and wearing only a lightweight jacket.

"What are you doing out here?" KC yelled through the open window.

"My car is stuck in the drift up ahead and the snow is piling up around it. I was afraid I would be buried," he replied.

"Hop in with us," KC offered. The man climbed in the back seat and I offered him a blanket that he gratefully pulled around him.

He explained that after his car got stuck in the drift, the falling snow piled up quickly, threatening to trap him inside. That's when he decided to get out and walk for fear he'd be buried along with his car. As he walked he came across that old abandoned truck on the side of the road. He climbed underneath it seeking shelter from the storm.

"I am sure glad you guys came by," he said.

"Me too," I said. Another twenty minutes and he might not have been found until spring thaw.

KC had a tow rope, and we decided we'd try to pull this young man's car out. KC pulled down to the car, which was almost in a snow tunnel now, and started turning around.

"Let me get out here and I can be hooking the tow rope while you back down," I offered.

KC slowed the car, and then changed his mind, "Why don't you wait until I pull forward and then back down. Then you can climb out." I agreed. Less of a walk for me.

As we were backing down, we noticed something very unusual. The car was in a different position. In fact, it was about six feet forward from where we had seen it only moments ago. The drifting snow was blowing so hard that visibility was difficult. As we got out, a man climbed over the top of the car. He had been coming from the other direction in his truck, and seeing the drift ahead, decided to gun it to make it through. Not seeing the car in the drift, he hit it, demolishing the back end.

I looked at KC with eyes wide. We had the same thought in both our heads. If he had let me out when I asked to get the rope ready, I would likely be mangled or dead.

Eventually we pulled the young man's totaled car out of the drift and dragged it to the highway where a wrecker could pick it up. All I could think of was how struggling pioneer families could have lived through storms like this. They did it without the warmth of a car heater and the convenience of a vehicle that made walking unnecessary.

Interestingly, the historians at the shoot site told us that the conditions that we were shooting in were very similar to the actual conditions the Willie Company had experienced in October 1856. I thought about this as I rode the mule past rows of handcarts that had just been delivered. Road crews with heavy equipment had been cutting a road into Rock Creek Hollow for the past couple of days, battling the huge blizzard and high winds. They couldn't rest, or the constantly blowing snow would make it impossible to get into the shooting location near South Pass. On the last day of the filming, a tunnel of snow ten feet tall on both sides had been cut into the last 200 yards of the road.

I was amazed that anyone in the Willie and Martin companies made it out alive. I feared for my life despite the fact I was most often in a warm car. I had plenty to eat and slept in a warm bed at night.

"She's more famous than you'll ever be," the wrangler repeated. I was lost in thought and came back trying to grasp the meaning of his words.

"Who?" I asked.

"The mule," he replied. "She's famous. Her name is Sheba and Tom Cruise rode her in the movie *Far and Away*. She's more famous than you'll ever be," he said again.

"Me?" I replied, "I am just the great-great-grandson of a poor farmer from Denmark. He's buried right over there, and all I really want to be is warm," I said jokingly.

Lee had asked me to play Joseph Elder that day, and we were reenacting a scene in which Joseph and Captain Willie desperately searched for the rescue party. The two were trapped in a blizzard and were out of food as they made a last desperate attempt to save the Willie Company.

As I rode the famous Sheba, I developed a deep respect for mules. She was great in snow up to her belly and any warmth she offered was appreciated.

Film crews had done scenes with men, women and children, pulling handcarts through the deep snow. I watched as people struggled to pull their carts forward and mused on the real difficulty the pioneers must have had, being at least a head shorter than the actors playing them and having had far less food to give them strength.

In one of the scenes, Lee asked us to ride out a quarter-mile with four wagons representing the rescue wagons and then turn back and ride in front of them as if we were bringing the wagons to the Willie Company. We did as instructed and turned away from the cameras, away from the trailers, away from the warm food and hot chocolate, and for a moment I was able to forget they were there. I rode behind the wagons as the sun was setting and all I could hear were the quiet sounds of the wind blowing snow across the sagebrush and the wagon wheels squeaking as they slowly turned.

Ahead was the snow-covered high plateau of South Pass. But underfoot was just smooth, white, drifting snow. The scene came alive. I felt suddenly transported back to 1856. I imagined there were people literally freezing to death, without food or adequate clothing, waiting, hoping and praying for a rescue. Sadness fell over me as I imagined how desperate and frightened they must have felt.

As we turned back toward the cameras, I was grateful I would be warm that night.

After filming that day, my 4-wheel-drive Tahoe got stuck in the same spot as the young man's car had on the previous day. I knew no one was ahead of us, but I didn't want anyone coming down the hill from behind me and having a repeat of the crash that totaled his vehicle. My two daughters and I could only get out of one side of the car, as the snow drifts were too high on the other side.

We dug with shovels for about an hour, moving the Tahoe only a few feet at a time. Each of us offered a silent prayer as we dug and pushed and the car's wheels spun.

We sat in the car and called for help. The closest wrecker was an hour away. The storm's intensity was building around us. We said a prayer, and were determined to have another go at digging the car out. After digging another fifteen minutes under the front axle and in the area behind the tires, I got out and pushed while Shaunee, my daughter, took the wheel. We gave it one last try, and this time we were able to spin our way out.

We got out of the car and stood in the bitter blowing snow. We were humbled and thankful to be driving to our warm rooms at a little bed and breakfast six miles away.

Jenny said with some emotion, "Dad how could anyone make it out of here alive pushing handcarts, with no way to get out of the cold snow and wind, and without warm clothes or enough to eat?"

I knew the question was rhetorical, so I said nothing and simply looked out over the frozen white landscape.

*   *   *

I lay in the darkness and listened to the relentless wind push on the windows of the motel in Casper, Wyoming. It was -35 degrees Fahrenheit, and the wind speed was 50 mph. That week, some of the gas pumps in Rock Springs had frozen. All I could think about was how I dreaded going back in the cold to Martin's Cove where Groberg planned that day to film the re-enactment of the Martin Company crossing the Sweetwater River.

The day was bright, clear and cold with a strong wind harping at us all day long.

A number of tents had been set up, and we quickly learned that it was a good idea to be huddled in one between the calls to shots. This made the cold almost bearable. We also had heavy coats to wear between shots.

By the time we arrived, the crew had already set up equipment around the Sweetwater River and up the hill to a simulated camp.

KC's main goal, above all else, was to know what it felt like to pull a handcart through a cold stream. We entered the wardrobe building and changed into our pioneer clothing. Those of us who were going into the water were given light neoprene waders to wear underneath our pants. When I saw this, I asked if I could do the scenes without the waders, as I wanted to get a sense of what Ole felt when he carried his children across. I was told it was my choice, but a few minutes prior to getting in the water, I was told they had changed their minds and I couldn't do it because it was too dangerous. I have to admit I was a little relieved. Just standing in the cold in thin pioneer clothing was brutal.

We did the scene and on the first take I stepped from the water and noticed that my pants and boots, along with the handcart wheel that had gotten wet, immediately froze. My heart went out to Ole.

Some of us were instructed to be in a sequence in which we were to carry a number of sisters across the river. After dropping one on the shore, we were to go back and get another and continue to do this while the cameras were rolling. It was exhausting and after the second time I was looking for the smallest sister I could find.

After the shooting ended, I went to a handcart and leaned against it for support. My head was down and I was panting, out of breath. I was also sweating. My shirt under my jacket was soaked. I was told to get someplace warm by a fire or in a tent. There was the risk that within a few minutes hypothermia would set in and I would be in trouble fast.

If Ole hadn't done what he did for his children, sparing them the crossing of the river, any one or all of them could have died on that trail. Ole securing room in a wagon to assist in the last long miles of their passage may have also saved Marie and Andrew. To think, if Ole hadn't made those sacrifices, I'd never have been where I was, leaning against a handcart in a punishing cold wind, out of breath and memorializing my great-great grandfather's final sacrifices on this earth. The experience was all too surreal.

I made my way to a tent to change and find warmth. As my legs began to thaw, I marveled again that anyone in the Willie Company made it out of there alive.

THEN

ଓ

November 9, 1856

T he wheels of the wagons made their last turn and came to an abrupt stop on Main Street in Great Salt Lake City. Zion did not fit the Willie Company's imaginings. Majestic mountains loomed to the east and occasionally strong winds raced down through the city's cross streets. The earth was dry here and the air crisp. The Great Salt Lake lapped the sandy shores far to the west. When the west winds blew, the air smelled and tasted of salt. Vegetation was sparse and sagebrush pervaded. With snow on their peaks the transcendent mountains were serene.

On the day the company arrived, the dry air was chilled. The sky was darkened by clouds, and threatened inclement weather. No snow yet covered the ground in this proposed area of the State of Deseret. It would threaten only to dump slush, not yet having made the transition to winter.

Typically, an arriving pioneer company would be met with a party and the streets would be filled with jubilant cheers, laughter and rejoicing.

Not today.

Throngs of women and men respectfully and mournfully advanced on the wagons. Sixty-seven of the 404 members of the Willie Company who continued from Florence had died on the journey, including two this day. Cries and whimpers were heard throughout the streets as men, women and children, left alive by God's grace, were pulled from the wagons.

They longed to be comforted, to be cared for. But their bodies, stiff and hurting, muscles sore and aching, shivered with pain and they wept as they were lifted from the wagons.

There would be lasting effects of the snowbound trail on many of the Willie Company survivors. Some would suffer impaired or lost vision from the blinding snowstorms and malnourishment. A woman's frozen scalp would lose all its hair, leaving her bald for life. Shoes would finally be slipped off only to have their frozen toenails fall off. A few who suffered severe frostbite would require limb amputation—most often with a kitchen knife.

Many of those who had come to help, upon seeing the conditions of the Willie Company people, couldn't help but join them in their weeping.

"Oh, you poor dear."

"God bless you."

"You are safe now."

They were met by strangers but treated like old friends. Some were escorted from the wagons to nearby houses while others were carried or put on horses or in carriages to be taken to a home farther away where they'd find food, shelter and warmth.

Kristina was pulled from their wagon first. She could have walked, but she surrendered to the arms that held her.

"Go with her," Ane ordered Johanna. She looked at her mother. Ane coughed a long dry cough. "They are taking us into their homes to care for us until we make a place of our own. You go with her."

Johanna did as she was told. She crawled to the open end of the wagon, and hands were there to receive her. They helped her down, and she thanked them in English. Then speaking in Danish, she pointed to the wagon, "My mother and her two youngest are in there." She wasn't sure if they understood.

Johanna looked through the crowd and found the man who cradled Kristina in his arms. He was talking to an older woman with black hair fastened in a bun, and droopy, almond-shaped eyes. Johanna limped toward him and watched as he carried her sister to the side of the road and laid her next to a young tree that had lost all its leaves. Johanna sat next to her. A stranger wrapped them both in a blanket and moved on. The outpouring of love and care they felt and saw was overwhelming. They were with their people now. They were in Zion. They longed to kiss the hands that caught their tears and then to collapse into a long and blissful rest.

The woman with the sweet almond-shaped eyes approached the girls. "Do you speak English?"

The girls shook their heads.

"Danish, then." She paused for a moment looking on them with pity. "Sister Ellen can take care of you," she said decidedly. "She will teach you our language. Come with me," she motioned. Johanna labored to stand and pull Kristina with her. The woman rushed to Kristina's side, and another woman grabbed Johanna's arm and pulled them up.

"It is close. You need to walk, your joints are too stiff." The girls didn't understand, but they followed her lead. Johanna clung to the stranger who held her arm as if she were her sister Karen. When they reached the sidewalk in front of a large brick house bearing a statue of a lion on an upper terrace, the other woman let go of Johanna and hurried back to the wagons. Johanna was unable to thank her.

Before entering the door, the girls looked back to see if they could find their mother but couldn't see her amidst the commotion.

"It will be fine," the woman said, sensing their concern. She led them through the front door. The floor beneath them was soft, covered with pleasing and fanciful rugs. Chairs had intricate woodcarvings and loveseats were covered in red satin. The ceiling dripped chandeliers. Fireplaces lit the walls and the windows were garnished with flowing white lace curtains. The girls were overcome by their luxurious surroundings.

They ascended the stairs on their left, trailing behind the bustling woman who lightly knocked on a nearby door, "Sister Ellen, I have need of you."

The door flung open, and a woman who looked to be in her twenties, tall and slim with fair skin, greeted them. She was dressed in a lovely deep blue gown and held a crochet hook in hand. She glanced from the woman to the girls, and then stood to the side as the girls were escorted into the room.

"They have just come in. These two seem fine, but they need food, drink and warmth. Start by getting them warm, change their clothes and wash them with water as hot as they can stand. Fit them into some of your old clothes and give them some food. Not too much though, their stomachs are in want of food, but they will have difficulty keeping it down. I will bring some herbs later when everyone is settled."

Ellen nodded, and the woman was off.

The girls glanced around the room, noting the ornate wood-carvings in the molding around the door and on the bed's head-board. Everything around them smelled fresh and new. They were completely unaware that they stood in the Lion House, one of the homes of Brigham Young, the prophet and leader of their church. They didn't know that the woman they stood before was one of Brigham's polygamous wives and that the woman who had escorted them to the room was Brigham's second wife, his first having passed away years before.

Ellen looked upon the poor creatures, but did not react. Their clothes were tattered, their faces browned with dirt, their hair ratted, their flesh frostbitten, their lips cracked and eyes blood red. She motioned for them to sit.

"I am Sister Ellen Rockwood Young," she said. "What are your names?"

The girls shook their heads.

"Ellen," she placed her hand over her heart, and then pointed to Johanna.

"Johanna," the girl said, then pointing to Kristina, "Metta."

Ellen smiled slightly. With no sense of urgency, she went to the bedside table and picked up a pitcher to fill with warm water. She discretely held a hand mirror at her side when she left.

The girls looked out the window and studied the landscape. Gardens surrounded them and farther off buildings were being constructed.

"The Temple is being built a block west from here," Ellen said returning with a small pitcher in hand. "They are using sandstone for the foundation. It is going to be beautiful. I cannot wait until it is finished."[1]

Ellen sat in a chair and motioned for one of the girls to take the seat across from her. Johanna helped Kristina forward. Ellen cleaned her face, then helped her out of her clothes and clothed her in a borrowed dressing gown. Then she washed her. Johanna sat at Kristina's feet, huddled in a blanket.

The warm water against Kristina's skin was like a gift, and her muscles began to ache as they relaxed.

Ellen had them sip on water, and then she lifted from her apron pocket a small loaf of bread and divided it equally between them. They ate quickly, hardly taking a breath. Ellen watched, thinking she should prompt them to slow down. But she had never hungered like that.

The girls ate beyond feeling satiated and were sick. Ellen was bathing Kristina when she saw her face turn pale, then flush. Kristina placed her hand over her stomach. Ellen dropped the cloth and lunged for a bedpan, bringing it to Kristina, who dry heaved and then vomited.

Johanna rubbed her sister's back and pulled her hair from her face.

Ellen set the pan down and wrung out the sponge. "Mother Young will be back soon," she said, "She will know exactly what you need. You will be feeling better in no time. You must keep faith. Everything will be fine." She knew they could not understand her, but empty silence was a heartbreaking void. *What had their experience been like? Had they lost anyone? Where were their parents and siblings? Would they really be okay?* She wondered.

---

1. The foundation was first laid with sandstone and later replaced when cracking was discovered.

"Mother Young will know exactly what to do," she repeated as she ran the damp cloth along Kristina's arm. "Mother Young has helped many in need. She is very knowledgeable. Her little girl, Mary, was once run over by a wagon wheel. The man in charge of the wagon swears the child should have died, but Mother Young said, 'Don't prophesy evil, brother,' and she knew just what to do, as if God were telling her. She shaped that baby's head back to normal, and you know what? She lived. Yes, Mother Young will know just what to do."

Mother Young returned hours later. The girls had been cleaned and lay on the floor wrapped in blankets. Fresh clothes hung over a chair and the tattered rags they had arrived in were taken out, along with the bedpan. Mother Young looked at the clothes Ellen had set out for them with a pained expression.

"Have you nothing else? These are a little out of date."

Ellen shook her head. The girls saw the look on Mother Young's face as she looked at the clothes and were glad they weren't the only ones who thought them dreadful. The skirts were short and hung just below the knees. Underneath the skirts were pantaloons that looked like bloomers, all to be worn with a long animal skin jacket. On top of it all, like a distasteful garnish to an even more awful meal, there were eight-inch-high top hats.

"I suppose they will have to do for now," Mother Young said.

"They are not keeping food down," Ellen informed her. Just then a bell rang, and Mother Young turned to Ellen, "How are your nerves? Can you eat?"

"Yes," she replied.

"I will stay here," Mother Young offered. "When you have finished with dinner, you can stay in my room tonight. Let these girls have your bed." Ellen nodded and left.

Mother Young lit some candles and took a good look at the girls, examining their eyes and touching their cold and sweaty foreheads with the back of her hand. She filled two cups with hot water and steeped some herbs. "Cayenne and ginger should do the trick. They will settle your stomachs and keep in the heat." She handed them each a cup and ordered them to drink.

They took small sips. When they were through, Mother Young motioned for them to get in bed. She tucked them in and sat in the chair at the base of the bed. She watched them for a few minutes, then gazed out the window and began to hum. Her hand rested over her stomach as she settled her own nerves.

The girls hadn't spoken to each other until Kristina asked, "*Hvor er Mor?*" Where is mother?

Johanna wished she knew.

Mother Young looked at them both, understanding she replied, "*Sikker.*" Safe.

The girls nodded as tears wet their cheeks. It finally sank in. They had arrived. No more hardships, no more persecution and no more losses. They had given up everything and stretched their bodies to the limit for what they believed, for what they dreamed of—for Zion. Now they were here. They were home.

NOW

ℰ℧

August 2006

"Now ponder for a time / All that you have done."
—*Along the Path*

NEPHI

"*Y*ou'll be right out here for the program," the president of the pageant said, motioning to the rodeo grounds. "We cleaned up all the beer cans and we're ready to dedicate the arena."

I walked out on the soft ploughed dirt of the Nephi rodeo grounds where the change from the loud, hard, fast life of the rodeo crowd—cowboys, rodeo clowns and loud country music—was about to become the quiet family crowds and a musical presentation of the annual Nephi Handcart Pageant, complete with horses, wagons, handcarts and actors in pioneer garb.

Prior to the presentation every year, the cast and leaders, about 150 strong, met to have a fireside, followed by a dedicatory prayer. The arena was cleaned and for the next week in the warm summer evenings the program played to packed crowds.

Every year the story of the handcart pioneers was reenacted. Directors casted local talent—singers and cowboys—and stayed authentic by using real horses and wagons.

Emily Christensen and I stood on the rich brown dirt of the arena as the performers sat in the rodeo stands. We had previously told some of the cast and crew how much we appreciated them sharing their talents with us.

This was the sixth fireside Emily and I had done together since our first program at Martin's Cove. Three of those six firesides had been earlier this year. I couldn't even remember why I had started doing these firesides. It was all so natural, and the messages and stories I got to hear and share were powerful—lessons in faith, sacrifice and courage. In time these firesides would take me around the country from Utah, Wyoming, Nebraska and as far as Washington D.C.

The format of the firesides usually went like this: I would play a song on my guitar, usually a medley of *A Poor Wayfaring Man of Grief/Come, Come, Ye Saints.* Then I talked about the story of my ancestors and their immigration to America. The wards and stakes we talked to had heard it all before and were usually hand-carted out of their minds, so I tried giving them stories that focused on what it means to us today. Emily's part was to add a feeling to the fireside that was warm and familiar. She did that well. Our relationship grew from "doing your part" to writing songs together.

It was very fulfilling after the firesides as many people came up to us, excited to ask us questions and tell us about their families and experiences. From the experiences we had and stories we heard, we were inspired to write new songs and add them to our growing media list of music. The requests for firesides and our commitment to do them increased.

We added a distributor for sheet music. BYU radio started playing one of the songs and Deseret Book put our music in their stores. Though we agreed that our intent in doing this was not commercial in nature, it sure seemed to be going in that direction.

While waiting for the Nephi show to get under way, I thought back on a recent fireside at Rock Creek Hollow. I remembered the pines and small draws, the creeks with marshy areas that sculpted the terrain. A feeling of empty solitude had settled over the green-gray sagebrush and dry yellow grass. As we drove out of the high plain of South Pass toward the familiar mountains of home, I had thought of how Marie might have remembered that part of her journey; those cold days in late October 1856. She went forward to Zion, leaving her father buried at Rock Creek, somehow moving on, somehow holding on. I thought, "What questions, besides survival, might have been in her mind? Why couldn't things have turned out differently? Why couldn't faith have preserved them from this, or the power of God and the leaders prevented such trials?"

I remembered looking out at the stunning natural architecture of the high plains of South Pass—the billowy white clouds set against a deep blue sky, accenting the dark green pines. Each element and shape drawn on the horizon had a red tint. Willows swayed by the clear stream water. I remembered it was very peaceful and welcoming. It had been a different season for Marie. She would have been rolling along at maybe five miles per hour in a crowded wagon in winter as they made their slow approach to the Salt Lake Valley. I think perhaps her lack of comfort was mitigated by the advantage of sharing the communal heat of many people crowded into the wagon.

Me? I had been cruising along at 70 miles per hour in July with the air conditioning on. I remembered looking up in the sky to see the contrail of a jet overhead. I thought how the harrowing journey that took Marie's family four months across the plains would take a little more than two hours in a plane. I marveled at how I was able to send an instant message over the Internet to people in Denmark who were helping me find my ancestors, how I could call them up and talk to them on the phone when I had immediate questions that needed answers. I tried to imagine what my great-grandchildren would see and say about my journey 150 years from now. I couldn't dream of what their futures might be like in this fast-paced modern world. The only thing I can say is that I hope those children will know Marie's story. And, perhaps, they will wonder about me, too. As normal and boring as my life is, perhaps they will want to know what motivated me to do what I have done in my life, how I handled the low parts, how my faith held out when dark storm clouds wrapped cold desperation around me, why I wrote this, why I went on a mission, how I treated my kids, if I was of service to those less fortunate around me and if I thanked God for what I had.

If there was one thing I learned from all my research, it was that the majority of the early pioneers didn't dwell on the hard times; they indeed related every aspect of their lives to their relationship with God, specifically in regards to this disastrous journey. They thanked Him for their lives and the fact that they made it through. Most didn't blame leaders or those around them. They learned to accept their plight and move forward with faith.

I don't think my journey has to be harrowing to be important. Simply doing the tasks of the day is enough. Such as getting up every morning to go to work to support my family and sacrificing personal time in service to others, teaching my children to give thanks for what they have and to care for others.

My musings on the past had taken me on into the future. Now it was time to return to the present. The Nephi program began and for the next hour or so, I was absorbed. I felt the spirit strongly and the audience was very reverent. Afterwards, we expected a short dedicatory prayer and then an hour and a half drive home. But this night things would be much longer.

After the program, the president of the pageant stood to speak. He was silent for a couple of minutes and when he attempted to speak, nothing came out. He became quite emotional and just stood silently in front of the group, unable to speak. Each time he tried to speak, the words eluded him. This went on for several minutes without a single word spoken! Finally he motioned to his brother, who stood up and thanked everyone for coming and thanked Emily and me for the program and talked for a few minutes about the pageant. He finished by offering gratitude to those involved in the pageant. Then he asked the president of the pageant to come back and give the dedicatory prayer.

Though he had been tongue-tied when he first faced the audience, the brother offered a dedicatory prayer that lasted, what felt like, thirty minutes. He made sure to thank every cast member by name, even the horses. By the time the prayer ended the sun was finishing its descent in the west.

Emily and I went to collect our equipment and many of the Saints came up and talked to us about the program and songs, which for us was always the best part of a performance.

Night was growing around us as we were leaving the arena. Then a brother came up to me and asked if I was in a hurry to leave. I replied that I wanted to leave pretty soon as we had a long drive home. He looked me directly in the eye and said, "I want you to give me a blessing. Will you do that?" I was quite taken aback and wasn't sure how to answer. After a few moments of silence I said, "Yes." But I needed to get my things to the car. I told him I'd come back.

I told Emily and Cheri about the request. Emily offered to stay but I told her to leave. Cheri was anxious to get home but she resigned herself to waiting in the car.

I walked back to a small circle of people who seemed to be gathered for the blessing and told them I was ready. They introduced themselves as friends of the brother who had asked for the blessing and a couple of missionaries from Martin's Cove. It was dark now and the only available light was a streetlight over a picnic table two hundred feet away. They suggested we go there.

I turned and recognized a good friend, Sherryl, who is a handcart expert and a missionary trainer. She informed me that John, the man who was going to receive the blessing, was her brother. I felt a little relief, because now I could get information about what was going on with him. She told me that John had a very serious form of cancer and that the prognosis was not good. She said he was going to a doctor the following week to see how long he had to live. That was hard for me to hear. As we walked to the picnic table under the dim shadowy lights, I felt a welling of sad concern and fear inside me. My mind raced back to my time as a full-time missionary.

I remembered one afternoon, when I was serving, we received a phone call about a church member's baby who was sick. The family asked if we could come and give her a blessing. I had been given blessings before and watched others receive them, but had never been involved in giving one.

When my companion and I arrived at the house we heard the baby crying. The parents were upset and tense. They informed us that their baby daughter was very sick with a fever and had been crying for a long time. They couldn't quiet her, even for the blessing. In my mind I was thinking, "What if we can't help her? What if we bless her to get better and she doesn't?" I thought about saying something in the blessing, such as "Thy will be done," just in case.

As the father held the infant I anointed her head with consecrated olive oil and then we gave her a blessing. My companion gave the prayer. It was simple and direct and scarcely audible above the screaming infant. But as my companion uttered the words that the baby would be able to rest, she immediately stopped crying, closed her eyes and drifted off to sleep. I opened my eyes in awe, even though the blessing had not ended. I glanced over to see the mother, head bent in prayer, holding one of her hands to her mouth as tears streamed down her cheeks.

Afterwards we handed the baby to the mother, who thanked us for coming, and we left. My companion and I didn't engage in any long discussion about the event, nor did I talk with the family about it. But as we drove to our next appointment I contemplated what had just happened. I wondered if everyone was as touched by it as I was. All through that week I thought about it. I wondered to myself, "What if it had not happened that way?" The next Sunday in church I saw the family, including their content baby girl. I greeted them and noted how pretty the infant looked. I had the feeling that maybe I was the only one who couldn't believe what I had seen earlier that week and wondered how this works. Not everyone who receives a blessing gets better.

What I later realized was that the call we got and the blessing we gave wasn't about us. We were simply vessels. Once I realized this, the worry of my saying the wrong thing and the family losing faith, left me. I learned that God's will would be done regardless of my weaknesses, and that I perhaps had a part in positive outcome by remaining faithful.

Now, somewhere in those two hundred steps it took to get to the illuminated picnic table, I lost my concern, and a little of my fear. Under the glow of a streetlight, we gave John a blessing. Like most priesthood blessings, it was simple, forthright and honest. We requested, backed by our faith and authority, help for John from our Heavenly Father. After the prayer I offered him some words of encouragement and left. I don't know why John approached me to give the blessing. I never asked him.

I didn't expect to hear anything back from John. Then the following week, on a Wednesday afternoon, I returned to my office and checked my phone messages. There was only one. It was Sherryl's voice on the recording. She was very emotional and had a hard time speaking. She explained that John had gone to the doctor and upon examination it was revealed that his cancer was gone. She went on to say that she was convinced that it was because of the blessing I had given that he was healed. I was thrilled and relieved to hear the news. But I wasn't going to take any credit for his healing. It was John's faith, supported by the faith of others, that healed him. Through such incidents in our lives, the understanding of the Gospel and the meaning of it all takes shape, if we have the commitment to recognize it when it comes.

My mind rolled over the events of the past week and drifted back to Ole and Marie as it often did. I leaned back in my chair and felt an overwhelming sense of gratitude for Ole's sacrifice and for Marie's life. Their sacrifices eventually led to my blessings. I thought of the sprawling effect of their choices and could hardly fathom the ripples it had created in my life and in the lives of so many others and how those ripples continue today. I was learning that life is a journey for all of us, whether across the prairies and mountains to Zion or through the confusing, evil-tainted, meandering paths of our modern world.

THEN

∞

Spring 1858

*"The only access / To unbreakable bonds /
...The place I call home."*
—Aspects

*J*t was just before dawn when Johanna and Kristina grasped each other's hands and dashed through the slush and mud of the city's streets. They slowed as they rounded the last corner and saw the wagon parked in front of the drugstore as expected. They quietly inched forward, taking cover in the darkness of early morning. The dark-haired man with slicked back hair, full beard and serious eyes, was the same man Johanna had seen yesterday. He stepped from the store carrying a trunk that he set in the back of the wagon already piled high with sacks of food and other goods.

"Thank you, Brother Godbe," the man called into the drugstore.

Kristina grabbed hold of Johanna's arm as they waited for the right moment. The man climbed onto the wagon and grasped the reins.

Johanna tugged on Kristina's arm as the wagon lurched forward. The girls ran behind the back end of the wagon, coming within arm's length. Kristina pushed Johanna, who grabbed hold of the wagon's back end and jumped, securing a foot on the lip. Johanna found her balance and pulled herself into the wagon. She turned and reached for Kristina, pulling her into the wagon with a thud.

The girls held their breaths, praying that the sound of the oxen's hooves against the ground had disguised the noise. Or perhaps the driver would assume his cargo had adjusted when he negotiated the turn. The man didn't look back and the wagon crept forward heading south. The girls tucked themselves securely in the back and stayed low.

The sun rose and they felt every bump on the trail, although it was wider and less pocked than the trails the Willie Company had taken. Johanna closed her eyes and remembered the last time she had been in a wagon with her family. Kristina had been sleeping with her head in Johanna's lap, her body contorted as she tried to find space to lie down among the others. Marie had one arm wrapped around Johanna's and the other hand holding Kristina's as she rested her head on Johanna's shoulder. Andrew had rested in their mother's arms. Johanna remembered the haunting image of her mother's leaden eyes as if it were yesterday. Never before had she seen her mother's gaze hold anything but determination. Johanna faintly recalled the feelings of numbness, emptiness and hopelessness they all had experienced at different points along the trail. The memories were no longer jarring to think upon. They had neatly knitted themselves into the tapestry of her life experience, and reminded her that she had the strength to endure and survive. But the feelings of loss were still fresh, as she had beheld them many times over the past two years.

Months earlier, Johanna, who was now 17 years old, and Kristina, aged 15, were separated from the rest of their family who had been assigned to settle in Fort Ephraim. The two older girls remained in the Salt Lake Valley where it was felt they would have more luck finding work, and possibly, husbands.

In the heart of the Mormon colonization efforts, they learned firsthand things that settlers in the outlying areas didn't know until later. They had been with others on the 24th of July 1857, when the Saints living in Great Salt Lake gathered in Big Cottonwood Canyon to commemorate the tenth anniversary of the Day of Deliverance when the first group of pioneers arrived in the Valley.

The Nauvoo Brass Band lit up the party with a rhythmic drumbeat and a chorus of horns and clarinets as they marched. They wore navy blue coats trimmed with gold-plated buttons and sported matching caps. Their blue-and-white striped flag, emblazoned with an all-seeing eye, whipped in the wind.

Johanna later recalled the moment when the dancing came to an abrupt stop and two men on horses rode into the canyon party, heading directly towards Brother Brigham.

"We came as fast as we could," Abraham Smoot said.

"We received word in Missouri that President Buchanan has ordered an army to march against us," said Porter Rockwell. "They intend to replace you in your post as governor."

Their message highlighted a wave of recent troubles that had engulfed Zion. In the past few months, missionaries had been recalled. Indian troubles raged as the Native Americans attacked Mormon posts. Confirmation that the federal government was sending troops to quell what they believed to be a Mormon rebellion, prompted quick responses by church leaders. The Salt Lake settlers prepared to evacuate and burn their homes if the federal troops actually invaded. Many families moved to outlying communities. Guns were made ready and scythes turned into bayonets. The Utah War had begun. It would end the next spring with only minor hit-and-run confrontations between the Saints and the soldiers. Negotiations had convinced federal officials that Utah Territory was not bent on seceding from the Union, and increasing concerns about a civil war turned the national attention elsewhere.

But Johanna and Kristina, without the support of their family, worried. They worried that all their sacrifices had simply led to more sacrifices. How much more could they bear? They fretted that they would have to leave everything behind and travel again. This time it was worse because they didn't have the strength and comfort of their family. They could take it no longer. They sat up sleepless nights thinking of their mother, wondering how much 7-year-old Andrew had grown and what kind of young woman Marie, almost 12 years old, was becoming. They missed them and had reached a breaking point. They were determined to go to their mother.

Another bump lifted Johanna, scattering her thoughts as her eyes flew open. She looked behind the wagon and watched the dust rise in a circle before settling back to earth. She looked at Kristina whose eyes were red with irritation.

Kristina covered her mouth and nose and her eyes squeezed shut. Johanna shook her head. She was about to stuff her skirt into her sister's face to muffle the sound, but it was too late.

"AAH-CHOO!" Kristina sneezed. The girls froze.

The driver turned his head slightly to one side as if he were considering whether his ears had heard right. Then he looked back. The girls ducked low behind the freight and stopped breathing. The wagon stopped. The girls looked at each other with wide eyes.

The man climbed off. Johanna hoped he was only relieving himself and stayed still. They heard his footsteps round the wagon. Kristina's eyes grew wider and Johanna shrank a little as if that would hide her.

"What are you misses doing?" the man said sternly as he turned the corner of the wagon and spotted them. They were close enough to Great Salt Lake that he could send them walking back on their own. Johanna couldn't let that happen. There was no way they could make this trip on their own. The territory was unsafe as relations with the Indians were tense.

"*Vi beder Dem hjaelpe.*" We need a ride, she pleaded with him in Danish, hoping some sense of shared background might induce him into helping.

"How did you know where I was traveling to?"

"I overheard you yesterday saying you were up here to get supplies and that you would be leaving before dawn, headed for Fort Ephraim once you had picked up your last load from the drugstore," Johanna explained.

"I see." The man nodded, "And what is it you're running from?"

"Not running from anything," Johanna blurted.

"Our mother and siblings live in Fort Ephraim," Kristina said.

"They were sent to settle there and we were to stay in Great Salt Lake, but we miss them dearly. It has been nearly a year since we have seen them. You must understand," Johanna pleaded.

He held up his hand to silence them, "Fine, I understand, but I am not going to Fort Ephraim. I am going to Nephi."

The girls looked at each other, confused. "We heard the fort was close by," Johanna said.

"About thirty or so miles southeast of Nephi. That is a day's walk—or more."

"We walked more than a thousand miles on foot before. I am sure such a walk will be easy," Johanna said. She heard her mother's determination in her own voice.

"In those shoes?" The man pointed to their moccasins, now covered in dry mud. "You will be walking in snow and mud. Besides, it's not safe with the Indians."

"We've had worse," Kristina said as an afterthought.

The man shook his head. "It's too dangerous."

The girls looked at each other. This might be their only chance to reunite with their family. How were they going to convince him?

"We will wait then," Kristina blurted. Johanna looked at her, confused. Kristina continued, "We will go to Nephi and we will wait until we find someone traveling to Fort Ephraim and we will travel with them. I promise. Please take us so we can be with our family."

"Please," Johanna pleaded.

The man looked at the girls. "Fine," he relented. "You okay sitting back here?"

They nodded.

"Don't touch anything."

"Yes, of course," they assured.

The man sighed, spat and climbed back on the wagon.

* * *

Polygamy had been a rude awakening for Ane and the family upon their arrival in Zion. But Hans Christensen was a good man who was assigned to care for Ane and the widow Annie Maria Ebbesen. Hans was a widower and had five children of his own. The oldest was twenty-five and the youngest sixteen. Three still lived with Hans—James was 22 years old, Lars was 18 years old, and Annie Catherine was 16 years old. His daughter Dorthe had wed a year earlier and Christen also was married. Sister Ebbesen had eleven children, all of them grown with families of their own. She was 77 years old now and needed looking after. They lived together in a small rock and adobe home near the edge of the fort with a fenced-in vegetable garden surrounding the property. Because of the small living quarters they all shared, it had been impossible for Ane to have Johanna and Kristina move to Fort Ephraim to join her, Marie and Andrew.

Ane's arrangement initially had the appearance of working. Hans had mothers for his younger children, Lars and Annie Catherine. Ane had a home for herself and her two youngest. Sister Ebbesen had shelter, food and someone to look after her. It was all a part of the plan.

Ane was not looking for a replacement for Ole. Nothing could replace the life she had with him. She often wondered if she had been a fool to dream. Or was that dream God's gift to her and to her children? Maybe some day the ideal they had dreamed of would be the reality for future generations. She wondered. But then she resigned herself to thinking that someday is all that idealists had to believe in. Someday. Someday, she believed, she would see her family again. Some would be seen on this side of existence and some after death.

These thoughts had repeated so many times that they had become little more than background noise. Ane picked up a bucket that was held together with birch hoops and poured water into the wooden tub where the washboard sat. She examined the water level and surmised she would need more to scrub the linens. "Marie," Ane called.

Marie was outside emptying the bedpan from last night. It was her least favorite chore. She tossed the contents of the pan and returned to their small one-bedroom home. She set the bedpan on the floor next to their only mattress which Sister Ebbesen and Hans slept on. Marie noticed a hole in the mattress with straw poking out. She would likely have to mend it or see if Sister Ebbesen could do it.

She turned on her heel and saw Mother steadying herself with a chair.

Ane pointed to the water buckets, "Fetch me some water for the washing."

Marie grabbed the empty buckets and carried them outside. She fastened them with a rope that hung from either side of a yoke. She lifted the yoke over her shoulders and held the two empty pails so they wouldn't swing as she walked to the creek. In the winter she carried the buckets on a wooden sled through the snow. She preferred that to this as the yoke always cut into her shoulders. She set the yoke down on the creek's edge and unfastened the buckets.

The wind blew loose hair into her eyes. She had forgotten to put on a bonnet. She let go of a bucket with one hand, tucked the hair behind her ears and listened to the whistle of the wind. Sometimes, at night, she would stay awake listening to the wind. She hated the wind. It reminded her of the wolves that howled the night after her father had been buried. The howling wind tormented her when she tried to sleep, reminding her of what horrors she had endured. She prayed. She prayed for silence, prayed for comfort and prayed for her sisters to be with her. It was the only thing that brought her some peace long enough to allow her to fall asleep. They had been promised so much, and now...

She finished smoothing her hair and yanked the bucket from the water. She filled the other bucket, and then tied them both back to the yoke. She fussed with the knots for several minutes, making sure they were strong enough. She had had her share of mishaps from weak knots.

"You are doing it wrong," Hans said, as he passed her on his way back to the house. His hair was white and long and he had a full and bushy beard. "Let me show you," he said, taking the rope from her. "This is easiest way to do it," he said, showing her how to loop the rope in such a way that it would secure the bucket to the yoke and make it easy to remove later. "You try with the other knot," he suggested.

Hans watched Marie as she fastened the other bucket to the rope with the knot he showed her. "That's a smart girl," Hans said and walked away.

Thank you, Marie thought. She stooped and laid the yoke across her shoulders and stood carefully. The buckets splashed a little. Marie steadied herself and walked back toward the house as she had done dozens of times before.

"Let me help you with that," James offered. He was 22 years old and very handsome. He spent most of his time working with his father cultivating the land and helping build the community. Crops had to be planted and cared for, canals dug and roads and bridges built. Everyone had their part to play. Stonecutters made tombstones from white oolite taken from nearby quarries. Houses built of rock and blue clay were continually being erected. Trees were cut down and carpenters hand-planed lumber to build doors, window frames, flooring and the mill. Each family had its own cow that was herded in the meadows during the day and corralled inside the fort in the town square at night. Everyone in the community had to work together to survive. Marie liked having James around but rarely saw him as he was often busy assisting in one of these areas.

Now, he effortlessly lifted the yoke off Marie's shoulders and onto his. He held tight to both ends as they walked toward the house.

Thank you, Marie thought.

*   *   *

Johanna and Kristina walked through the sopping mud in their moccasins and pretended they didn't mind. They had hoped to procure better shoes for their escape, but it didn't matter. They were headed home at last. They had spent a week in Nephi, staying with other Saints and helping with chores, before they found a man who was taking a cow to Fort Ephraim and was willing to escort them.

The trail at first was winding and small. Johanna led the charge, letting the Brother direct them when she was unsure of the trail. When they came to a river, Johanna stopped. The last time she had meant to cross a river, her father had stopped her and insisted on carrying her across. This act had saved all their lives and taken his. Kristina paused next to Johanna and grabbed her hand. Nothing needed to be said.

Johanna stepped into the cold glass of the river when the brother caught up to them, "Wait." He pulled his cow forward, "Do not cross. You will freeze your feet and catch a cold. The old cow here will carry you."

He grabbed Kristina's waist and lifted her onto the cow. He waited until she felt steady before lifting Johanna on behind her. They sat with their legs dangling off the sides, their torsos turned forward and their hands grabbing hold of either side for balance as the cow moved through the river. They felt unsteady and laughed nervously. They held the backside of the cow until it finished carrying them safely across.

* * *

"Are you finished with your chores?" Ane asked. Marie nodded. They were alone. Hans and James were out working and Sister Ebbesen was visiting a neighbor. "How are you feeling today?" Ane asked.

Marie said nothing.

"This is getting worse, you not speaking," Ane said.

Marie's gaze turned to the floor.

"I will not tolerate this."

Marie looked at her mother and saw desperation and anger in her eyes.

"Why will you not talk to me?"

Marie was amazed. How could her mother not know?

"Every day you speak less and less, and it concerns me."

Marie turned around and looked out the window at the muddy yellow landscape.

"Maybe you could tell us a story tonight after dinner?" Ane approached Marie cautiously until she stood by her side. "Maybe you can tell us the story of *The Girl Clad in Mouse Skin.* It is your favorite."

Marie's eyes grew hot with tears.

"I am sorry," Ane said, stepping back, "but you cannot feel sorry for yourself forever. We all lost something."

Marie remembered back to sitting in the room with her sisters the night before the family left Denmark to travel to Zion. How scared she was, and how they reassured her.

We are going on a big adventure, Kristina had told her.

We will all be there, Johanna had assured her.

I want all my sisters with me, Marie had said.

She knew what had happened since wasn't their fault. They could not have foreseen what would become of their family. They simply didn't know any better. It was supposed to be for the best.

Quietly she muttered, "They promised me we would be together."

"Who did?"

"Metta, Hanna. They promised we would be in Zion together as a family. That we would all be here." Ane bit her lip. "Why are we here?!" Marie yelled with more force than she had realized she had in her. "We gave up everything and now we have lost Metta and Hanna too!"

Ane could not argue. Her heartbreak was the same as Marie's, but this was the way it had to be and she accepted it. She stepped toward her daughter, arms extended.

Marie spurned the invitation and ran out the door. A few tears escaped from Ane's eyes but she quickly wiped them away and pulled herself together. Marie did not come home for dinner. Ane was concerned but knew the girl would be safe so long as she stayed inside the Fort.

*   *   *

Johanna and Kristina were grateful for a clear sky and full moon as they traveled on into the night. It was well after dark when they reached Fort Ephraim. The brother who had accompanied them had told them the history of the Fort on their journey. He said it was seventeen acres and cost near $13,000 dollars to build. The walls ranged from seven to fourteen feet high.

They were met at the west entrance by a guard who let them enter. The brother suggested they stay with his family for the night, but the girls wouldn't consider it. They knew they wouldn't be able to rest until they had found home.

Had they been less excited, they may have been more polite and respectfully declined the invitation. Instead, they ignored his request and asked where Hans Christensen lived.

"I am not sure," he said.

The girls, without uttering a thank you or even an explanation, ran off.

The first house they came to was completely dark. Should they skip over it? But what if their mother was inside? Johanna banged on the front door. A lantern was lit and they saw its glow from the side window. They heard footsteps, and the door swung open. A man in his long underwear stood in the doorframe. The lantern sat on a table in the room and didn't provide enough to light his face. Was it Hans, their stepfather? They had met him briefly in Salt Lake when he married their mother, but it had been a long time since they had seen him.

"Ane Madsen—" Kristina muttered.

"Is she here?" Johanna asked.

The man, alarmed and confused, likely still recovering from the rude awakening, said no.

The girls didn't wait for him to say anything else, but raced off toward the next house in sight.

Again they banged on the front door of the darkened house. It took more time for someone to answer. This time it was a woman with a red shawl draped around her shoulders. Her brown hair, sprinkled with gray, hung in two braids and she carried a lantern.

"We are looking for Ane Madsen," Kristina blurted.

"Hans Christensen," Johanna added.

"She is three houses down," the woman pointed.

The girls smiled, and with their hearts beating fast, they ran. The house came into view. A single window held a flickering light.

"Mama," Kristina yelled as they ran faster.

Marie sat up in bed. She lay next to Andrew and her mother. Their bed consisted of a few blankets serving as mattress and a thin pillow they shared among them. She threw off her blanket and ran to the window, not caring whose sleep she disturbed. She heard voices. It wasn't the wind this time. Her mother, who lay nearest the fireplace, had been asleep with a blanket draped over her. She sat up when she heard the cries. The door burst open.

"Metta! Hanna!" Ane held out her arms.

The girls fell into their mother's arms. Andrew awoke and clung to his sisters. Marie stood hesitantly near the doorway, disbelieving her eyes. Isn't this what she had asked God for every night?

She watched as they held each other, tears running from their eyes.

"How did you get here?" Ane asked. The girls cried, unable to answer.

Hans, his children and Sister Ebbesen awoke and upon seeing the reunion, allowed the family some privacy by turning over and pretending to sleep.

Kristina glanced up and saw Marie standing in the shadows. "My dear sister," she opened her arms toward her.

Johanna turned also, wiping tears from her face. "Marie!" she cried.

Marie stumbled forward, feeling the bottled emotions pour from her as she fell into their embrace and wept.

Holding each other, they cried for their losses, their sorrows and their joys. The love they had for each other enveloped them in a sense of forever. This was their Zion moment, the family unity for which they had prayed. Together they wept and were happy.

NOW

&

Winter 2007

"With these strong arms /
I'll carry you / To Zion."
—Legacy

$\mathcal{T}$he shoreline of my thoughts disappeared as I drifted upon an open ocean of reflection. I hung up the phone, grabbed my jacket, and walked out the door into the brisk winter air. I needed to think.

The call was a result of a walk I made up Rocky Ridge on October 23, 2006. The hike commemorated the 150th anniversary of the ascent up that trail by my great-great-grandfather Ole and his family. Members of our families were determined to hike it that day, despite a large storm that had blown through two days prior. Luckily, it had cleared the day before we arrived, and we drove in over snow, slush and mud.

Wyoming mud is interesting. It coats your car like paint and doesn't come off easily. I had bet KC a malt (if it's a malt, it's not really betting) that we would see others on that anniversary, since the media had recently generated so much interest about the 1856 rescue. The anticipated release of the Groberg film about the rescue, which he had created for PBS, had been announced. I won the bet with KC, but not by much, as we saw only one other person. He was walking toward us with a backpack, heading up the ridge. He stopped to talk for a moment and told us he was making the trek with his brother. They had started from the ice slough a few miles back, but his brother had given out and he had gone on ahead. I wondered facetiously, "Did he leave his brother on the trail, in a car, or, as my ancestors had, did he bury him?" He didn't seem worried about their situation, so I guessed we didn't need to be worried either.

The wind was blowing and it was very cold. We parked by the monument marking the base of Rocky Ridge and got out with everyone dressed like Eskimos. The group headed up the ridge, but I lingered behind. I put on a light jacket because I wanted to feel the cold. I wasn't completely stupid. I also stuffed a heavy parka in my backpack and I had a ski cap and gloves as backup.

We took the walk slowly and spoke little. The sound of the wind pushed against my thoughts as I tried to visualize that day 150 years ago. After several miles, when we got to the top of the ridge, I told KC I would meet them at Rock Creek Hollow. He wisely talked me out of it, convincing me it was already too late in the afternoon.

As we walked back down the trail, I noticed there were places where people had stacked flat rocks together into tall peaks. These rock piles, or cairns, marked the trail along Rocky Ridge. They also served as monuments to honor those who had battled the ridge in that awful pioneer crucible. As we got closer to one of the monuments, I decided to walk along the ridge above it. When I arrived at the top I looked out over the landscape and the view was unbelievable.

I looked to the east and could see the path of the Sweetwater winding up its corridor. In my mind's eye I could see my ancestral family struggling desperately to survive as they crossed it and continued to climb.

To the west, I could see the trail winding up Rocky Ridge, heading toward Utah. I could see my children, but instead of fighting up a ridge pulling a handcart, I saw them struggling through life away from me and my wife, leaving home with what we had given them and heading into the future. I momentarily thought about my grandson, Joshua. The loss was still there, but it didn't have the overwhelming ripping feeling it had before. I will always wonder about Joshua, and feel that loss—just as Marie must have reflected often upon those little ones she had lost—but I am grateful for my daughter's courage.

I took out a small notebook I had with me and contemplated where I had been and what it meant to me and to my family. As I watched the scene unfold below me, some words for a song came to me. It became *Rock Creek Hollow.*

I didn't understand the meaning of some of the words at first. One part of the lyrics didn't seem to fit. It talked about stopping to turn around and look. During the trip that day and afterward, I tried to write that part out of each chorus, but it wouldn't let me.

After we finished at Rocky Ridge, we drove to Rock Creek Hollow. I had been there last with the Groberg film crew when the hillside was covered with snow. It was cold now, but there was no storm, and I could see a clear orange tint of light upon the horizon, a remnant from the setting sun. I walked alone down to the area where my cousin Janet had taken me during our Ole Madsen reunion, and where she had had her spiritual experience. It was so quiet and still; a sharp contrast to the roaring wind on the ridge.

The stillness was so tangible I felt as though I could reach out and touch it. I opened my little black book again and tried to write my feelings into song.

Later, I sent these lyrics to President Lorimer. This was before I had decided I was done with song writing. Emily had quit doing the firesides with me as she needed to devote more time to her family and I grew tired of doing the firesides alone. So after much thought and prayer about what I should do, I loaded up all the media I had in my truck and dropped it off to my friend Jolene Allphin.

I had met Jolene during my search for Ole and was immediately touched by her spirit and the love she had for the handcart people. She had written a book, *Tell My Story, Too*. It was a compilation of stories of the handcart pioneers. Jolene cannot talk about any one of the pioneers without getting very emotional. Families flock to her to tell their stories and to listen to hers.

Emily and I had just completed a website for our music and I turned the website over to Jolene. I told Jolene she could do with the website as she saw fit. I was through with it all.

"Are you sure?" Jolene asked.

I replied, "Thanks for doing this. I am done for good."

"What about the new CD you've been working on?"

"I'm not going to finish it," I said very decidedly.

My plan was to let Jolene distribute the media. I would let the handcart story go and just move back into the folds of life, my family and the church. I would play my guitar to relax as I used to.

I spent the next year playing music in my room to an audience of one. Now, I walked down a little scenic trail near my home pondering the phone call of a few minutes ago.

At the other end of the line was the familiar voice of President Lorimer. He was no longer a stake president, but I can't help but call him President still. It's simply the level of respect I have for him. The funny thing about the call was that he and I had both decided that we were done with the handcart story. It took up too much of our time, we agreed. He had put a lot more into it than I had, but we both felt there wasn't much more to do and there were plenty of souls willing to take up the cause and move it along. It appeared we were both wrong about quitting.

He called to ask me if I would send him the music for *Rock Creek Hollow* as the Riverton Stake wanted to use the song in a production. Truth be told, I could only vaguely remember the melody. I hadn't heard it since a year earlier as I sat above the Sweetwater. But at Lorimer's request, I went home and set myself to the task of finishing the song. I pulled out the lyrics and read over the words a few times.

I continued to stop at the part that read, "She can't stop / To look or turn around / Where she steps / Is hallowed ground." Again I tried writing that part out as it didn't seem to fit or make sense. I couldn't. Sometimes songs have minds of their own.

One evening, after working on the song, I went to the Bountiful Temple. I was one of many who had volunteered to clean the building that night. I was to arrive at about nine p.m. and work until midnight. I had done this a few times, and my main goal was always to get a vacuum. I think the question as to why I wanted a vacuum goes without saying when the possibility of cleaning bathrooms is taken into consideration.

This night I missed the vacuum squad and was assigned to go to the third floor of the temple. While riding the elevator I tried not to think about what cleaning assignment I might get. The elevator doors opened, and I noticed three vacuums sitting in the hall. I pointed and declared, "I want one of those."

The sister in charge gave me a vacuum. I sighed with relief. She assigned me to one of the endowment rooms and the celestial room. I hurried through the endowment room and moved on to the celestial room.

There I was in the dark of night, alone in the celestial room of a temple, the dearest place on earth for Latter-day Saints. As I moved with the vacuum, I stopped in the middle of the room and stared into mirrors that lined the walls. Because the mirrors faced each other from either side of the room, I could look into them on either side and see my reflection going backward into infinity. I vacuumed the same spot repeatedly and looked into the mirror, letting my thoughts drift.

I did this for some time, just looking forward. Then, I turned around to look at the opposing mirror. The reflection looked the same. I couldn't tell what was in front and what was behind me.

In my mind, past, present and future became a blur as I stood in the middle of the celestial room, in the middle of forever. It was as if I were to take a rope that went on forever in both directions and cut it anywhere then the cut would always be exactly in the middle. And if I cut it twice I would have a beginning and an end, but eternity would continue in both directions.

In my mind I was at Rocky Ridge, looking down across the Sweetwater, imagining a rag-tag handcart group struggling to move forward. The steps they took without giving up, the hallowed ground they walked on and the place where I now stood felt the same.

Then it came to me: my song, *Rock Creek Hollow,* was a metaphor for the temple. The song was about the temple, about the possibilities of eternal family ties stretching backward and forward in time. I thought about the bonds that were made in the Temple, where individuals can be sealed together in family units forever.

As I stood in the temple contemplating these things, my mind drifted to my family. I thought about how I had the opportunity to serve them. I didn't have to carry them across a freezing river in the middle of a snowstorm or give them my food when they didn't have enough. There would be other streams they would need help to cross, and I'd be there for them, always and in whatever way they needed me.

I had thought for some time that my purpose was tied up in playing music and touching the lives of complete strangers. Standing in that room, wearing down a patch of carpet, I wondered: "For what purpose was I really made?" I looked in the mirror again.

The things that matter most to me are eternal. The bonds of love shared within a family I believe to be eternal. The song was not only a metaphor for the temple, but a metaphor for my life. I suddenly felt that everything that had happened to me, good or bad, along my path, had led me to this realization.

I can assure you, there was a very clean and perhaps slightly worn spot in that carpet from prolonged vacuuming.

As I mused, the sister in charge came in with the rest of the group and said we were done. I unplugged my vacuum and walked toward them. She told us that before we left she wanted to show us something special about the celestial room chandelier. She was about to turn it off and then back on again. I asked her if I could go back to my vacuum spot before she did. She said "Yes."

The light went out and it was very dark and then she turned the chandelier on. Instead of coming on all at once, it came on a few small bulbs at a time. Looking in the forever mirrors, it was like watching the birth of a universe.

I knew in that moment that everything happens for a reason, but we can't always know the reason when the journey begins. Some things we can only understand at the end of our journey. Everything is connected and I truly believe we can either see the connections, celebrate them, and express gratitude for our blessings, or we can see life as a string of coincidences that have no meaning or connection.

For me, I'm going to believe in miracles, celebrate life, rejoice in the views of eternity and hope my choices will create a positive ripple effect in the lives of others. This is my choice. This is the legacy of my ancestors.

The End

EPILOGUE

Kristina (Metta)

ॐ

Kristina Metta Madsen

Shortly after Johanna and Kristina arrived at the Fort on that spring night in 1858, they secured work helping with household chores and went to live with their employers. Kristina met and married James, the son of her stepfather Hans. Kristina and James were married in December 1859 at Fort Ephraim. Together, James and Kristina had seven children. Only five lived to be adults. In 1860 they moved to Mt. Pleasant to settle the area. James helped to build the fort and many bridges in the area. Kristina continued to suffer ill health throughout her life due to the physical stresses from the trek. Andrew and Marie lived with Kristina for many years. They lived in a log cabin with a dirt roof and had little in the way of furniture.

It was said that kindness, tenderness, and love filled their hearts and home each day. James worked the fields and sometimes worked day and night to irrigate their acres of land. In 1867 James became a Minute Man during the Blackhawk Indian War—standing guard to protect property or riding out to retrieve stolen cattle. The family was happy, but poor. James hired out his oldest daughter at fifty cents per week to work for others—cleaning, help-

James Christensen

ing with children, or with other necessary chores. James often made trips to mining camps to sell grain to pay taxes. While traveling night and day he grew ill with a severe cold. While James was away Kristina lost her infant daughter. When James heard of this he came home immediately and in his grief-stricken state remarked, "I see you are all here but one." After this he became very ill with typhoid fever. He passed away at the age of 45. Kristina passed away on the 15th of November, 1900 after a short illness. She was 57 years old.

Karen

ℰↄ

Karen returned home to Tornved to discover the premonition of her dream was true. Her aunt had died. Karen stayed with the family, helping her uncle raise the children. She eventually left and traveled from city to city, having no home to return to. Shortly thereafter she was excommunicated from the church. She also became pregnant out of wedlock. No further information about her has been discovered.

Andrew

ഇ

Andrew was baptized in the spring of 1859 in Mt. Pleasant, where he lived with his sister Kristina. He was later employed as a logger in Big Cottonwood Canyon for homes being built in Salt Lake. Later he worked on the railroad. He witnessed the driving of the last spike knitting the east and west railroads at Promontory Point, May

Andrew Madsen with wife Maria

10, 1869. He assisted in bringing immigrants into the valley and in mining. As a young man during the Blackhawk war, he searched for cattle taken during the Indian raids. In 1873 he was called to help build the St. George Temple. In 1874 he married Anna Maria Jensen in the Endowment House in Salt Lake. In the spring of 1875 Andrew purchased a forty-acre farm in Chester, Utah where he raised sheep and cattle. Andrew and Maria lived in a one-room log cabin. Maria washed and carded wool from their sheep to make quilts. Andrew later moved his family to Spring City where he built a beautiful home and was president of the Spring City Milling Company for twenty-seven years. Together they had eleven children, nine of whom grew to adulthood. Andrew went blind in his later years. He was considered to be a man of faith who never wavered, with character that stood above reproach. On May 13, 1936 at the age of 85, Andrew died. He is buried along with his wife of sixty-two years in the Spring City Cemetery.

Johanna (Hanna)

એ૦

Johanna (Hanna) Madsen

As a young woman Johanna had many suitors due to her charm and vivacious nature, but there was only one who caught her attention. In the winter of 1860 Johanna married Martin Aldrich. Together they settled in Mt. Pleasant and had eight children. The first child, a son, died shortly after birth. They were later asked to settle Piute County but due to food shortages and Indian raids they eventually returned to Mt. Pleasant. Martin served as a Minute Man in the Blackhawk War. They worked a farm and raised sheep. Johanna was a member of the Daughters of Utah Pioneers and active in the Mt. Pleasant Relief Society. She was said to be brave and was not one to complain. She was a woman of strict routine, lived frugally and stayed up to date with current events. Her philosophy of life was to avoid worry. She was said to store up reservoirs of courage and power ready for any emergency and was a devoted mother. She remained active and self-reliant in her old age. She died in 1942 at the age of 101.

Peter Madsen

ဆာ

Peter Madsen, at the age of 62, died when the remnant of the company limped down Echo Canyon, only a few days before the company arrived in Salt Lake. Peter traveled with his daughter Petrea, his wife having died years earlier. Petrea made it safely into the promised valley.

Captain James Willie

ဆာ

James Willie's eight-year-old son, whom he had not seen since he was four, met his father at the mouth of Emigration Canyon. It was an emotional reunion for Willie and his son. Willie stumbled from the wagon to embrace his son with burlap sacks swaddling his frostbitten feet and legs. He lifted his son into the wagon and they rode into the valley together. Willie arrived to greet his wife and other two children in Salt Lake City

James G. Willie

but was in poor health. The feet that had led by example, walking over a thousand miles with his company, being the first to enter streams and carry women and children across to spare them from the icy water, these same feet were afflicted with frostbite. A doctor recommended his feet be amputated, but his wife nursed his black and bleeding feet back to health.

After his brother's death he inherited a large sum of money. The majority of his inheritance was donated to the Perpetual Emigration Fund. Seven weeks after returning home he was called to be bishop of the Salt Lake 7th ward. Willie later became an early settler of Mendon, Utah. He was the superintendent of the cooperative store and also served as mayor, water master and postmaster. He had two more children, one with a plural wife. He also served as first counselor in the bishopric, and founded the first Sunday School in Mendon. He died September 9, 1895 at the age of 85.

Johan Ahmanson

℘

Johan Ahmanson
Photo courtesy of
Ahmanson family, Nebraska

Johan Ahmanson had intentions to travel by wagon until he was called as sub-captain in the Willie Company. Not wanting his wife and young son to bear the affliction of pulling a handcart, he arranged for them to travel by wagon with the Hodgett Wagon Company that was traveling a month behind him.

He safely made it to Utah Territory with the remnant of the Willie Company. Upon his arrival, he was anxious to see his family and assure they were safe. On the seventeenth of December, Ahmanson left on his own to find his family out on the trail. He writes, "Who could describe my joy at finding both of my dear ones in the best of health." However, Ahmanson was distraught when he learned that his belongings had been thrown from the wagon to make room for members of the Martin Hand-cart Company.

After living in Utah for several months, Ahmanson became dis-illusioned with his faith and left the church. Unable to recover his personal items left in the canyon that had been discarded from the Hodgett wagon train, Ahmanson filed a lawsuit against Brigham Young demanding a compensation for his missing belongings, as well as for his time serving as sub-captain. It was settled out of court and Ahmanson received $1,000 in reparation. He relocated to St. Joseph, Missouri, then later moved to Omaha where he lived the rest of his life working as a hardware merchant, a grocer, and later a doctor of homeopathic medicine. He wrote and pub-lished a book in 1876 about his time with the Mormons.

Levi Savage

ಖಾ

Levi returned to his son in Salt Lake and later was appointed one of the presidents of the Fifty-seventh Quorum of the seventies and also worked as a school teacher. Most could not pay him for his teaching services and he struggled financially. He was active in defending Salt Lake during the Utah War, and in October 1858 he wed the widow Ann Brummel

Levi Savage

Cooper, whom he had met in the Willie Handcart Company. He moved around the territory in the 1860s, starting in Lehi where he sold lumber. In 1865 he settled in Toquerville, Utah, where he took Ann's two daughters, Mary Ann and Adelaide, as plural wives. Mary Ann bore three children. In 1885 he was imprisoned for three years for violating the Edmunds Act, which outlawed plural marriage. Once released from prison in 1888 he returned to his family and lived the rest of his life in Toquerville, raising fruit. He died on the 13th of December, 1910 at 91 years of age.

Ane Marie (Marie)

〜

Ane Marie Madsen

When Marie was younger she felt compelled to work for others and always gave her pay to her mother. Ane Marie married Hans Peter Ericksen in the spring of 1865. Hans had emigrated from Denmark in 1863 and settled in Mt. Pleasant in 1865. They lived in Mt. Pleasant shortly before migrating to Nebraska Territory where diphtheria struck and took the lives of so many of their children. When the doctor suggested they return to Utah, they waited through the winter, and in 1881 they boarded a train that took them home. They purchased a farm of 120 acres in Mt. Pleasant, and they had three more sons in Utah, two of whom died of pneumonia. Of the ten children she bore, only two sons lived to adulthood—Christian, and my grandfather Leonard.

Hans bought a drugstore and later went into the sheep business. He and Ane Marie were sealed in the Manti Temple on May 23, 1899. Hans died December 23, 1928 of pneumonia. Marie joined him nine months later when she passed away in Leonard's home in Hamer, Idaho. Despite her trials, she was said to be a woman of affable courage with a wistful smile that inspired life.

Hans Peter Ericksen

Ane
ঙ্গ

Ane never recovered completely from the physical and emotional hardships of the trail to Zion. She lived in Fort Ephraim and then Mount Pleasant until she died in 1864 at the age of 54. She was later sealed to Ole in the Manti Temple, assuring the eternal family circle they had envisioned when they left their Danish homeland and headed into an unknowable future in a distant land. Their Zion was accomplished not as they had envisioned, but as the Lord had known all along.

Ole Madsen and wife Ane Jensen

Notes

ℬℭ

*A*lthough the story of the Madsen family has been fictionalized for the purposes of story telling, their experiences are true. We pulled as much information as we could from records and old journals from the time. We relied heavily on Johan Ahmanson's account in discovering how missionary work was conducted in Denmark and Elder Lars Madsen's journal, which mentions his involvement with Ole Madsen and his family several times. Other stories were passed on through the family.

The stories of the trail were taken from many differing accounts as many journals were kept about the experiences of the Willie Handcart Company. Information about the trail was mainly taken from accounts or journals written by Johan Ahmanson, Peter Madsen, Levi Savage, William Woodward and John Chislett, as well as newspaper articles from the era. Many of the speeches given by Franklin D. Richards, Millen Atwood, Levi Savage, and James Willie were taken as direct quotes as documented in various journals or accounts written by company members. Information was also gathered from pioneer museums, interviews, personal histories and Nick Ericksen's careful compiling and caretaking of the family record and stories. Helpful books written about the Willie and Martin Handcart companies include: *Tell my*

Story, Too, by Jolene Allphin, *The Price We Paid* by Andrew Olsen, *Handcarts to Zion* by LeRoy and Ann Hafen, *More Than Miracles* by T.C. Christensen with Jolene Allphin and *Emigrating Journals of The Willie and Martin Handcart Companies* by Lynne Slater Turner. This list is not all-inclusive, but a reference for any who have questions or would like more information regarding these accounts.

There are varying accounts and lingering questions as to what happened to the oxen on September 3, 1856. Some say it was a stampede while others think it may have been Indians. Some believe that Porter Rockwell, who was hired to take Babbitt's wagon train into Salt Lake City, took the oxen to carry Babbitt's supplies and was later paid by a Judge Appleby for bringing the cargo in. We were unable to discover enough hard evidence to write it one way or another, so we wrote it how the pioneers experienced it and left the rest for you, the reader, to ponder.

Some things were difficult to write as we only had limited information. One lingering question was why Peter Madsen resigned as Danish company clerk. We drew different conclusions on possible reasons, debated on whether to include the information or write it out, and eventually kept it. Peter Madsen's stopping his writing in mid-sentence, while recounting a horrific Indian attack, portrays the emotions of the uncertain times. In some trek journals, the worse things became for the company, the fewer details people wrote; perhaps because they didn't have time, or perhaps because they lost their ability to look upon and recount the atrocities that were before them.

One particular part that was difficult to write because of the lack of records was what happened to the family when they reached Salt Lake. We had stories of what other pioneers had experienced and upon learning that some stayed with the Young family upon their arrival, we decided to write the story in that way, although it is unlikely that Johanna and Kristina were guests of the Youngs.

The Willie and Martin handcart fiasco was looked upon as a dark time in LDS Church history. Many were frustrated by how it unfolded. Five more companies traveled with handcarts from 1857–1860. They learned from the failures of the Willie and Martin Handcart Companies, and were sure to make arrangements for supplies to be replenished at different points along the way. They also changed the construction of the handcarts, making them stronger, reducing the need for repairs. The Willie and Martin Companies were the fourth and fifth of the ten groups to travel with handcarts in this era, and the only ones to encounter serious problems. Many of the unfortunate companies' members used the handcart experience to draw on their faith and found meaning from their hardship and sacrifice, while others held bitterness toward their leaders.

Light up the Land became the dedicated song of the Second Rescue of the handcart pioneers as stated by Scott Lorimer who was the Riverton, Wyoming Stake President at the time and the one who organized and secured the handcart sites in Wyoming for the church. The song also was used at several Native American events in recent years. Jenny Jordan Frogley, who sang the song on the Olympic album, later performed it for one of these occasions. Here are her words regarding the song:

"This song in both lyric and melody stirs greatness and inspiration. Carefully written, this song could be used in many ways, to lift and inspire the individual, or lift an entire nation, even the world!"

The film, *Sweetwater Rescue,* was released on PBS and received much acclaim. The documentary focusing on my ancestors, and written by screenwriter James Jordan, *Walking in Obedience: The Ole Madsen Story,* was debuted at the Bountiful, Utah Handcart Days. Since then the film has played at other events and festivals along the Wasatch Front, including being featured in the LDS film festival, and winning best documentary at the Westates film awards.

I am grateful for the experiences with which the Lord has blessed me and my family that drew us closer to our ancestors and their tragic, thought-provoking, and altogether inspiring story of faith, courage, sacrifice and love.

Deleted Scenes & Extras

℘

*M*ike Ericksen and Sage Steadman wrote many scenes about Ane Marie's later life and experiences that happened along the trail that didn't make it to print. They would love to share these stories with you at the book's website **www.UponDestinys-Song.com.** Enter keyword **Sojourn 1856** to unlock these hidden chapters.

Acknowledgements
ഇ

$\mathcal{I}$ value my life based on those who have crossed my path and had a profound influence on the way I think and who I am.

In writing this book I wish to thank my wife Cheri, for putting up with the countless hours of talking about the stories I found and the many miles we traveled as we learned about and experienced the trail of Ane Marie. I also appreciate her listening to every version of my songs many times.

Thanks to my Father and Mother for encouragement and my Dad's stories about the past. My grandmother Jennette who took the time to tell me stories and the Spirit who brought them to mind and set my course.

Big thanks to my brother KC for starting our family down the road to understanding where we came from. Thanks to my brother, Steven, for his research and desire to find the truth, and my brother, Greg, for his musical talent and encouragement with mine.

Thanks to my children, Amy, Jennifer, Shaunee and Luke for not only listening but being a part of the journey.

Thank you to the following: Sage Steadman for being the perfect writing partner and friend. Jolene Allphin for her devotion to the stories and love for the pioneers, and for taking the time to help us with the story. Scott Lorimer for his friendship and knowledge of the trail. Lee Groberg for his friendship, fabulous talent, and including my family in his production, and his generous permission for use of Groberg Films photos and film clips. Emily Christensen for her friendship and musical talent. Nick Ericksen for his dedication to family history. Henrietta Fredricksen for being our Danish contact and guide. Twila Van Leer for her editing talent and encouragement. Lauren Horsley for the discussion guide. Sandra Rast for the book's cover photo. Shaunee Lamb for the trail map and for posing as the model for the cover. Jaime Singer from Fluid Studios for the book cover design. Bob and Barbara Townsend for their encouragement and helpful information on early Mormon history.

I'd like to thank my band, Cedar Breaks, including Rebecca Croft, Michael Gibbons, Diana Glissmeyer, and Keith Behunin, for taking our music to a new level.

Thanks to Norm Bosworth for his artistry and believing in our sound.

The following organizations were very helpful in my search for Ane Marie: the LDS History Department, the LDS Family History Center, Snow College Archives, the Hall County Nebraska Archives, Daughters of Utah Pioneers Museum, the Mount Pleasant Pioneer Museum and Relic Home and the Mormon Trail Center at Historic Winter Quarters.

I'd also like to thank Ronnie O'Brien, Lyndia Carter, Kaye Watson, Sherryl Fowers, Julie Rogers, Rick France, Lynn Gourley Allen, Bill Slaughter, Shirley Porath, Louise Johansen, Doug Nielsen, Robyn Beck, Gary Horlacher, Janet Leonardson, John Peterson, Lynne Turner, Mark Goodman, Don Smith, James Jordan, Sandra Rast, Brad Wardle, and Lane Ward.

Discussion Guide

෨

1. What unexpected things did you learn from this book?

2. (a) While most of the book's happenings occurred in two major time-periods, several chapters took place in other decades (ex. 1968 and 1997). Why might the author(s) have chosen to include these brief snippets in time? (b) Did it enhance your understanding of the characters?

3. (a) The Madsen family immigrated to America based on a commandment from the prophet to gather in Zion. Would you be willing today to leave your home and belongings behind and travel to an unknown place if asked by church leaders? (b) What sorts of sacrifices do our modern-day leaders ask of us that can be difficult to obey? How do they compare to what was asked of the pioneers?

4. (a) On pages 83–84 Ole and Ane must face their oldest daughter Karen's last-minute decision to remain in Denmark. Would you have been willing or even able to leave a child behind on the docks as they did? (b) Could they have done anything differently?

5. (a) Mormons are often accused of following their leaders with "blind faith," or obeying without questioning or thinking for themselves. Was this the case with the Willie Handcart Company? (b) What role should personal revelation play in our desire to follow the religious leaders in our own lives?

6. Is it important to know and understand our family heritage? Why or why not?

7. The Willie Handcart Company was very strictly controlled, and exact obedience was demanded. Was this necessary and if so, why?

8. (a) One of the remarkable scenes in the story of the Willie Handcart Company is the public rebuke of Levi Savage (pg. 162) for the "rebellious words" he spoke when urging the company not to start their journey so late in the season. Was this appropriate? (b) If the Willie Handcart Company had not encountered the trials of hunger, blizzards and death, would you feel differently about Levi's warning and subsequent chastisement?

9. (a) Why is it important to know and understand the history of the LDS church? (b) How does this particular piece of Mormon history affect your view of the LDS faith?

10. Should blame be laid on anyone's shoulders for the devastating hardships the Willie Handcart Company endured? If so, who was responsible?

11. Is there always a reason or silver lining to the difficult trials we encounter in our own lives?

12. (a) When you read KC's interviews with the author's great aunts, were you surprised to learn that Marie felt bitter about the hardships she had encountered during her lifetime? (b) If you were in her shoes, do you think you would feel the same way?

13. (a) On page 195–196 the author realizes that everyone's faith looks different. Do we, as individuals or as a religious culture, expect others to express their faith in the same way we do? (b) Is the path to faith and righteousness the same for all?

14. If you were to write a *What I Owe My Mother* essay as Leonard did for Marie, what might it say?

15. In what ways did the 'Now' present-day portions of the story enhance the 'Then' telling of the Madsen family's ordeals?

16. (a) The author viewed the chandelier in the celestial room of the temple (pg. 290–291) as a symbol of the gradual gaining of spiritual knowledge as the lights came on one bulb at a time versus all at once. How do you relate this to your own life?

17. (a) Music plays a strong role in *Upon Destiny's Song,* as it was a way for the author to connect with his ancestors' experiences. In what way did the lyrical excerpts at the heading of each chapter assist in setting the mood as you read? (b) If your book came with a CD, Did you listen to the music? If so, how did it affect you as you read the book?

Mike Ericksen has been a devout student of the trail of the hand-cart pioneers since learning of his family's trek from Denmark to Utah in 1856. In the past 10 years he has spoken in many programs and firesides across the country and has produced films and music related to the stories and events of the pioneers. The documentary *Walking in Obedience* produced by Ericksen in conjunction with Groberg Films and Dreamchaser, has been heralded as a "historical masterpiece" and has been shown around the country receiving acclamations and awards at film festivals and firesides. An accomplished classical guitarist, Mike has produced four musical albums to date, and is currently playing with the band Cedar Breaks. He is passionate about music, writing, faith and family. He enjoys nature, tennis and yoga, and currently resides in Utah with his wife Cheri. Together they have four children and eight grandchildren.

Visit Mike online at **www.musicforthetrail.com** & **www.cedarbreaksband.com**

Sage Steadman has a Masters in Social Work from the University of Utah. She became a licensed mental health therapist while pursuing her passion for writing. She is the author of the inspirational self-help teen novel, *Snowflake Obsidian: Memoir of a Cutter,* written under her pen name, The Hippie. She has been heralded as a talented new writer who tackles her novels with a witty, raw and honest approach. She currently lives near Salt Lake City, Utah.

Visit Sage online at **www.thehippiewriter.com** & **www.snowflakeobsidianbook.com**

www.UponDestinysSong.com

The CD containing the music of *Upon Destiny's Song*

1. *Light Up the Land* - 1997
   Album: Unsung, Music for the Trail
   Song: Greg Ericksen
   Arrangement: Carol Jones
   Copyright © Greg Ericksen, used by permission

2. *Jenny's Lullaby* - 1997
   Album: Unsung, Music for the Trail
   Song: Mike Ericksen
   Arrangement: Mike Ericksen
   Guitar: Mike Ericksen
   Cello: Kristiana Silver
   Copyright © Empath Media, LLC

3. *Rock Creek Hollow* - 2007
   Album: Sojourn, Along the Path
   Song: Mike Ericksen
   Arrangement: Mike Ericksen
   Vocal: Diana Glissmeyer
   Guitars: Mike Ericksen
   Banjo: Keith Behunin
   Copyright © Empath Media, LLC

4. *Aspects* - 2012
   Band: Cedar Breaks
   Album: Tyme, Aspects of Home.
   Song: Mike Ericksen & Sage Steadman
   Arrangement: Mike Ericksen
   Vocals: Rebecca Croft, Michael Gibbons, Diana Glissmeyer
   Guitars: Mike Ericksen & Michael Gibbons
   Banjo: Keith Behunin
   Copyright © Empath Media, LLC

Find all the music from *Upon Destiny's Song* at:
www.CedarBreaksBand.com

Related Media: Albums

Unsung, Music for the Trail (CD album)

Unsung, with its somber chords and wistful lyrics, leaves you pensive and inspired to look beyond the dull and routine, and to remember those who have gone before us with sacrifice and courage, and paved the way for a better tomorrow. *Unsung* also invites you to explore your own path as it gently guides you into introspection.

> *"Unsung is my new favorite... The music stayed in my soul."*

Sojourn, Along the Path (CD album)

Sojourn, Along the Path is a variety of instrumental and vocal arrangements, layered with soulful lyrics, and provocative melodies. *Sojourn* is a good companion for a walk alone in the fresh air or a quiet evening of introspection by the fire.

> *"Haunting and beautiful. It makes me feel quiet in my soul."*

Tyme, Aspects of Home (CD album)

Tyme, Aspects of Home is the debut album from the new band Cedar Breaks. The album is a groundbreaking musical tribute to the exploration of life and home. It examines our relationships with each other, and with the world around us. The album is a collage of strong harmonies, beautiful instrumentation, and thought provoking lyrics.

> *"Tyme makes a lasting impression. I love the music*
> *and the feeling that consumed me while listening."*

Hymns Plus, (CD/notation and tablature book)

Written for classical finger picking style with detailed notation and tablature. The pieces are set for easy to intermediate level guitarists and a CD is included with popular favorites such as: *Amazing Grace, How Great Thou Art*, and *I Am a Child of God*. The CD includes fourteen songs in all.

> *"Fun to play...great melody adaptation and variations."*

> *"The Poor Wayfaring Man of Grief/Come*
> *Come Ye Saints medley is amazing."*

Related Media: Videos

Westates Award Winner for Best Documentary
Walking in Obedience: The Ole Madsen Story, (*DVD documentary film, 40 min.*)

Walking in Obedience contains dramatic scenes and incredible scenery depicting the journey of a Danish family traveling with the Willie Handcart Company in 1856. The story is told through the words of those who lived through the experience with both the Willie and Martin Handcart Companies.

Walking in Obedience: The Ole Madsen Story is visually spectacular, historically accurate, and reverently told. Both touching and faith promoting, it is recreated and told through Ole Madsen's daughter, Ane Marie.

"Historical masterpiece..."

*"I have just finished this magnificent
production. It is truly wonderful."*

Empath, Music for the Trail (*DVD, two music videos*)

Empath takes you on a visual journey with the Willie Handcart Company, emphasizing the rescue. Hear the designated song of the second rescue, *Light Up the Land,* and the song of the third rescue, *Walk the Path of Faith.* *Empath* was directed by Lee Groberg and uses dramatic scenes from his acclaimed documentary *Sweetwater Rescue: The Willie and Martin Handcart Story,* along with never before seen footage from the film. *Empath* includes both songs with the performing artists in the video as an extra feature.

*"Watched the DVD several times and am moved by the beauty and
spirit of the music. What a contrast with music videos these days."*

"It was a little hard holding back the tears."

Tyme, Aspects of Home (*DVD musical documentary, 64 min*)

This musical art film is a stunning compilation of music videos interwoven with a thought provoking narrative that offers a treatise on the concept of home, family, and heritage. Set against the stunning visual imagery of Utah and the music of Cedar Breaks.

"It is so beautiful and filled with passion and love. "

visit:
upondestinyssong.com | cedarbreaksband.com | musicforthetrail.com

Jenny's Lullaby

Written by Mike Ericksen

It might be all right
If she just holds on tight
Then closing her eyes to hide
The hopeless tide inside
Oh for a subtle illusion
To hide away this confusion
On this dark and lonely night
Without an end in sight
Then I heard her whisper

"Sleep for both of us

All the night long
Dream for both of us
On my song
Please remember as you
Listen to my heart

Please remember me."

In her eyes I see
A tear exposed to me
As she searches her soul to find
A simple peace of mind
Oh for the clear light
of truth now
Step back away from the shadow
Let it rush to the open day
And hold the world at bay
Then I had to whisper,

"Sleep for both of us

All the night long
Dream for both of us
On her song
Please remember as you
Listen to her heart

Please remember her."

Mama hold on don't cry
Just hold me tight to say goodbye
When we meet another day

No word we'll have to say

Because the rhythm
of your heart
Has been the song from the start
From the beginning back again
Reaching out to draw me in

Mama hold on don't cry

Just let me feel your lullaby
From the beginning back again
Reaching out to draw me in.

Fall out of darkness
Reach hard to feel the light

She's clutching her heart to find

A giving so divine
Oh bring that melody to me
The one heard low and carefree
To carry me along its song
Because it sounds like home
On the breeze it whispers,

"Sleep for both of us

All the night long
Dream for both of us
On my song
Please remember as you
Listen to my heart

Please remember me."

Aspects
Written by Mike Ericksen & Sage Steadman

Mother's womb was the ground

A stepping stone till wings are found
Mama wakes as baby cries
Sister smiles and grandma sighs
Innocence moves in front of us all
Everything that matters is right
before your eyes
Centered around a bouncing ball
A day is spent just waiting for
A simple smile and nothing more
More is known than has been said

Quiet now, it's time for bed

Borrowed moments in space and
time
You will hold forever, what you have
found
Set together in a nursery rhyme

Okay in darkness, warm in the light
Sad in the winter, safe through the
night

Share the sadness, ease the pain
Feel my gladness, and keep me
sane

The spirit surrounds me, I can't soon
forget
Open up to feel it, and never let it go
Always myself, not always my best
Now lift me up, I need to feel
Hold me close, you love me still
Place in my heart, deep in my chest
Heart of my soul, above the rest
The only access to unbreakable
bonds

The key that will open it, you will
always have
Left deep within the place I call
home.

Laughing hard I fall apart
To then uncover connected hearts
Place to run to more than from

Eutaw
Written by Mike Ericksen

Take my hand, don't walk too fast
Down the trail of ages past
Quiet sounds in rhythm fall

Broken by the thunder's call
I wrote it down
Never to get it right
She looks so young in the morning
sun
Made no sense to struggle on
For his time was over
He dropped his head and humbly
said

I'm sorry, for all that I have done

With my horse and gun
I will fight you no more forever.

Stayed with her through the night
To view the stars till morning light
Then we climbed, she took my hand
On colored rock where angels land
I set my mind
Across the great beyond
For I was alone, I just sang alone
Caught between the right and wrong
He brought with him a dream
He raised his head and softly said,

"Drive on."

Not all would see the light
But it will be all right

There's more than your heart can
hold.

I walked along without a care
I felt her breath and touched her hair
So it was from the start
She set herself into my heart
I moved ahead
Knowing she was with me
We just strolled along, lost in her
song

When I stand on sacred ground
I can hear their voices

Soft and low they seem to say, "look

up."
Beautiful are her feet
Upon the mountain peak
For she is called Eutaw.

Set to Wander
Written by Mike Ericksen

She set herself to wander
As she opened up her eyes
I thought as I held her
How the time would surely fly
And I wanted to tell her
She was born among the free
What I had to give her
Was given once to me
Like the gentle spring rain
That lets the flowers grow
Without provocation
Into the even flow

I set myself to wander
When I opened up my mind
As I helped my brother
It was joy that I would find

And I wanted to tell him
He could set his spirit free
To look for the answer
To all that he could be
Like looking at the stars

On a warm summer's night

Felt through inspiration
Your soul takes flight

The time passed away with us,

Our lives passed away...As a dream.

We set ourselves to wander
Across the span of years
Take time to remember
The cost to us in tears

The Children of tomorrow
Will know a brighter day
Look back to find you
And what you have to say
Like the moonlight shining
So bright at harvest time

Set up by laughter
With your hand in mine

The time passed away with us,

Our lives passed away... As a

dream...